W9-AMB-554

Also by David Lozell Martin

Losing Everything
Tethered
The Crying Heart Tattoo
Final Harbor
The Beginning of Sorrows
Lie to Me
Bring Me Children
Tap, Tap
Cul-de-Sac
Pelikan
Facing Rushmore
Our American King

CRAZY LOVE

A Novel

David Lozell Martin

Simon & Schuster Paperbacks
New York · London · Toronto · Sydney

Simon & Schuster Paperbacks
1230 Avenue of the Americas
New York, NY 10020

This book is a work of fiction. Names, characters, places, and incidents either are products of the author's imagination or are used fictitiously. Any resemblance to actual events or locales or persons, living or dead, is entirely coincidental.

This Simon & Schuster trade paperback edition January 2009

SIMON & SCHUSTER PAPERBACKS and colophon are registered trademarks of Simon & Schuster, Inc.

For information about special discounts for bulk purchases, please contact Simon & Schuster Special Sales at 1-800-456-6798 or business@simonandschuster.com.

Designed by Lauren Simonetti

Manufactured in the United States of America

1 3 5 7 9 10 8 6 4 2

The Library of Congress has cataloged the hardcover edition as follows:
Martin, David Lozell.
Crazy Love/David Martin.
p. cm.
1. Farmers—Fiction. 2. Businesswomen—Fiction. I. Title
PS3563.A72329 C67 2002
813'.54—dc21 2001054235

ISBN-13: 978-1-4165-6663-2
ISBN-10:1-4165-6663-5

To Samuel

I fear animals regard man as a creature of their own kind which has in a highly dangerous fashion lost its healthy animal reason—as the mad animal, as the laughing animal, as the weeping animal, as the unhappy animal.

—FRIEDRICH NIETZSCHE

1

Watch time. At 8:30 A.M. on April 19, a farmer named Joseph David Long, known locally as Bear, was on his way into town when he saw two men standing over a cow. Bear stopped his truck to the side of the county road and looked out across the pasture—a fringe of grassland, a background of forest. Both men laughed. They were far enough away for him to see their heads go back before he heard their laughter, which came a disconnected moment later, as in a poorly dubbed movie. Bear knew that one of the men must be Phil Scrudde because Scrudde's big blue Cadillac was parked right out there in the pasture, next to the cow, which was lying down. Scrudde was famous for driving his Cadillac into pastures and fields, like maybe he thought he was Hud. From this distance, Bear couldn't recognize the other man, taller and thinner.

Quickly now, Scrudde, the shorter fatter man, grabbed up a pitchfork and stuck the cow's flank. Bear's mouth dropped at the sudden cruelty of it and he once again saw movement—the cow stretching its neck and raising its muzzle at being impaled—before hearing the cow's sound, a sad trumpet on this empty-stage, frost-chilled April morning. Bear exited his truck and crossed the fence.

More than a fence was crossed of course. To enter that pasture was one of those decisions fat with fate, leading to mayhem. But even if he'd known it at the time, Bear still would've crossed that fence: he was a dangerously uncomplicated man; on occasion he was inevitable.

When they saw him coming, Bear counting steps, Scrudde handed the pitchfork to the taller man, who turned out to be Carl Coote, twenty-five years old and considered handsome by the women. Carl preferred you hold the final *e* silent when pronouncing his last name, but it was a campaign he had waged without success from first grade on. Carl was called Cootie. He worked for Scrudde because no one else would have him, Carl known as a thief and fistfighter. Word was he wanted to be a rock star, though how he hoped to accomplish this, here in Appalachia, was anyone's guess.

"Hello there, Bear," Scrudde said with a smile like false dawn. "You're just the man we need." Scrudde had a problem with the pronunciation of his last name, too. He wanted you to call him "Scrud," rhymes with *Hud* and sounds tough, but people who did business with him pronounced it "Screwed," as in *I have been . . .* He was a sneaky little man, age fifty-six, who had acquired a fortune through deceit—cheating widows, for example. He seldom attacked directly but was relentless on the back end of a deal, stabbing you with a lawyer if it came to that. In his younger days he'd been notorious as a dog-poisoner.

"Unless we get this cow to stand," Scrudde continued in that falsely jaunty voice, "she'll die for sure. Now, everybody knows Bear has a way with animals. *You* get her on her feet for us, what do you say?"

Bear looked down at the cow's rump and counted a dozen puncture wounds oozing thick dark blood. Bear counted things; he was also a name-giver.

"I'll get her up," Coote announced. He wore black jeans and a black cowboy shirt and an open letter-jacket from high school. At his skinny neck you could see the tops of chest tattoos. Coote stuck the cow with two short jabs of the pitchfork, adding six additional puncture wounds and eliciting from the creature another pained bellow.

Bear reached over and took the pitchfork from Coote, who started to protest but was interrupted by Scrudde telling Bear this was all the cow's fault. "No use trying to doctor 'em, Bear, unless you get 'em to stand first, you know that. This one's being contrary." Scrudde wore lizard cowboy boots, wool pants so thick they looked inflated, a denim jacket, and a white cowboy hat. All the other farmers around here called themselves farmers but Scrudde said he was a rancher.

"Gimme that fork back," Coote demanded.

Bear didn't.

As Coote weighed the issue, his tongue squeezed together until it was real fat and then the tip came out between his lips—a lifelong tic. He was thin but ropy strong, long redneck hair greasy over the shirt collar, his face cut on angles and planes that caught light and cast shadows. Sometimes he played electric guitar with a garage band, more loud than good. Coote practiced sticking out his tongue onstage. He had eyes sleepy with luxury lashes and the lids halfway down, what the women called bedroom eyes, but many men took as insolence. In fact, those eyes and what he did with his tongue made some men want to slap his face on principle, which is what had turned the boy into a fistfighter.

Scrudde, seeing the two men weren't going to engage, at least not just yet, mocked the peacemaker by saying what's important here is not our petty differences, what's important here is saving this poor cow, God's creature. "Bear, can't you get her to stand? That'll save her life, you know it will, give me your opinion."

There was truth to it, a sick cow that's down and won't get up will surrender on the whole idea of living and before you can do any good with food or water or medication, first you got to get that cow on her feet.

Bear, still holding the pitchfork out of Coote's reach, bent to this particular cow, black with a white face, a cross between an Angus bull and a Hereford cow. She was old and had suffered a winter of low-quality hay and no supplemental grain, Scrudde squeezing a few cents more out of each pound of his cattle's flesh. This one was also in severe dehydration owing to the lateness of spring rains. With only a few pools of mud-fouled water in the creeks, cows didn't drink as much as they should. Bear knew that if you cut open this cow right now you'd find bushel baskets of crumbly dry feces blocking her bowels. New green grass could save her, could liquefy and clean her bowels, but it was April and the spring grass hadn't come in earnest yet.

"What'da you say, Bear?" Scrudde urged.

"Shoot her," was what Bear finally said . . . which surprised the other two because Bear seldom spoke. If you knew this, then pressing him to speak, as Scrudde had been doing, became a form of ridicule.

"Shoot her?" Scrudde took off his cowboy hat, used the inside of his forearm to wipe at his high white forehead, then replaced the hat. "That's fine advice coming from a animal-lover like you." This was not meant as a compliment. "Get her on her feet, she'll be fine."

Bear shook his head because sometimes a failure to stand is not a matter of lethargy or contrariness, sometimes the cow is all but dead but simply won't die, which was the case with this one.

"You wanna buy her?" Scrudde asked. "Everything I own is for sale at the right price, so if you want to buy this cow and save her your own way, let's dicker."

"Shoot her," Bear repeated. Shoot this cow and put her out of misery's reach. Bear had a revolver in his truck, Scrudde undoubtedly had one in that Cadillac there. Just shoot her.

"Company," Coote said.

Bear and Scrudde looked toward the road where another vehicle, an old green Chevy Nova, was parked facing Bear's truck. A woman had crossed the same fence as Bear and was heading toward the three men at a measured pace, almost as if she, like Bear, counted her steps.

❦

At eight-thirty that morning, precisely the time Bear first stopped his truck to see what the men were doing with the cow, Katherine Renault had been awakened by a phone call.

"Hi, hope I didn't wake you."

"Who is this?"

"Don't you know? It's Barbara."

Barbara? Katherine had been living in this small town for five months and still wasn't accustomed to the reality that everyone knew her, the expectation that she should know everyone. Who was Barbara? Must be one of the women from the library.

"I did wake you, didn't I?"

Katherine looked at the bedside clock and lied, saying she'd been awake for hours. "What's up?"

Barbara drove a school bus and this morning had seen something nasty, two men sticking a cow with a pitchfork. She told Katherine where, exactly, on the bus route this had happened and said she hoped Katherine would go out there and make the men stop, it was a terrible thing to see.

"How can I make them stop?" Katherine asked, sitting up, wide awake now.

"At the library you were talking about rescuing animals."

"I meant strays, abandoned animals."

"Well that cow needs rescuing more than any stray, those men sticking it with a pitchfork."

Katherine asked why the men would be doing something like that.

Barbara said she didn't know and suggested Katherine go there and find out.

"Can you come with me?"

The woman said no, sorry, she was due back home to make breakfast for her husband. "This is more up your alley," she said. "You know, one of them rescue missions you were talking about."

Katherine started to explain again that she didn't mean rescuing animals from their owners, she meant rescuing strays and putting them up for adoption, but Barbara was already saying good-bye, hope you're able to do some good and save that cow, gotta go, I did my duty by telling you.

It was last year at Thanksgiving that Katherine Renault came here, moved into a little furnished cottage owned by her fiancé. He was always apologizing for owning property in the heart of Appalachia, explaining that he had inherited it from an uncle and decided to keep it as a vacation place, fix it up, diversifying his property portfolio. After Katherine's illness, after the operation, after she got out of the hospital, when she started going crazy because all her friends were so constantly *there,* doing what friends are supposed to do, offering advice and comfort and company, what Katherine most wanted in the world was some time alone. So her fiancé offered his little hillbilly cottage, as he called it, and Katherine came here intending to stay a few weeks. It had been five months.

Here, people left her alone. Katherine was the one who finally made contact after going stir-crazy, too much TV. She started taking walks around town, seeing notices about meetings at the library: book groups, civic improvement, self-esteem, weight loss. It was at one of the library meetings, attended by women and a few old men, that Katherine mentioned rescuing stray animals. For the last eight years she'd worked as a lobbyist in Washington, D.C., representing nonprofit fund-raising organizations, but before that, back when she got out of college, Katherine had volunteered with groups like Greenpeace and PETA—People for the Ethical Treatment of Animals. A person would have to be careful about mentioning animal rights here, Katherine thought—here in Appalachian farm country where animals are considered personal property, where violence is commonplace and farmers go armed in their fields. Katherine was interested in finding homes for strays, nothing more than that; she was here only temporarily, would be going back to D.C. soon and getting married.

She got out of bed, washed, dressed, and wondered how to approach men who were torturing a cow, what to say to them. Back in D.C., in Katherine's circles, a woman could say something wiseass or provocative to a man, he'd laugh and think the woman was great fun. But not here. Katherine had seen how men here reacted when a woman was smart-alecky, acted flippant or defiant; men would get their backs up and give the woman a bad look under bristly eyes that warned her, you'd better watch your mouth.

Katherine didn't want any part of that throwback behavior. She was here to recover, recuperate, then go home.

Heating water for tea, Katherine watched the two parrots she was caring for as they sidestepped back and forth the lengths of their perches. Outside in the fenced yard, eight dogs were awakening, stretching, walking the perimeter. All these animals had come to her in the past month, since she opened her big mouth at the library about rescuing strays.

The kettle whistled and Katherine thought, *damn.*

❦

"Hell's bells," Scrudde muttered as he watched Katherine approach.

"Katherine *Reee-no,*" Coote said, faking the French and sticking out that fat tongue-tip.

The other two apparently knew her but Bear had never seen the woman before: hovering around thirty, average height, thin and straight, with thick red hair cut short, wide mouth, green eyes, and freckles; she looked a little scared and she wore an oversized corduroy coat and boots too big, an outfit that appeared to have been borrowed from a larger brother.

When Katherine reached the men she didn't know what to say; she had no authority here and it wasn't in her nature to berate people, yet when she saw the cow, suffering and bleeding, her face went red with anger. She looked now at Bear, holding the fork, and told him softly, "You should be ashamed of yourself."

He was appalled that she thought *he* was the one who put puncture holes in that cow. Bear wanted to explain. He's got the pitchfork because he'd taken it away from Coote. But Bear said nothing. He had three problems in life and one of them was happening right now: his mind in a muddle when emotions ran high and an explanation was needed.

Scrudde grinned that Bear was being falsely accused, but Coote, lacking Scrudde's instinct for the devious, came out and told Katie, "Bear's a big animal-lover like you, he was trying to stop us, is why he's got the fork."

Bear thought, thank you, Cootie, thank you for telling the truth.

Katherine was glad to hear it. She liked the looks of the big man, over six feet and over two hundred pounds but appearing to take up even more space than that because his shoulders were ax-handle broad and his chest barrel deep, neck thick and hands like big mitts made for a shovel. He had a wide, high-cheeked face that was lovely and open and round and innocent, soft blue eyes, a trimmed black goatee, and long black hair that he combed straight back and tied with a string. Unusual for a country man around here, he didn't wear an ounce of denim, neither jeans nor jacket, but instead had on a pair of worn gray dress pants, an old tweed jacket. He looked like he could've been an eccentric professor or funky jazz musician, maybe even an oversized poet. Katherine figured him at about her age or maybe a little older. She had a soft spot for oddballs; it was too bad this one stood there with his mouth hanging open because it made him appear moronic. (This was the second of Bear's three problems: forgetting to close his mouth.)

"My name is Katherine Renault," she said to Bear. "Kate."

Coote asked her, "Who told you we was out here, *Kate?* It was that school bus driver, wasn't it. I saw her slowing down when she went by."

"I'd rather not say—"

Coote cut in, "It's all you women hanging out at that library, trying to cook up things to do with your time 'cause you ain't got to work or nothing." He let the wet tip of his tongue show and said, "I know about you women."

"What?"

Coote held two fingers, V for victory, to his mouth and obscenely worked that tongue in and out between those fingers.

Scrudde laughed.

Bear didn't get it.

Katherine was unsettled and remembered that she'd read once about tribal women who would, upon hearing the enemy approach, hurry down to water's edge and gather up sand and work it into their vaginas, packing themselves against the prospect of rape. It was said that when *white* soldiers came, the women learned to pack themselves front and back. Now Katherine thought that here in this hard country, maybe everywhere in the world, if a woman has to go out alone among men, she should start every day with sand.

She knew Scrudde and Coote, knew them from what the women at the library told her. Scrudde cheated people and mistreated his animals; he raised veal calves in the worst possible conditions. Coote beat up women and was capable of dragging Katherine back into the woods where they wouldn't be seen from the road, and Scrudde wouldn't try to stop him, Scrudde would be happy to watch. But Katherine didn't know the big man with the pitchfork, where he fit on the spectrum of what men will and won't do to a woman, and she turned to him now and asked his name.

Bear couldn't find a voice.

"He's Bear," Scrudde told her.

"Bear?" She stayed riveted on him. "Is that your last name?"

Coote laughed. "Bear's his nickname 'cause he shuffles like a big ol' bear, ain't that right, Bear?"

Bear didn't answer.

"Lives in that farm up the road there," Coote continued.

Katherine finally stopped looking at Bear and turned toward the younger man. "You're the one they call Cootie."

"Coot," he corrected her. "Carl *Coot.*"

"I don't mean to interfere where it's not my business, but can you just tell me what's happening here, why this animal is being stuck with a pitchfork?"

Coote, disarmed by her soft manner, nodded toward Scrudde and said, "His cow."

All grease and grin, Scrudde told her, "We're trying to *save* this animal. She won't live unless she stands and she won't stand unless we force her to. If you knew anything about cows, you'd know that."

Before Katherine could reply, Coote said he knew a guaranteed way to get the cow to stand up. He went around gathering twigs and dry sticks. Oddly, perversely, he was doing this to impress the woman.

She didn't know what Coote intended but Bear did. He'd raised beef cattle all his life. On occasion he had forced cows to stand by shouting at them, pulling on their tails, kicking them in the ass. But stabbing them with a pitchfork was wrong and what Coote did now was even worse: lifting the cow's tail and piling kindling right there at her tender vulva, then leaning down with a butane lighter.

Watching Coote, the other three waited as the air around them acquired shoulders, tensed up for what might happen next.

"Hey, Bear," Coote asked as he took out a generic cigarette, lit it, then returned the butane flame to that pile of sticks, "you smoke?"

Bear didn't answer.

"Well, this cow don't know it but she's about to *start* smoking." He held the flame to the sticks until they ignited.

Katherine couldn't believe it, the cruelty of it. She stepped forward to put the flames out but was grabbed around the waist by Scrudde.

Then it was Bear who kicked away the fire.

And time got up on a bicycle.

Katherine held down on Scrudde's wrists to keep him away from her chest.

Coote cursed as he stood, throwing the cigarette from his mouth and making fists of both hands.

Scrudde waited there behind Katherine, excitement glistening in his eyes, he wanted to see a fight and sneak a feel when the woman struggled. But fists didn't get thrown and Katherine didn't struggle except to keep her hands firmly on Scrudde's wrists. He released her and said to the two men, squared off, "Now boys."

Coote cursed some more, then regathered the sticks and twigs, repiling them beneath the cow's tail, reigniting the tinder.

"Both of you," Scrudde said to Bear and Katherine as he positioned himself to keep them away from what Coote was doing to the downed animal, "this ain't your cow and this ain't your land."

For Bear it was a powerful argument here where men worshiped at the altar of private property.

But Katherine, recognizing a higher authority, asked Bear, "Are you going to let this happen?"

He threw down the pitchfork.

"If a little heat will cause this cow to stand," Scrudde continued in that oily voice he used when reading at church on Sundays and Wednesdays, "well, then, that's just a way of saving her life, any reasonable person would see it that way."

Coote was leaning over and blowing on the fire, burning quickly with everything so dry this time of year. "Smells like barbecue!" he shouted, standing with Scrudde to block interference.

These are black-hearted men, Bear thought, that's what Robert would call them. Robert was Bear's beloved older brother, and he had a way with words. Their father used to say Bear was born with the bulk, Robert with the brains. Robert got all A's in school and had so many girlfriends you couldn't keep track of them without a scorecard, also something their father used to say. Robert was normal size. Bear started as a big baby and kept on growing, reaching six feet and two hundred pounds barely into his teens. It was because this growth embarrassed him that he started to hunch his shoulders and walk with a lumbering gait, giving rise to his nickname, which in later years he didn't regret because it was a good name for someone bred by the forest's *barely people.*

The third of his three problems (along with his mind getting in a muddle at critical times and that propensity for mouth breathing) was inappropriate behavior, but whether Bear was officially retarded was a topic of some debate in the local town of Briars. He had dropped out of school when it was legal, age sixteen. He went to work full-time on the farm, just him and his father because the mother had run off years and years ago and then Robert left as soon as he could too, went to Chicago and got himself a big job.

The flames were terrible now, Coote adding fresh fuel. All

four people could smell the flesh cooking and so could the suffering cow. Although her anal-genital area was being burned alive, she was still too weak to stand and could only endure, stretching her neck, moaning pitifully like a trombone played in hell, rolling her eyes to white, enduring this horror because that's all she could do, endure.

Even during the worst parts of her illness, the horrors of the operation, Katherine had stayed in control of her emotions, but now, as she watched that cow being burned alive, she went a little crazy and shouted for Coote and Scrudde to stop, please stop burning that poor animal, then she pleaded for Bear to do something.

Which he did, shoving the men aside and kicking out the fire.

Coote came around and got in a sucker punch. Bear grabbed him by the throat.

"Retard!" was all Coote managed to say before Bear squeezed, choking off further insult as Coote's tongue emerged in earnest now.

When Scrudde picked up the pitchfork and stabbed, Bear grabbed *him* by the neck and lifted both men off the ground, one in each hand, suspending them in death grips.

Time rode faster as Katherine watched wide-eyed. She considered herself equal to most men she'd met, perhaps their better in perception, in endurance, empathy, but she yielded to males in this one category: violence. Her roommate in college had a boyfriend who, in Katherine's presence, struck the roommate in the face with his fist—which stunned Katherine who'd been raised in a gentle family and had never seen violence up close. Several times in the five months she'd lived here, Katherine had witnessed local men striking their wives or children in public. It was scary the way a man could transform from what appeared to be a normal father and husband into something so terribly ready to kill.

This man here, this Bear, blue eyes no longer soft, he clearly intended homicide. Lowering his victims to the ground to get better grips on their throats, he shook them and shook them, his hands like two terriers, Scrudde and Coote the rats. Both men tried desperately to escape Bear's grip as their faces turned a terrible purple and they voided their bladders, bulged their eyes.

I have to do something, Katherine thought, though she was already stepping backwards to put distance between herself and this man who was committing murder.

"They're not worth it," she said softly, retracing steps to place a gentle hand on Bear's left arm, the one he was using to power that choke hold on Phil Scrudde. (Katherine felt something amazing when she touched Bear: the big man was actually vibrating.)

As if coming out of a trance, Bear dropped them in a gasping heap, Scrudde atop Coote, then reached into his front left pocket and took out an immense folding knife, ten inches when open. *"No,"* she said softly, Scrudde and Coote untangling from each other to shrink back in mortal fear.

Bear went around to the cow. Before slitting the animal's throat, he looked up at Katherine wanting to explain what he was doing, why he had to do it, but she already understood and nodded for him to go ahead.

When he made puncture-slits in two places on the neck, the cow jolted each time as if Bear's blade was connected to electricity. But it would take her another minute or so to die. Unlike horses and sheep, which are always rushing toward mortality, cows seem to get right up to the edge and then refuse to go over no matter the size of their suffering or the unlikeliness of their prospects.

While the cow was thus dying, Bear stood guard to make sure no more fires got started. Scrudde and Coote were on their feet, voices raw as Coote cursed Bear with terrible words and Scrudde called Bear a clay-eater.

Bear looked to the woman to see if she'd heard that slander, but the only thing on her freckled face was anguish for an animal's suffering.

He knelt down to see if it was over yet, covering the cow's closed eye with his hand, then pulling back her eyelid. That big brown eye fixed Bear and, just before dipping into oblivion, the cow told him, *God bless you* . . . and time stopped.

2

Katherine and Bear walked together out of the pasture and crossed the fence. He held the wire for her and then they didn't know what to do with each other as they stood between their vehicles. Meaning to thank him, to apologize for whatever role she had played in this morning's trouble, Katherine took Bear's right hand and rose up on her toes to kiss him on the cheek. But Bear didn't get her intention and stood out of reach like a statue. Finally she made a self-conscious murmur. He raised his eyebrows: *What?* Turning red, thinking this shouldn't be this difficult, she whispered, "Bend down." He did and Katherine kissed him on the cheek while still holding his hand, kneading it in hers, telling him, "You were magnificent." He smelled clean.

Bear stayed bending down, fighting an urge to embrace her. He was so desperate for human touch that when getting a haircut he would try to lean against the barber's hands—until the guy told him to stop doing that, it was creepy. Bear was so embarrassed that he let his hair grow long, tying it in the back.

Katherine released his hand and made gestures—*up, up*—encouraging Bear to stand upright again. She was a little scared of him still, especially when he acted weird like this.

His hanging-open mouth seemed about to say something, ask her a question, but nothing came out.

Katherine had been surprised, while kissing his cheek, to feel that he was still vibrating. She'd assumed that his trembling had come from the way he'd been choking those two men, yet now here he was standing peacefully next to her, still vibrating like his chest cavity contained a large wobbly machine.

"I'm sorry if I got you in trouble with your friends," she said.

Bear didn't answer, didn't say what was on his mind, they're no friends of mine.

Katherine thought, he's better as a verb.

Then once again she told Bear, "You were magnificent."

"Katie," he said.

"What?"

Bear nodded, meaning that's the name he was giving her. Not Katherine or Kate but *Katie.*

"Did you want to say something?" she asked.

When he still didn't reply, she got into her old green car and drove home to the little cottage owned by her fiancé.

ॐ

Katherine had been engaged to marry William Trent for more than two years and though all their friends called them the perfect couple, neither Katherine nor William was in a hurry to wed. With William you got the idea he was keeping his options open, maybe someone even prettier than Katherine might come along, someone younger, with a more prestigious career. This makes him sound cold-blooded, and at times that was so, but then again William was tall and good-looking and perfectly in shape, plus he had a great job working with overseas investors *and* he was moderately wealthy from family inheritances. Katherine's hesitancy about marriage arose from the old myth that you should be crazy in love with the guy you're marrying, not just compatible with him, as Katherine was with William . . . so maybe she was keeping her options open, too, waiting for that old black magic. Meanwhile, the illness and operation had intervened, and now Katherine was recuperating here at his cottage in the heart of Appalachia.

Almost all the men she knew back in D.C. were like William: They dressed nicely, were well versed in wines, kept in shape, didn't smoke, didn't drink to excess, invested wisely, and were surprisingly free of demons. William had decorated his cottage to make it look English by way of Martha Stewart, all bright prints and colorful rooms, sunlit windows, vines and trellises outside, winding flagstone paths through flower gardens (which unfortunately had been trashed by the eight dogs that Katherine was caring for until they could be adopted).

Coming home to those dogs was like arriving by limousine, and when Katherine got out of the Nova to greet them, she felt like waving. Sorry, William, she thought, seeing the new holes that had been dug. She opened the gate, swarmed by her fans, the dogs wagging and barking and spinning in circles, eager for Katherine's attention and happy for her smell. They were a battered crew with injured legs and ears and tails and eyes, one little white Jack Russell completely blind but managing quite well now that he'd sniffed out the yard's particulars.

Katherine bent down to accept their attention and thought she'd like to see that man again whose only word to her was *Katie.*

3

When Bear got back to his farm, he stopped the old Ford pickup in a skid. After shutting off the engine, he stared through the windshield as if waiting for a train to pass.

Also waiting, sitting outside near the driver's door and looking up at the closed window where they could see but not smell Bear, were his two German shepherds.

That cow talked to me, Bear said to himself. As his mind tried to outstare the impossibility of it, Bear recalled another miracle, how the woman took his hand and reached up and kissed him on the cheek, said he was *magnificent* . . . kept squeezing his hand and called him magnificent again. This must be how Robert feels all the time, Bear thought, being made much of by women.

Still sitting in the truck, Bear realized his mouth was open and wondered if it had been hanging open the entire time he was with her. All Bear's life, his father would tell him, "Shut your mouth, retard." Bear's mother, before she ran off, would tell him, too, though she did it more nicely: "Close your mouth, you'll catch flies." Even his brother Robert would occasionally remind him to shut his mouth. When he was reading of an evening, Bear would sometimes embarrass himself when a line of drool dropped onto the page.

Why can't I keep my g-d mouth closed?

Outside, his two dogs whined and barked. He'd always gotten out of the truck before, why wasn't he getting out now?

When he finally climbed down from the cab, both dogs sniffed anxiously at his pants. Bear saw a thick stain of blood high on his right leg. At first he thought it was the cow's, then realized he was bleeding from a hole in his leg. Scrudde must've stuck him with that pitchfork.

I didn't even feel it, Bear thought. So much was going on. A cow said something to me, a woman kissed me and called me magnificent twice. (Bear knew what the word meant but intended to look it up tonight and roll in the details.)

He started for the farmhouse making his way through a receiving line of ducks and dogs and chickens and cats, counting them as he went, the cats staying up out of the way on porch railings and reaching for Bear with friendly paws as he passed. Not letting any of the animals into the kitchen with him, Bear could feel the leg wound vividly and dropped his pants to look more closely: eight inches above his right knee, in heavy thigh meat, a hole oozed blood exactly the way those puncture wounds on the cow had. He shuffled over to the gas stove, lit a burner, kicked off his pants. He was trembling.

Bear had never been with a woman, had never in his thirty-two years been kissed with passion upon the mouth, had never made love. How you can go thirty-two years so bereft, you'd have to live his life to find out.

In the back room he found a coil of electrical cable and ripped loose a bare ground-wire, which he then snipped off with a pair of pliers kept on the water heater. He took this eighteen-inch length of twelve-gauge copper wire back into the kitchen, wrapped one end around a big wooden spoon, and held the free end over that propane flame.

The copper heated quickly to a glow, Bear sitting on a kitchen chair he'd dragged to the stove. Holding the spoon end, he kept the wire in the fire, using the thumb and forefinger of the other hand to spread his puncture wound, a neat round hole filled with rich red blood. He quivered until the chair could barely contain him.

When Bear was growing up, his father would inflict pain with games the old man called oogies and Dutch rubs, Indian burns and charley horses, six-inch pokes and "megahurts." Here's how megahurts worked: After grabbing a tender spot such as Bear's inner thigh or the upper part of his arm, his father would squeeze with increasing pressure as he counted off megahurts and challenged Bear to take as many as he could—one megahurt, two megahurts, three megahurts. The deal was, his father would stop when the boy cried uncle. Try as he might, steeling himself against the pain, Bear as a little boy could seldom endure more than five or six megahurts. And now he wondered how many megahurts it might count to plunge a glowing wire into your own wounded flesh.

Part of this was to cauterize the wound against infection and part of it was to shock himself out of vibrating. Bear didn't want to be hauled away in a straitjacket.

For as long as he could remember, he had feared insanity, that it could happen any time and without warning, the way fat men fear a second heart attack, and now here it was: *A cow talked to me, I've gone crazy.* He felt tight in the chest and short of breath. Years ago a neighbor woman tried to serve hay to her husband and two sons for dinner; eventually she was taken away in an actual straitjacket, her open mouth drooling, her wild eyes rolling. Bear remembered it vividly, though he never gave a name to the woman and thought of her only as the Woman Who Fed Hay to Her Family. Bear's father was always predicting Bear would end up the same way, carted off to the loony bin. Even beloved brother Robert wasn't above using the Woman Who Fed Hay to Her Family as a warning whenever Bear acted inappropriately. ("Inappropriate behavior," as the term for one of Bear's three problems, came from comments teachers used to write on his report card: "Occasionally Joseph engages in inappropriate behavior." "What the hell does that mean?" his father would ask before the beating. Bear admitted that sometimes he would hug little girls in the playground and keep hugging them even after they hollered to be let go—in fact, sometimes a teacher would have to come over and pry Bear's arms apart—and also he would get up in the middle of class for no reason at all and do a little shuffle dance, pirouetting with both hands in the air, pretending to tap, provoking the other kids to hysterical laughter as the bewildered teacher shouted for order.)

How did Scrudde know to call me a clay-eater? Bear wondered. Dad must've said something to him. Maybe everyone in town knows, though apparently the woman, Katie, new to town, hasn't heard the gossip or else she wouldn't have squeezed my hand, kissed my face, called me magnificent twice—those were not things you did to a clay-eater.

"Clay-eater," Bear murmured with self-disgust as he took the wire from the fire and held the glowing end just above the puncture wound. *Keep your mouth closed you damn old clay-eating retard.* When wire touched wound, there was a quick sizzle followed by the smoke-smell of meat burning, reminiscent of Coote burning that cow. Bear pushed so hard that the jagged end of the wire plunged through the bottom of the puncture wound and gouged its own channel another inch deeper. Pain bloomed, radiating from his leg, causing Bear to tremble all the more, to resonate. He jerked the wire out and threw it, spoon and all, across the room and held his leg—*on fire!*—with both hands. Dishes in the cupboards rattled and, outside, dogs barked.

4

Sitting in the Cadillac still parked in the pasture next to that throat-cut cow, now at peace, Scrudde and Coote sucked at revenge, passing its possibilities back and forth like two drunks with a bottle of Everclear. Coote suggested Scrudde could hold a gun on Bear while he, Coote, broke Bear's legs with a shovel or sledgehammer, whatever Scrudde had in the trunk of this Cadillac. "Or we could poison his dogs, Bear dotes on those two police dogs of his."

The prospect of poisoning dogs again after all these years made Scrudde go all syrupy. But he had a better—that is, more destructive—idea. "Burn his barn."

Coote liked that one right away. "I'll do it tonight."

Scrudde shook his head. "We're near at the end of the hay season, Bear's barn'll be all but empty. You'll hurt him the more if you do it when his barn is full up again, burn the barn *and* the hay."

"You mean wait 'til *summer*?"

"No I mean wait until next fall or better yet winter, the price of hay'll be at its highest and if Bear wants to replace hay and rebuild his barn, he'll have to go into debt. It's cancer for a ragtag operation like his, debt is. He'll have to sell his cattle, maybe lose the farm."

Coote took out one of his generic cigarettes. "I won't even still be mad at him come next winter."

"I will." Like a troll under a bridge, Scrudde was willing to wait. When Coote flashed his lighter, Scrudde told him, "Don't smoke in here."

Coote stuck out his tongue tip and lit the cigarette anyway.

The older man powered down his window. Employing Coote

was like owning a vicious, untrustworthy dog that you could sic on others to great effect though he might just as likely take a bite out of your own sweet ass.

"Made me piss my pants," Coote said guilelessly, holding the cigarette in his mouth so he could use both hands to pull the sticky jeans away from his legs.

While being choked, Scrudde had fouled himself, too, but the stain didn't show through his thick wool pants and he wasn't admitting to it, occupying his mind with speculation that if Bear went bankrupt after a barn burning and had to sell his farm, Scrudde could buy it at public auction or, even better, make a low-ball offer to Bear before the auction. Then Scrudde could add Bear's 320 acres to his own farm (the properties adjoined) and hire Bear for four dollars an hour to work cattle, because, weird as that clay-eating retard might be, he had a genius for animals.

" . . . mistake of birth," Coote was saying.

"What?"

"Bear."

"Oh Lord yes," Scrudde agreed, nodding somberly. "A throwback, an abomination, a freak of nature, and a danger to others. He should be institutionalized, he could've killed us both; you burning his barn down next winter would be a community service."

"Except if he's so dumb, how come everybody brags on his cattle? Exactly what kind of retard is he?"

"Clay-eater."

"Say what?" Coote asked.

"He was fathered by one of the *barely people.* Please throw that cigarette away."

Coote lowered his window and tossed out the cigarette, then turned to his employer. "The who?"

"What the rumor is," Scrudde said, "Bear's mother got herself knocked up by one of the *barely people* and—"

"The who?"

"You know about the *barely people* live around here?"

Coote shook his head.

"Good Lord," Scrudde said. "You youngsters don't learn nothing about your heritage or surroundings, sit in front of the damn television and—"

"Hey turn on the heat will you, freezing in here."

Scrudde started the Cadillac. "*Barely people* are like what you'd call a tribe. They live back in the hills and mountains around here, so far back no roads go there and it ain't even been timbered and these *barely people* aren't on no government rolls, the kids don't go to school, no marriage ceremonies or families as we know them, they all live together in caves and trees and breed *indiscriminately.*" Scrudde waited to see if that word registered, then continued, "And they're so inbred and so"—Scrudde searched for the right words—"so *before the flood,* that they go backwards on the scale of civilization, primitive and hairy, rumored that a few of them have tails, little remnant ones. I saw a dead body once when I was a kid but it was decayed and coulda been what was left of a black bear."

"You going to turn on the heater or not?"

Scrudde slid the lever over to hot and flipped the fan on full blast, the sudden warm air causing smells to swirl about the car's interior, cow shit and blood and drying urine. "You never even heard of the *barely people*?" he asked Coote. "Your family's lived here for generations and nobody's ever told you about—"

"Sounds like bullshit to me."

"Your ignorance is—"

"My what?"

"I don't blame you for what you ain't been told but it's a crying shame all this is being lost, our heritage."

"Backward people living out in the woods and screwing each other, got tails, and you're saying Bear's old lady got knocked up by one of them."

"It's the clay eating gives Bear away."

Coote shook his head, he was weary of this topic.

"The *barely people* lack certain nutrients and they develop a craving for clay and if you go far enough back in the woods where there's no roads or trails, you'll come across clay deposits that have been fingernailed out by *barely people,* who eat little bits of the clay to get those missing nutrients and minerals."

"If you say so."

"Sometimes traders from the city make contact with them and bargain mirrors and knives for forest products the *barely people* collect, ferns and moss, lizards for bait, and—"

"Let's go to the café for breakfast, I'm starving."

"The way Bear's mother attracted one, she laid out in the woods after midnight stripped naked from the waist down under a waxing moon for six nights running, that's the tradition if you want to attract a *barely people* male to father your child."

Coote laughed. This was the kind of bullshit he heard from older relatives, rumors and myths involving moons waxing and waning.

"That male will sniff out the woman," Scrudde said, "and come to her from downwind."

Laughing again, Coote asked, "Why would any woman want to get knocked up by some old throwback who's got a tail?"

"Sometimes it's because the woman's husband's got something wrong and can't get her in a family way or sometimes the woman is just strange and wants to be bred by an exotic—you know how women are that way, attracted to the exotic."

"Like rock stars."

"I was thinking more along the lines of Siamese twins or professional basketball players."

Coote's tongue went fat in his mouth, then the pink tip showed between his lips as he considered something. He asked Scrudde, "What do you know about that woman, little Miss Katrina *Reee-no?*"

"She's staying in that cutesy-pie bungalow at the edge of town, people tell me it's her fiancé's but I always thought it was a three-dollar bill that owned that place. Don't know what she's doing here, must be rich, 'cause she don't work."

"Maybe I'll pay her a visit some night at that cutesy-pie bungalow."

"Really?"

"For what those two done to me today . . ." Coote touched his neck, which was vividly marked, thumbprint and finger bruises. "Bear gets his barn burned down to the ground—"

"Next winter when it's full of hay."

"—and that library bunny-hugger gets a midnight visit she won't forget."

Scrudde asked what Coote meant.

"You know." The younger man smiled, taking out a cigarette and pushing in the dashboard lighter.

"Tell me what you'd do to her, you got the chance."

Coote said, "Come on, buy us breakfast."

"Wait a second, have you ever, you know . . ." Scrudde didn't want to say *raped.* "Have you ever taken a woman against her will?"

The kid smirked. "You come along with me when I go visit that Miss High 'n' Mighty, see for yourself what I do to her."

"Mmm, I don't think . . . mmm, maybe."

"Help yourself to sloppy seconds."

"Oh, I couldn't do that!" Scrudde was grinning, his eyes were wet. "I'm a Christian."

"You like to watch though, don't you?"

"Oh golly . . ." Scrudde rubbed softly where Bear had choked him. "You think she'll struggle much?"

"You don't know the half of it."

The lighter clicked and Scrudde quickly pulled it out and held the trembling glow to the tip of Coote's cigarette. *"Tell me."*

5

That night Bear called his brother Robert to tell him about Katie Renault. *Ri-KNOW* was the way she pronounced her last name and Bear was the one who named her Katie. He planned to say: Guess what, Robert, she kissed me and called me magnificent twice, it means splendid and exalted and virtuous and grand. Bear had filled dozens of lined tablets with vocabulary. Although he read slowly with lips moving and blunt fingers following the text, once Bear finished a book or learned a word, he owned it.

Lifting the phone, carefully pressing numbers he knew by heart, Bear counted seconds while waiting excitedly for his brother's voice, then immediately said, "Hey Robert, guess what, it's your *little* brother Bear." It was one of their jokes. Bear might be younger than Robert by four years but he towered over him and outweighed him by about fifty pounds.

"Who?" Robert asked. This was another of their jokes, Robert pretending he didn't know who Bear was.

"It's me, your brother."

"My *brother.*"

Bear was smiling. "Come on, Robert, you know who this is, it's me, Bear."

"Oh, I thought you said it was my brother."

"It is."

"I have a brother who's a bear?"

"It's *Joey,*" Bear said, grinning widely now.

"Oh, hi, Bear."

"Hi, Robert, what's up?"

"The sun, the moon, the stars, prices."

I told you he had a way with words. Bear was still grinning. Sometimes after one of these talks with Robert, Bear's mouth would actually ache from the smiling.

"You got your cows on spring pasture?" Robert asked.

"Guess what, Robert, it's only April nineteen, no grass to speak of yet, you know that." Sometimes Robert showed a willful ignorance about the farm, as if he had blotted out all he once knew about pastures and cows and machinery. One time he told Bear he didn't even change his own oil, he took his cars to a place that did it in about five minutes while you waited in air-conditioning and read magazines.

"How come you didn't call collect like I told you?" Robert asked.

"Now, Robert. I got money for these calls, don't you worry. You have to save every penny to send your boys to college."

"Yeah, before you know it." Robert's two sons were thirteen and fifteen.

"I'm looking out the window at the old barn," Bear told Robert. It was the same window Robert and Bear had looked out of back when they were growing up in this house, sharing this bed. To the east of the farmhouse a gap in the surrounding hills allowed the moonrise, at certain times of the year, to illuminate the barn from behind. "Remember how we used to lay here and look out at that old barn, watch the moon come up over the top of the roof?"

"I didn't know you had a phone upstairs there in our old room."

"Oh sure." Bear must've told him a dozen times where the phone was.

"Are you're still sleeping in that little room?"

Bear said he was, thirty-two years, each and every night of his life in this room.

"You should've moved into the old man's bedroom, it's bigger and better heated."

"I don't want to sleep where he slept."

"I don't blame you," Robert said. "He was a sadistic bastard."

But that wasn't the reason Bear didn't stay in his father's room. It stunk, yellow in smell and stain from the old man's constant Lucky Strikes. Still, Bear missed him. The old man might've been a terror but at least when he was alive the house wasn't empty of an evening like it was now.

"Bear?"

"Yes, Robert."

"I gotta go."

Bear started trembling because he still hadn't told Robert about Katie. And if he tried to tell him now, Robert would get mad because he absolutely hated it when Bear tried to continue a conversation after Robert said it was time to go.

"Bear?" Robert said sternly.

"Okay, Robert . . . tell those boys of yours that their Uncle Bear said hello, and tell that pretty wife of yours I said hello, too."

"I will. One of these days I'm going to surprise you and bring them all to the farm."

"Oh Robert that would be the best thing ever."

"Don't know when though. Money's tight. All the things you gotta have for two boys, then with the wife spending like there's no tomorrow . . . You don't know how good you got it, Bear, no one but yourself to care for."

It's *you* who don't know how good you got it, Bear thought as he looked out the window. "Hey, Robert, is it the full moon tonight?"

"How the hell am I supposed to know, I live in Chicago."

"I don't think it's full until next week but right now that old moon's coming up behind the barn so bright and yellow you'd think it was the sun."

"I gotta go."

"Sorry, Robert, bye."

"Take care of yourself, bye."

Bear sat on the bed. Here's the part he hated: this abiding silence that always followed hanging up with Robert. He wanted to pick up the phone and call his brother back and say, I forgot to tell you about Katie. Bear used to do this, calling Robert back claiming there was something he forgot to tell him, making stuff up just to keep the conversation going, until Robert lost his patience and told Bear he had to stop. And Bear did. Whatever Robert said, went. If Robert told him to call only once every four years on leap year's February 29 between the hours of 7 and 8 P.M., Bear would mark it on calendars and count days until that old leap year came around. Whatever Robert said, went, because Bear didn't want to risk making Robert mad because never being able to talk to Robert again was easily more horrifying to Bear than the prospect of death.

He lay back on the bed. His hand and ear were sweaty from the phone. Now what, he wondered. Another long night. I should've told Robert about Katie right at the beginning. Using a finger, Bear worked and worked until he got under the bandage and found that puncture wound. When he stuck his fingertip in, the pain popped out so large and quick that for a moment Bear was unable to breathe.

Removing his hand from the bandage and waiting for the pain to subside, he thought maybe he'd just stay here and go to sleep, wouldn't bother washing his face or taking off his clothes or even saying his prayer, which every night was a variation on the same theme: "I'm ready, Lord."

He sat up to look out the window: that big yellow moon was so bright it made the old barn look like it was on fire.

6

The town's only restaurant, Briars Café, had been opened up at this predawn hour to serve men who had fought the big barn fire out at Bear's place. Bear sat at the head of a big table with twelve men, their teeth especially white and all their eyes unusually bright in contrast to their faces darkened by hay soot, which none of them had washed off because who wanted to be the only man there with a clean face? For the first time in his life, Bear was the center of attention, his face also blackened with soot. Unlike the other men, however, Bear had been injured, both of his hands so badly burned they looked cooked, cracked open like sausages.

The mood was hearty even though the barn hadn't been saved. Of the three hundred or so bales of hay only thirty bales were salvaged, those that Bear threw down from the loft before the volunteer firefighters talked him out of the barn so they could start spraying it with water from the five-hundred-gallon tank carried on their pumper—like peeing on a volcano, one of them admitted at the time. If each of those volunteer firefighters had climbed up to the loft and helped Bear, all the hay would've been saved, but they told Bear their first priority was keeping the fire from spreading. With the barn sitting out there by itself in a pasture you had to wonder where the fire might go. After squirting their little bit of water, the firefighters were content to stand around smoking cigarettes and drinking coffee and watching Bear's barn burn. *That's* the way they operated.

He didn't care. If it took a barn burning to put Bear at the center of all this attention, men telling stories about him throwing out hay bales with the whole world burning around him, others laughing on his behalf and pouring him coffee, Bear thinking this is how Robert, always popular with people, must feel, then let's burn a barn every night, was Bear's opinion.

Also swept away by tonight's bonhomie was Ronny Ward, the manager of Briars Café and a passionate volunteer firefighter. "I got something to say," he told the men. "This *sense of community* is what we've lost over the years." Ronny was one of those civic-duty men, volunteering for the Fourth of July committee and complaining there was nothing for the young people to do, nowhere for them to go, that's why they stood around smoking cigarettes, they needed a community center. "It's a crying shame," Ward continued, "that it takes a tragedy like a fire to bring us together." He felt stirred, as if this could be one of those great speeches you see in movies. But then Ward couldn't think of anything more to say and abruptly announced he was going to serve free breakfast.

The men cheered and raised their arms and praised Ward, though some among them would later note that the restaurant was owned by Ward's wife's parents and therefore Ronny Ward was like the politician extending a generosity that's coming out of someone else's pocket.

Ronny said that instead of taking individual orders he'd go into the kitchen and make bacon and eggs and pancakes and toast, then bring everything out on platters and people could take what they wanted. The men, even the cynics among them, cheered him again.

While Ward was in the kitchen, Bear listened closely as the firefighters talked among themselves. He had been to this café several times as a child—Robert used to take him—but seldom as an adult with his father, and after the old man died, Bear never came in here on his own. Driving by the restaurant, Bear would see men sitting, drinking coffee, talking. He wondered what in the world they could be saying to one another. Now he would find out.

They talked about barn fires they'd seen before or heard about or how they had a cousin who died in one up to New England somewheres, about how well the pumper worked tonight and also about its shortcomings, about trucks and beef prices . . . and then Katherine Renault came in.

Bright eyes in sooty faces followed her as she walked toward the table. She wore jeans and a bulky blue sweater. Yesterday morning out in that pasture she hadn't worn makeup, but tonight she had on red lipstick and green eye shadow and wore earrings painted bright yellow and red, hanging so far down they almost brushed her collarbone—they swung as she walked. It wasn't until she was standing next to him that Bear saw that the earrings were carvings of little parrots on perches. He had never seen anything like it. She had red hair. She had really big green eyes opened so wide you could see a lot of white around the green. Her nose was straight, her mouth large, and seeing so many freckles on her face was, to a natural-born counter like Bear, overwhelming. Where would you start and how would you keep track? Staring at Katherine's face flanked by those long colorful earrings, Bear felt like that time he went to a carnival at night and kept murmuring *wow* under his breath.

She put her hands on Bear's sooty face: he was vibrating again.

"Did any of your animals get hurt in the fire?"

He shook his head.

"How about you, Bear?" she asked, removing her hands from his face. "Did you get hurt?"

He didn't answer, but one of the volunteers volunteered that Bear was a hell of a firefighter tonight. "Throwing bales out of that barn, one in each hand, some of those bales already on fire, ol' Bear ignoring the flames."

"Hell of a thing to see," another agreed. "He's got grit."

Everyone waited to see where this was going.

"You got grit?" she asked him.

Bear held up his hands.

"Good God," Katherine gasped.

They were red and black and swollen and cracked open in bloody seams. More shocking than the condition of his hands was Bear's behavior. He held those hands aloft like prizes as he stood and turned, raising his knees high, then doing a little shuffle, grinning in a manner that all the men at that table would later describe the same way: *like a moron, grinning like a big moron.*

After the silent turning circle dance finished, Katherine told him: "We have to take care of your hands. I have a first aid kit out in the car."

"Breakfast is coming," he said, indicating the kitchen where frying could be smelled and sizzling could be heard.

"Your hands should be taken care of first. I really ought to drive you to the emergency room."

"Breakfast is coming," he repeated plaintively.

"I'll tell you what. Let's go out and see what's left of your barn, I'll wrap your hands, then make you breakfast."

He looked around at all the men, his mind in a muddle.

"Come on," she said, taking him by the upper arm.

They exited the café, and when they got out by Katherine's old green car she said, "You're *quivering.*"

Bear ignored this, he was concentrating on remembering to keep his mouth closed.

Katherine figured that Bear's barn got burned down because of what he did to those two men who were torturing that cow and she felt responsible to whatever extent her presence provoked the situation. "I really would like to help, if you'll let me . . . wrap your hands, come with you to see what's left of your barn . . . Is that all right?"

He nodded.

"I also have something to ask you," she said, opening the front passenger door and holding it for Bear.

She's going to ask me to marry her, Bear speculated wildly. And why not, times had become crazy. A cow talked to me, my barn burned to the ground, now she's going to ask me to marry her.

Katherine got in behind the steering wheel and sat a moment before turning to Bear. "Are you okay? Your hands burned like that, you could go into shock."

"I will," he announced.

"Pardon me?"

"What you were going to ask . . . I will."

"But you haven't heard the question yet."

"I will."

❦

Out at his farm, after Kate bandaged Bear's hands, she took a flashlight and walked to where the old barn was gone but still smoldering. The dogs went with her. Staying inside the house waiting until it was a decent hour to call his brother, Bear managed to delay gratification until 6 A.M., forgetting that would make it just 5 A.M. in Chicago.

"Hello?" Robert asked sleepily.

"Guess what, Robert."

"Bear?"

"Our barn burned down." He frequently used the plural possessive when referring to the farm and its properties and equipment, emphasizing that he still believed Robert had an ownership position, seeing as how their father had really left the farm to Robert.

"And guess what too," Bear said.

"The barn burned down?" Robert didn't sound completely awake.

"And guess what too!"

"Bear, are you okay?"

He was practically jumping up and down, insisting to his brother, *"And guess what too!"*

"What?"

"I met the most wonderful, *wonderful* woman in the whole wide world!"

"What?"

"And I'm going to help her rescue animals!" Bear shouted.

Robert got mad at all this 5 A.M. silliness and told his brother to calm down right this instant—stop talking nonsense or you'll end up carted off to the loony bin.

"Do you want that, to be carted off to the loony bin?" Robert asked, not waiting for an answer before asking another question: "Have you gone completely crazy?"

I don't want to be carted off to the loony bin, Bear thought, watching out the window as the sun came up where the barn used to be, seeing Kate walking there with his two dogs, but, in answer to Robert's other question, Bear thought, yes, apparently it's true, I've gone crazy. A cow said something to me right before it died and some woman claims I'm magnificent, so yes, Bear thought, yes, Robert, I guess it's true, I've gone completely crazy.

7

Later that same morning, arriving for his appointment to check one of Bear's cows, the old vet, Richard Setton, drove carefully past vehicles parked on both sides of the road, past sightseers gathered around the barn's smoldering ruins. Some people waved at him, but some turned their backs. At age eighty, Doc Setton should've retired a decade ago but was still looking, hoping, for someone to take over his practice. He tried modest recruiting efforts all over the country, but veterinarians didn't want to come here where you couldn't charge much for your services, had to travel long distances between clients, and were called out only when an animal was near death because people here preferred home remedies to vet care, no matter how cheap it was. For forty of the fifty years he'd practiced in this area, Setton was well liked—did his job and never lectured anyone about how they cared for their animals. But over the last ten years, he'd changed. Maybe it was getting old, feeling death nudging you, or maybe he'd simply seen too much cruelty in his life, but gradually over the last decade Setton had become an advocate for the humane treatment of animals. His position on this issue had grown increasingly strident until now he couldn't abide cruelty in any form to any animal. That didn't sit well with farmers. Setton's new attitude had a fractionalizing effect as his practice declined and seemed destined to go out of existence. A few locals, mostly townspeople and mostly women, welcomed his interventions on behalf of abused animals, but the majority thought him meddlesome and farmers demonized him.

Setton drove to the house and gingerly, creakily, got out of his truck. The vet was short, slim, and dapper; up until ten years ago he'd been spry, too, but he was feeling his age now. He bent painfully to greet Bear's two German shepherds, who were sitting together like matched statuary, the big male with a head like a grizzly bear's, the female much smaller, almost foxy looking. Other animals, cats and ducks and chickens and peahens, wandered the yard. Ever since his father died, Bear had opened his heart and farm to a growing nonprofit menagerie, which endeared Bear to Doc Setton even as neighboring farmers took this zoo as further evidence of retardation.

Katherine Renault walked out of the house, surprising Setton, who'd become friends with her from those library meetings where he tried to recruit volunteers to help him at various free clinics.

While still petting Bear's two dogs, POTUS and Jamaica, Doc Setton smiled at Katherine and said, "Well, look who's here."

"Hello, Mother Setton," Katherine replied pleasantly.

"That's supposed to be an insult," Doc said, straightening up with a wince. Some of the locals had started calling him "Mother" when the vet went soft on the treatment of animals.

"How in the world can calling someone *Mother* be an insult?" The old man started to explain but Katherine went on, "I meant it as a compliment."

"I know you did. What're you doing here, hon?" he asked.

"Bear burned his hands and I came over to bandage them." She turned as Bear emerged from his house with both hands wrapped in heavily padded bandages like thick white oven mitts.

"The man of the hour," Doc Setton said. "Son, I'm sorry about your barn."

Repeating his strange predawn performance in the café, Bea held his hands over his head and slowly turned in a circle, rai ing one leg, then the other—an odd, slow-motion parody c victory dance. Doc Setton and Katherine exchanged glance

Bear was freshly washed and shampooed, his long blac combed back but not tied. He wore dark gray trousers lowing white shirt, and a tweed jacket.

"I covered his hands with antibacterial cream," Katherine said, "but I think he should go see a doctor."

Setton agreed. "I don't know if he's current on his tetanus."

"I don't know, either," Katherine answered, the two of them discussing Bear as if he were a child.

Setton asked him, "Will you go to the hospital and get those hands looked after?"

Bear offered a noncommittal shrug.

"He won't," Katherine said as if she'd known him for years.

Doc Setton told Bear, "You probably forgot with the fire and all, but I was scheduled to come out here this morning and check one of your cows."

Bear lost his smile. He had dedicated himself to remembering appointments, meeting obligations, being on time. He used to have nightmares, after his father died, Bear waking up in the middle of the night with a dread that he'd forgotten something, to feed and water the chickens, for example, and they were all lying stretched out dead up in the chicken house. Nothing like that ever happened but he worried about it constantly and now he'd forgotten for real about the vet. This was terrible.

"It's all right," Setton told him, putting a hand on the big man's trembling shoulder. "You want me to come back later this week?"

He didn't know, he was in a muddle. If he went now with the vet to check the cow, did that mean Katie would leave?

"What's wrong with the cow?" she asked.

"I think she's lost a calf," the vet replied. "Isn't that what you said, Bear?"

He nodded.

"Let's go check," Katherine said to Setton. Then, to Bear: "Is it all right if I come along?"

He nodded and set off with the dogs to fetch the cow as Katherine and Doc Setton got into the vet's truck.

"What do you think happened?" Setton asked her, indicating the barn ruins where people still milled. "Not the right time of season for green hay to catch fire and I bet Bear's never put up a bale of wet hay in his life. No power to that barn, so it wasn't an electrical short."

"Carl Coote and Phil Scrudde did it," Katherine announced. She told Setton in vivid detail what had happened yesterday morning with the downed cow tortured by Coote and Scrudde and how Bear had choked the two of them. "One or both of those men came out last night and torched Bear's barn."

"You got to be careful saying that, hon. If they hear you were trying to blame an arson on them . . . they'll find a way to make you shut up about it."

"I haven't told anyone except you, but considering what happened yesterday with that cow, it's obvious, isn't it?"

"Let Bear report it to the sheriff's office, let them handle it."

Katherine thought the vet was probably right, the last thing in the world she wanted was getting involved in a local feud.

After driving to the corral, which was in the pasture near the county road, Doc Setton and Katherine waited as Bear and his two dogs walked an old red cow up a long hill, down through a small creek, working her toward the corral. Meanwhile, ducks and chickens and cats from the house wandered out to watch.

Katherine got down from the truck and opened the corral gate for the cow. Then Doc went over to Bear and said, "Katherine was telling me about Coote and Scrudde. Do you think they torched your barn?"

He nodded.

"But you didn't see them?"

Bear shook his head, then chanced speaking. "Cootie is mean to your face but that Scrudde is like a yellow dog that'll wag his tail until you turn, then bites the back of your leg."

Setton told him he should call Deputy Miller at the county sheriff's.

Bear didn't say anything.

"He's been good to you in the past, he'll look into it."

Bear nodded.

"You should've seen Bear," Katherine said, "yesterday morning with those two creeps—he was magnificent."

"I've *always* thought he was a pretty magnificent kind of guy," Setton added.

Bear colored and tried to cross his arms, but his hands hurt too much for that. Should he tell them, Katie and the Doc, that that cow talked to him? What might they make of such a confession? He turned and kicked at two ducks who were screwing.

"Why'd you do that?" Katherine asked crossly, then immediately apologized. "I'm sorry, I keep putting my two cents in."

"Both boys," Bear told her. The big white duck was forever mounting the little brown one, who sometimes squawked and struggled and ran away, but other times just sat down and took it like a man. Bear wanted to explain, in case Katie didn't know, that when the opposite sex ain't around, animals of the same sex will mount each other, it's commonplace, but he wasn't sure how to word the explanation.

Doc Setton began bragging on Bear, pointing out to Katherine how Bear built his own head gate using thick padding to protect the cows' necks even though most farmers never bother with the subtleties of cow comfort. The vet said Bear practiced wise farming techniques such as intensive grazing, which was how the bison grazed the Great Plains, making them the richest grasslands in the world. Bear reads extensively about farming and is careful with his animals, which is why they're so gentle, like this red cow, Setton said. "He loves his animals."

"I know he does," Kate agreed. "That's why I think he should work with us, rescuing animals."

The vet pondered this a moment before asking Bear if this red cow was his oldest.

"Yes," he said, "she's the first one Dad let me buy on my own, I named her Red Cow."

The vet laughed carefully the way old men do. "Well she's red and she's a cow, you can't go wrong with that name."

"Robert says I'm good at naming." Bear bent down and, being careful with his bandaged hands, hugged the big German shepherd male. "Robert helped me name this one . . . POTUS."

"Otis?" Katherine asked.

Bear smiled. "Everyone thinks it's Otis but it's POTUS. Robert knows stuff about the White House most people don't and I told him this here dog had more dignity than the President."

The vet went back to his truck and opened a side compartment. Working tenderly, as if every movement hurt, Doc Setton slipped on a plastic sleeve that covered his arm to the shoulder and then squirted a lubricant up and down the length of that sleeve and reentered the corral.

"Doesn't *look* pregnant," Setton said as he held the cow's tail aside and gently began inserting his hand and arm into her rectum, up to where he eventually could palpate, through the intestinal wall, her uterus.

Bear had his arm around the cow's neck, hugging rather than subduing her, and as she made a little moan and took a step forward, Bear used his bulk to hold her steady.

"She's not carrying a calf," the vet announced, arm still up the cow all the way to the shoulder. "At least not one that was conceived last fall. It would be big enough by now that I could feel it."

Bear shook his head. "I had this cow all her life, bred her fourteen times, got fourteen calves, this'd be the first time she ever lost one. I'll take her to the stock auction in the morning." He tsked.

Doc Setton removed his arm from the cow and stripped off the plastic sleeve, agreeing with Bear that it was a shame. "I know she was your favorite."

Turning to Bear, Katherine asked, "Am I missing something here? Why are you sending her to slaughter?"

"Well, hon," Doc answered for Bear, "if a cow, especially an old one like this, loses a calf, it doesn't make sense to keep her open and wait for next year."

"Make sense?"

"You lose a year's production," the vet said. "You and I talked about this at the library. Either you accept raising animals for food or you don't. If you don't, that's one situation. But if you do, and I thought you said you did, then you have to accept certain realities. What I've been trying to do these past few years is make sure animals get treated right within the reality that they're being raised for food."

But Katherine wasn't ready to give up on the topic, asking Bear, "How much money have you made from this cow?"

He couldn't tell her right off the top of his head.

"If you had a horse that served you faithfully for fourteen years, would you send *it* off to slaughter?"

"Red Cow ain't a horse," Bear told her. This distinction struck him as so fundamental that he thought he must've missed Katie's point. Was he supposed to keep a cow, which could easily live into its twenties, keep it on pasture and feed it precious hay even though it wasn't producing any income, just keep it as a pet? That seemed unnatural to Bear.

"How much is enough?" she pressed him.

Bear felt terrible. He'd do anything to stop Katie from being upset, he'd bring Red Cow in the house and let her live in his father's old bedroom if that's what Katie wanted, if that would make her stop being mad at him.

Before Doc Setton could intervene, Katherine was suddenly apologizing once again to Bear. "It's none of my business, I had no right to say anything. I'm sorry."

"Get in my truck, hon," the vet told her. "We'll go up to town and get a cup of coffee."

Katherine nodded. When she reached the truck, she said to Bear, "I'll be back for my car. I know you have to take that cow to market, I know that's what you do for a living . . . I was out of line saying anything."

Setton patted Bear's arm. "You go get your hands checked, okay?"

"Okay."

After watching the vet's truck drive off, Bear went over to Red Cow and stood with his bandaged hands resting on her back. She really was a gentle old soul, there probably wasn't one beef cow in a thousand you could pregnancy-check without securing her in a head gate. This cow never gave him a lick of trouble and he loved her as much as you can a cow.

The gawkers over where the barn used to be couldn't hear him from that far away, so Bear spoke aloud, telling Red Cow how happy he was with her all these years, that's why he kept her beyond the age a cow is normally kept to raise beef calves, she was his first, his favorite, he had intended to keep her as long as she produced calves. Now that she's lost one he's sorry he has to put her off to auction but that's how things are, especially now with his barn gone. He's going to have to build another one or get out of the cattle business.

When she swung her head up and looked Bear in the eye, he got the strangest feeling she wanted to say something back to him.

8

At the café, Katherine headed for a booth but Doc Setton said let's sit here at a table, I'm too old to slide in and out of booths. The waitress, Diane, brought and poured coffee without being asked.

Katherine asked her, "Do you have any nondairy creamer?"

Diane was over forty and henna-haired. She arched her plucked brows and answered, "Most want half-and-half, complain if all we got is the nondairy, you lactose intolerant?"

"In a way," Katherine said, still surprised at how rudely she, as an outsider, had been treated in the five months she'd lived here . . . except at the library.

Doc Setton was telling her that Bear, in spite of the initial impression people got of him, had a lot on the ball. "He's smart about things, he reads all the time, some women might even consider him a handsome man, but . . . I'm sure you noticed, there's something off-kilter about him."

"Eccentric."

"More than eccentric. But whatever Bear is, he's accepted around here because he's considered harmless, a danger to no one."

"He was a danger to Coote and Scrudde."

"I don't know how that happened, hon, but it's exactly that sort of thing that'll ruin Bear."

"Ruin him?" Katherine asked.

The old vet paused to think how he could explain it. "A few years ago his brother Robert was supposed to come out for a visit, bring his two sons. Bear had never met his nephews, had no experience around children, so apparently he got this brainstorm that he'd stop at that Lutheran home and ask if he could 'borrow' a couple little boys to play with for the day, to find out what little boys liked to do, how late they stayed up at night, if you had to feed them any special foods, how gentle you had to treat them—you know, Bear trying to get ready for Robert's sons. You can imagine the commotion it caused out at the Lutheran home, this big strange farmer wanting two little boys to play with. There's a sheriff's deputy who was Robert's best friend in high school, Miller, and Miller went to talk with Bear, told him he couldn't show up at Lutheran homes or anywhere else asking for little boys to play with, his intentions would be misunderstood. Bear didn't know why that should be the case but he promised to stay away from kids. The point is, nothing ever came of this incident, people around here didn't push for Bear to be arrested or undergo psychiatric evaluation. And the reason is, he's never hurt or threatened anyone in his entire life. Being considered harmless is what protects him. But now, if he goes around choking people, Bear will lose that protection."

"His protection being that he's considered harmless?"

"Yes."

Katherine thought of her own life, how harmless she's been and how little protection it has afforded her. She sipped at the coffee but it tasted bitter and the waitress hadn't returned with the nondairy creamer.

"I appreciate you taking care of those dogs and the two birds," Setton said, "but when we talked at the library about rescuing animals I didn't think you'd be going around interfering with farmers who—"

"Doc, I *didn't.* At least I didn't plan on it. The bus driver, Barbara, told me about a cow being tortured and I went out there just to see what was happening. Bear was there and—"

"I know, hon. My point is, I get away with criticizing the locals about their animals because I'm eighty years old and if they don't respect my age, at least they think I'm harmless enough, just an old vet who's gone soft. You don't have that protection. You're a woman and you're an outsider, they won't take criticism from you, they just won't."

"And I don't intend to give it to them," Katherine insisted. "I've been talking with women at the library about going out and rescuing *stray* animals. I don't intend to become a crusader."

"Not that we don't *need* a few crusaders around here—"

"Mother Setton, are you listening to me?"

The vet smiled. "Don't call me that." Even though age had wizened him, you could still see the spark he'd had when he was younger, a tough bantam, one of those little guys that the Texas Rangers say will always beat a big guy if the little guy's cause is right and he keeps on coming. "I know you intend it as a compliment but I don't take it that way."

"Fair enough," she said, looking around for the waitress. Then she admitted to Doc, "While I was bandaging Bear's hands, I asked him if he'd help me adopting strays, rescuing animals."

"What he'd say?"

"He said yes." She laughed a little. "Actually, he said yes before I asked him the question."

"How's that?"

"I said I have a question to ask, and he said yes . . . before I even asked it."

"That's Bear for you."

She nodded.

He told her, "Well, like I was saying, there are a lot of animals that need to be rescued around here. I could tell you stories that'd bring tears to your eyes."

Katherine didn't need tears brought to her eyes, she'd had enough.

"There's a pair of horses, for example, that are starving to death," Doc Setton started to say.

Katherine reached across the table and put her hand on his. "Doc? First you tell me I'd be out of line if I interfere with how people around here treat their animals, that Bear is at risk if he does things like choke those two guys so he can put a cow out of its misery, now you're going to tell me about horses that need to be rescued because they're starving to death."

"I just want you to know what you're getting into."

Though she was smiling at the old man, Katherine spoke bluntly. "This isn't my home. I don't even know how much longer I'm going to be living here."

"That little bungalow you're in, it's your boyfriend's from back in D.C.?"

"My fiancé, yes. We're going to get married soon and I'll be gone from here and it wouldn't be fair to start some big rescue crusade and then leave."

"Why'd you come to Briars in the first place?"

She shrugged. "Rest and recuperation."

"From what?"

Katherine smiled and shook her finger at the little man.

He smiled, too. "One of the few compensations being eighty years old, you ask impertinent questions and people just shake their fingers at you instead of slugging you for being nosy."

"I've been recovering from an illness. My fiancé offered his cottage and I had some accumulated vacation time from work so here I am . . . but not for much longer, I don't think."

"If I was your boyfriend, I wouldn't let you out of my sight."

"I'm the one who insisted on getting away. William—that's my fiancé, William Trent—he's been a saint."

"Hard having a saint for a boyfriend?"

"Doc . . ."

"Sorry."

It *was* hard. William always being right, correct, logical. *You tell me to stop calling you so often, Kath-er-ine, but if I skip a few days, you say I'm ignoring you, it's not logical, Kath-er-ine. I can't win.* He was fond of pronouncing all three of her syllables.

Katherine thought of Bear, how much easier, looser-feeling, it was to be around him, how he called her Katie.

Doc Setton asked what she was thinking.

"How much I miss William."

He laughed. "You want to hear another impertinent crack from an old veterinarian?"

"Sure, why not."

"Liar, liar."

9

When Bear woke up the next morning, his burned hands hurt the worst but the puncture wound in his leg was a close second. Also his teeth hurt. In times of trouble he ground his molars, they were almost down to the gum line. The prospect of waking up in pain every morning was another reason that, every night, he suggested to the Lord he was ready to put his burdens down. But this morning as always the Lord had declined the offer.

Bear went downstairs to make coffee. He lived in a classic American farmhouse shaped in a T with the top of the T being the front of the house, two rooms up and two rooms down, a chimney on each end. The shaft of the T was one story: the dining room and then, in the back, the kitchen. Bear walked through the house as he did every morning feeling spiritually cold because there was no one living here with him and a house seems to grow cold of spirit if enough people, you'd have to say at least two, don't move through it with some regularity.

For weeks after his father died, Bear imagined he could still smell his old man lighting a Lucky Strike, could hear him banging around in the room where he had slept, and died—another reason Bear would never take that room as his own, too much of his father still left in there.

While waiting for water to boil, Bear remembered a dream from last night: a little girl about five years old is standing by the side of his bed and Bear asks, "Who are you, little girl?" and she says, "I'm your daughter waiting to get born." Even though this clearly was a ridiculous dream (Bear knew he would never marry or have children, he didn't harbor any illusions about that), Bear in the dream didn't dispute the little girl's claim. Instead he asked her, why are you so sad? She never answered him.

It was a dream. Bear knew what was real, what wasn't. He'd better stop fooling around with women from out of town, with talking cows. He'd better get back to farming, he had a barn to replace.

Today's first job was taking his red cow to the stock auction and that meant putting on cattle racks and loading her by himself with two bandaged hands. But he got it done, got her loaded. With Red Cow in the back of the truck, Bear stood a moment admiring her, a long leggy cow that had some Brahmin in her, you could tell by the long ears that stuck out to the sides and also her cowl-like dewlap. She was so perfectly uniform in color that it seemed someone had spray-painted her a dark burgundy red, a red deeper than Hereford red, and she didn't have a single mark of white. Bear didn't speak to the cow, he had had his say yesterday.

He drove to the stock sale on the outskirts of the town of Briars. After unloading the cow into a holding pen, he parked the truck and returned to the auction barn just as Red Cow was being weighed. She hit one thousand pounds exactly, a big cow. If she were being sold as a breeder she might've brought $600 because she didn't look her age. But sold to slaughter as an old canner cow, she'd be lucky to bring forty-five cents to the pound, $450.

The men here at the stock sale had heard about Bear's barn burning down and they figured it was only a matter of time now before the big retard lost that farm they thought he didn't deserve in the first place, his father having left the farm to Bear's brother, who turned around and gave it to Bear on a tray. The consensus was, Bear had been lucky not to lose it before now.

There had been incidents and rumors about Bear all his life, starting with his paternity. The men here had already heard about the day before yesterday, Bear almost strangling Scrudde and Coote, but, years before, people had also heard how he tried to get those little boys out of the Lutheran home so he could take them back to the farm and "play with them," is what he told the lady there. The local barber tells people he's glad Bear stopped coming in for a haircut because it was creepy the way he kept leaning into the barber's hands like he wanted to be nuzzled or something. The gal who delivered mail out Bear's way said that one time he grabbed her and kept hugging and hugging until she thought she was going to be raped. And then there was that incident at the public library almost two years ago and still being discussed.

The Briars Public Library showed old movies every Friday night and Bear used to attend during the winter months when the sun dropped behind the ridges around his farm while the clock was still working on afternoon and you'd finish your chores and spend hours inside and *still* it wasn't time for bed. To burn up a few of those hours, Bear would on occasion come to town and slink into the library to sit in the back and watch the old movies being shown in the darkened main room, donation one dollar. This one January, the library was showing the old *Lassie Come Home* movie with Roddy McDowall as the little boy over there in some country where they speak English but not like we do here, and halfway through the movie, Bear was biting hard on his lower lip to keep from crying, especially when the little boy asked his father if he was mad at him and the father said something that sounded like *Nay, a father can no be angry at his own lad, not truly angry at his own lad . . .* Bear concluding that those movie people never met a man like his father. As Lassie had more adventures trying to come home, Bear bit down all the harder on his lip, drawing blood, the pain a dam to tears, which held until the end of the movie when little Roddy McDowall (and Bear) thought that Lassie was gone for good, but here she is all limping and dirty from her travels to get back to the boy she loves, and at that moment when the boy comes out of the school and sees his dog waiting there by the tree like always, Roddy McDowall gets this expression on his face of pure joy. But before he can say anything, it's Bear crying out from the back of the library, "Lassie! Lassie!"—standing now full height in the darkened room and crying out in a voice most people there had never heard—"Lassie!" He was sobbing. The other moviegoers looked back in shock as Bear left without seeing the last few minutes. The story has been around town for a couple years now, Bear crying over Lassie.

After getting his ticket for Red Cow, Bear went in to where the auction was held around a square pit, thirty feet to a side, with the auctioneer's booth elevated in front and tiers of seating rising on the other three sides. Bear sat ringside where he could get a good look at the stock. Like the hedgehog, Bear knew one great thing—in his case, cattle. If a high-quality cow-calf pair came through, he might bid on them as a replacement for Red Cow, though he cautioned himself not to be thinking too hard about new cows when he hadn't even figured out yet where he would put up hay this summer with no barn.

Sheep got auctioned off first, then orphaned calves. Bear considered buying one but the prices were crazy, one three-day-old black calf went for $230 even though it would have to be bottle raised and still had a good chance of dying.

Ten cow-calf pairs came through, Bear bidding on three separate pairs but dropping out each time when the prices went too high above $750. Then came the pregnant cows, the months of their pregnancies chalked on their rumps, from 1 to 9. After that came the slaughter cows, old animals and ones that were crippled or had disease or were open, not bred for one reason or the other, having lost their calves. Red Cow was the last of this group.

Starting at an optimistic sixty dollars per hundredweight, the auctioneer had to slide down to thirty dollars before he got a bid and could start climbing up again. The auctioneer solicited two-dollar increments from three bidders until he hit thirty-six dollars per hundredweight and one bidder dropped out, the remaining two trading one-dollar increases until they stopped at forty dollars, which Bear multiplied by ten in his head—not as much as he had hoped she would bring.

Seeing Bear, the red cow walked over to him and looked up right at his face the way she did yesterday when he was telling her what a great cow she'd been.

"No secret who that cow belongs to," the auctioneer said,

getting a big laugh that colored Bear's face as Red Cow continued staring up at him from the auction ring.

Taking pity on Bear, considering his barn loss, the auctioneer gave a little spiel on behalf of the cow in question: "Boys, this cow shouldn't be sold as a canner, she's got a little age on her but take her on home and turn her out with your bull, she'll still raise you a good calf or two before she's finished."

Bear shook his head to get Red Cow to stop staring and move on, but she stayed right there below him, looking at his eyes.

"No reason in the world for her to get sold at canning prices," the auctioneer was repeating. "Everybody here knows how Bear keeps his stock, ain't no bad cow ever come off his farm, and you-all've heard about his barn burning down. So what say we show a little generosity here and try selling her by the head, I got four hundred who'll give me four-forty?"

He eventually worked Red Cow up to $430 and then, unusually, a new bidder came in late and offered $440 (Was it Scrudde? Bear thought he recognized the voice but didn't turn around to see) and one of the two original bidders countered this new bid with $450. After that, no one agreed to any further increases in spite of the auctioneer's singsong pleading.

"Are we all finished?" the auctioneer asked.

There was a pause in the proceedings while the bidders considered the auctioneer's question . . . which is when the cow begged Bear not to sell her off to slaughter.

10

Bear coughed explosively, as if a piece of food had got caught going down the wrong way. Everyone in the auction barn stared at him.

"You okay?" the auctioneer asked over the loudspeaker system.

Bear nodded and raised a bandaged hand.

"Choked on that low price, did you?" the auctioneer asked, getting a laugh.

Bear nodded again and raised both hands. A few men here had fought the barn fire and been with Bear afterward at the café, and now they wondered if he was going to stand up and dance a slow circle while grinning like an idiot.

But Bear stayed put, paralyzed with embarrassment.

"Come on, boys," the auctioneer said, "let's get Bear four sixty for this cow, what say?"

Because of the raised seating around the ring, Red Cow's head was at the level of Bear's feet, her nose about six inches from the toes of his boots, which he now wiggled frantically, hoping the sudden movement would scare her away. It didn't.

The cow told him she was pregnant.

He shook his head, it wasn't true. Doc Setton had checked her for pregnancy just yesterday, but mainly it wasn't true that the cow was talking to him, Bear knew that, he knew it was him *thinking* the cow might be pregnant because he saw the bull cover her a few weeks ago, maybe she lost her original calf and is pregnant with another one, Bear looking at her big brown eyes and praying, *please God* don't let me go crazy here, it was bad enough crying out two years ago in a darkened library where there were mainly women and children to witness the shame of it, please don't let me go crazy here in front of *farmers.*

While the auctioneer was haggling for another five dollars, Red Cow said Bear's name plaintively: *Bear.*

Putting a bandaged hand to the side of his mouth so the man closest to him wouldn't hear, Bear whispered back, "Shut up . . . *please shut up.*"

Somehow in the face of all reluctance the auctioneer finally got that five dollars and then five more. Four sixty for the cow . . . who would pay four sixty-five?

Bid, Red Cow begged Bear.

He stayed paralyzed.

Singing the final stanza of his song by repeating the bid over and over, the auctioneer finally asked if everyone was done. "All done . . . all done . . . all done?"

Please, Red Cow said and, insanely, Bear was about to raise his arm and bid on his own animal, which would've made him a laughingstock, when the auctioneer cried his finale: "Sold for four sixty to G. Tracking. Move her out, boys."

One of the ring boys came over and prodded Red Cow with a stock cane, but she refused to move, looking intently at Bear until someone in the crowd hollered, "Oh for crying out loud, Bear, climb down there and give her a kiss good-bye!" Which also got a big laugh.

Good-bye, Bear told her, mouthing the words in quiet shame so none of the men would hear him talk to a cow.

With the ring boy beating on her rump, Red Cow gave Bear one last panicked look and then went trotting out a gate being held open for her.

Bear sat stunned. Finally, walking as if in a daze, he went up to the office and waited for his check to be cut. The $460 sale price minus commission and yardage and insurance and beef checkoff netted out $448 plus change. The check stub named the buyer, Gerald Tracking.

Bear went down to the pens where the cows that Tracking

had bought were being held. Gerald shipped cows all over and his trucking company had a funny name, Tracking Trucking.

Hearing his own name being called frantically, Bear looked over the top board of a pen in time to see Red Cow pushing her way through the herd.

She wanted to know if Bear had bought her back. When he shook his head she seemed more sad than mad. Did she point out that she'd given him fourteen calves or was Bear just thinking it? How much profit is enough from one animal? She had lost her calf this winter and Bear never found its body, apportioned among foxes. But then she came into heat just recently, got bred, and conceived a new calf, number fifteen, still too small for the vet to palpate. *You're sending me off to slaughter with life inside me,* the cow told Bear. *When they cut me open at the slaughterhouse, my baby will fall out, squirming.*

He stood there in dumb wonderment.

"Hey, Bear," Gerald Tracking said, startling Bear who wheeled around and almost asked Gerald if he'd heard this cow say anything just now.

"You burn your hands fighting the fire?" Tracking asked.

Bear nodded.

"That was funny, the way your cow just stood there and kept looking up at you," Tracking said. He had a big round face and wavy red hair, more orange than Katie's, whose red hair was redder. "You going build a new barn?" Tracking was asking Bear.

"I'll buy that red cow back from you," Bear said.

This surprised Tracking, first to hear Bear speak at all and then to hear him making such an extraordinary offer. Looking over the top board, Tracking saw Red Cow standing there, then turned to Bear. "Why would you want to do that?"

He shrugged.

"Sorry, Bear, but I already got her on the manifest."

"I'll give you what you paid."

"Why?"

Bear couldn't think of an acceptable answer.

"If you didn't get the price you wanted," Tracking was saying, losing his patience now, "you could've no-saled her."

"I'll buy her back for what you paid plus some extra."

"I already made out the paperwork, four-sixty was a good price, them other canners in there with her didn't bring forty a hundred. I thought I was doing you a favor."

"I'll give you five hundred."

"You just sold her for four-sixty and now you want to buy her back for five? Hell of a way to run a cattle business."

Pressing his point without looking Tracking in the face, Bear said, "Five hundred, what do you say?"

"I say you're crazy."

"Five-twenty!"

"Bear, I knew your old man, he had a temper on him but he was a cattleman and he kept that farm going all those years and if he knew—"

"Five-sixty!"

"What?"

"Hundred more than you paid."

"You *are* crazy."

"Deal?" Bear was reaching in a pocket for the check he'd just been given upstairs, intending to sign it over and then pay the difference in cash.

"What'd you net out?" Tracking asked him.

Bear showed the check.

With a sigh Tracking said, "Sign it over to me, I'll take a loss on your deductions and you keep that extra hundred you're so hot to pay me, keep it in your pocket because I don't want it . . . ain't Christian to turn a dollar on another man's misery." Then he told Bear, "I feel sorry for you."

After signing the check and thrusting it at Tracking, Bear hurried into the holding pen to cut Red Cow out of the herd and put her in the aisle that led to a ramp where he could back up his truck and load her.

"You're welcome!" Tracking called out sarcastically.

Bear raised an arm in acknowledgment. He was grinning.

Gerald Tracking said it wasn't Christian to turn a dollar on another man's misery but Bear didn't feel miserable. Think of the possibilities. If you live by yourself out on a farm, so lonely you feel like life is leaking out of you every day, no one to speak to, to tell, *Hey, guess what I saw today,* then suddenly cows start talking to you . . . think of the possibilities for company, for comfort, for joy.

11

In the cottage's little living room, shades down against the sun that amplified the unrelenting cheeriness of the decor, Katherine sat on a couch that smelled of dog. She held a mug of tea with both hands. The parrots were quiet in the dark, one with its head tucked. Outside, all the dogs were also quiet, it was a bright April day and each according to its coat was either sunning in the open or panting in the shade. This is why she came here, to be alone, no visitors expected, no outings planned.

If she were back in D.C. right now, Katherine would be in constant touch with friends—*How are you feeling, anything I can do?*—and her fiancé would be organizing petite excursions, cappuccino at a sidewalk café, a stroll through the zoo. In matters of taste and accommodation, you could hardly fault William.

Being alone was what Kate wanted but here in Appalachia it came with a price. Alone in a town where no one knows you, there are questions you begin to ask, why me and what now and, really, how solid was the universe, supposedly organized in solar systems and galaxies, gravity just right to hold it all together and keep it all apart, but then what happens if everything starts to *wobble?* Sitting on the couch clutching that mug of tea, Katherine felt the gut-suck wobble of her own life, once so vibrant and busy and active, a handsome fiancé and a hot career. Would she be going back to all that, *as if nothing had happened*?

At the end of the month, her fiancé has suggested, she should return to D.C. and let him rent out the cottage again, she should be recuperated by then: I mean, really, Kath-er-ine, it's been *five months.*

And of course he was right, was being logical . . . but Katherine played out scenarios that were terribly illogical, of having children, of ever being happy, of hot water and open veins.

She tasted the tea, feeling betrayed by its coolness, as if the tea were mocking her: *See what I did while you weren't paying attention? I cooled off.* And isn't this what's happening to the universe, cooling toward cinder, and isn't this what's happening to me? Katherine thought. I'm cooling toward something—what, she wasn't sure, an inert mass, something leaden. She ran her little finger along her eyebrows.

You'd have to have known her *before* to appreciate how Katherine hated being needy like this, hated feeling small and dark and unloved.

Her car was still at Bear's farm, she could call someone, the school bus driver, to get a ride out there. She could also put on a cute dress first and fix her face, *smile.* Wasn't that what her mother was always encouraging her to do? *Smile, Katherine, you look like the world is coming to an end.*

She'd been a serious student in college, pursued her career relentlessly. People would ask, are you happy? And Katherine would tell them, I am, I really am.

She placed the mug of cold tea on the floor and laid her head back on a pillow—covered, of course, in dog hair. I'll get up in a minute, she told herself. Get dressed, wear something nice. Put on a big smile.

But Katherine didn't move. Always before in her life she'd been a go-getter, but now the effort to get up and go, get dressed, and smile—but especially the effort to smile—seemed huge, undoable.

12

Back at his farm Bear didn't unload Red Cow into the pasture with the rest of his herd, he put her in a small shed he called the new shed though it had been eight years since he built it. After fetching water and a bucket of sweetfeed and several leaves of hay from a bale he'd rescued out of the burning barn, Bear told the cow, "You're home now!" She made no reply, her mouth was full of sweetfeed.

Bear hurried back to the farmhouse, trailed by his female German shepherd, named Jamaica after Robert took his pretty wife to that island for a vacation and hinted that maybe the boys could stay on the farm for those two weeks but it didn't happen and all Bear got out of that wonderful possibility was a name for his new dog. Jamaica sensed Bear's excitement and barked, ran in circles, occasionally leaping up trying to catch Bear's bandaged hand in her mouth. POTUS, the male shepherd, also aware of agitation in the air, held more tightly to his dignity by retiring to a favorite spot on the front porch where he would sit for hours, his gray muzzle elevated the better to smell, frowning a little as he surveyed his territory, always on alert but also profoundly composed, as if composition were the higher duty.

Even as a puppy, when Bear first brought him home eleven years ago, the dog had been acutely aware of his dignity, agreeing to foolish puppy games only at Bear's insistence. Talking by phone to Robert, Bear had said the new puppy had more dignity than the President of the United States. As a young dog, before Jamaica came along, POTUS would sometimes sit out in the yard and look up at flying birds, and one time Bear saw POTUS following the overhead flight of a crow so intently that he kept bending his head farther and farther back until he unbalanced himself and fell over. After immediately regaining the sitting position, young POTUS glanced at the porch to see if Bear had witnessed this small humiliation. And now, in the final portion of his life, the big German shepherd had refined dignity until it became him no matter what—that he was attended by two male ducks frequently in coitus or that to escape summer's heat he would dig holes in the creek and then sit there like an old gator with only his massive head showing. Even in water and mud and accompanied by ducks he still had more dignity than the President of the United States.

It was only after Bear had rushed into the house that he realized he didn't know why he was rushing, where he was heading, what he intended to do next. He couldn't talk to Robert, he'd been forbidden to call him at work during the day.

He made a pot of coffee and sat at the kitchen table while the coffee perked.

Bear's hands had bled through the bandages, which he now removed, using his teeth. Those big burned hands were ugly. They smelled bad, too. And hurt.

Years before his father died, the pain games had stopped because Bear was too big and his father was too old for Dutch rubs (which meant you got put in a headlock and had the top of your skull rubbed hard with Dad's knuckles) or six-inch pokes (Dad held his fist six inches away from Bear's shoulder and hit as hard as he could from that distance) or milk-the-mouse or oogies or smoke-gets-in-your-eyes, which was played with a lighted cigarette. In old age, Bear's father replaced these games of physical pain with hateful comments, telling Bear he was a retard who'd end up in an asylum, that he wasn't half the son his brother was, making comments about clay eating even though Bear hadn't indulged in clay since his teen years. Bear would never answer these insults, but sometimes when his father started in on him as the two of them sat here at the kitchen table, Bear would hold a fork up in front of one eye so he could see what the old man looked like behind bars.

Oddly, though, it was Robert who hated their father more than Bear did. Bear had a difficult time explaining to Robert why he missed their father, bad company better than no company, feeling pain better than feeling nothing. Besides, the old man's main complaint in life had always been regretting that Bear wasn't more like Robert, and since Bear regretted the same thing, how could he resent his father for it?

The coffee was boiling now. Bear poured a third-cup of sugar and a third-cup of milk into a big white mug, then added scalding black coffee. Carrying this potent mixture, he went outside, making his way among dogs and ducks back to the new shed. Red Cow had finished her sweetfeed, a mixture of oats and cracked corn and barley, with blackstrap molasses holding the grains together. Cows love it beyond all measure. She had also finished her water and was working on the hay, her appetite apparently undiminished by the excitement of very nearly being sold to slaughter.

Bear leaned over the top board of the stall, drinking his sugary hot coffee. He loved the smell of cows, maybe it was the fermenting contents of their multiple stomachs that made them so toothache sweet. "I bought you back," he told her.

The cow looked at him.

Bear smiled waiting to hear a comment, a thank-you, an expression of relief.

Red Cow stepped away from the hay and nosed the empty water bucket.

"You want some more water?"

She didn't answer but Bear went to fetch her a fresh bucketful anyway. By the time he got back with it, Red Cow was lying down chewing her cud, and Bear's coffee had cooled, bitter to the tongue.

"Anything else I can get you?"

She didn't reply.

"Oh . . . I get it." Red Cow wasn't going to talk to him (or, rather, his insanity wasn't going to have her talking to him) on a regular or reliable basis. This was frustrating because the compensation for going crazy would have been having someone to talk with.

"I bought you back from Gerald Tracking," Bear tried again.

She got up, raising her back end first (horses get up the other way, front end first), and went over to drink from the bucket in long sucking draughts. Then she came to the boards against which Bear was leaning and looked at him with her muzzle dripping water. He was almost sure she was about to speak. But the cow said nothing, just kept staring at Bear. He'd seen this look before: a cow hoping to get another scoop of sweetfeed.

"The last time Robert was on the farm was when Dad died," Bear said to the cow. The funeral was terrible because no one came . . . just Bear and Robert and the guy from the funeral home. As a child, Bear had been taken to many funerals, some of them spectacular in attendance, the church so filled that people had to stand outside by the open windows to hear the tributes, and then there was a long headlighted procession to the cemetery. You got the feeling from such funerals that something significant had passed, that a void was left in many lives. Not so Bear's and Robert's father, no one there. He was a mean-spirited soul and his passing left a hole in only one life, Bear's.

"And do you know what I told Robert?" said Bear, still speaking to the cow. "I told him, 'I guess the next visit you'll make home is when I die and you come to *my* funeral.' I thought he was going to say, 'Oh no, Bear, I'll come visit you real soon and I'll bring my two boys along.' Which is what he always says on the phone. But at Dad's funeral Robert was in a bad mood about the will and said I was probably right, he might not be back again until I died. Robert said every time he sees these mountains his stomach gets all tight inside and doesn't loosen up again until he's back on flat ground, that's how much he hates the farm. I can't understand why though. He left as soon as he turned eighteen, it's not like farming's been a burden he's had to carry all these years. Me, I love this farm . . . how about you?"

Bear had slipped that question in hoping to trick the cow into speaking, but it didn't work.

"I would've never sold you," continued Bear, who even without the cow's participation was warming to the task of talking, growing as loquacious as he did in those telephone conversations with Robert, "if the vet hadn't said you lost your calf. Which I guess you did, except now you're pregnant with another one. Right?"

No answer.

Bear tucked his burned hands into his armpits. "Well, like I said before, you've been a great old cow."

"And you've been a good farmer to me."

This reply didn't surprise Bear because he had supplied it himself, talking out of the side of his mouth to give voice to the cow that was steadfastly refusing to speak to him.

"I do my best," Bear said.

"Better than most farmers around here," Bear answered himself. "Bear's cows get wormed and deloused twice a year, all their shots, green grass and spring water in the summer and, in winter, that delicious sweetfeed along with hay—what more could a cow ask for?"

"I've sent all your children off to feed lots where they get fattened up for slaughter."

"Well, that's a cow's reality, isn't it?" Bear said, forgiving himself on the cow's behalf. "If we lived out in nature we'd get pulled down by predators or laid low by disease or starve to death. At least you let my babies run free and romp while they were here on the farm, you never penned them up the way Scrudde does his veal calves."

"It's awful how those calves have to live," Bear agreed with himself. "Chained in a box where they can't even move a step much less run and kick up their heals."

"And I wouldn't want to be their mother, either; a milk cow is grotesque the way she's been engineered to overproduce milk."

"Yeah, I wouldn't be a dairy farmer, either. Well, I got to go now."

"Okay," Bear said out of the side of his mouth. "Come back and we'll talk again."

Bear thought he heard someone behind him laugh but when he turned no one was there, just the German shepherd bitch. Even so, Bear had embarrassed himself pretending he was talking to a cow, so he didn't tell Red Cow good-bye upon leaving the shed, didn't pet or acknowledge Jamaica, either.

He returned to the house and got the .22 rifle from the closet where he kept all his long guns upside down, muzzles resting on folded pieces of cloth. Bear carried the rifle onto the porch where the two German shepherds went a little crazy. They loved hunting with Bear and would whine like puppies whenever a rifle or shotgun came out. After hurriedly shooing the two ducks into a pen so they wouldn't follow along on the hunt, Bear brought the rifle to his shoulder and aimed off into the woods, saying, "Pow! Pow!" This made the dogs even crazier because they wondered, what the hell was he pretending to shoot at? Bear aimed up into the sky. "Pow! Pow! Pow!" The dogs had never seen him act like this. He had shot groundhogs and deer and crows and possum and raccoons and snakes and stray cats and even a few stray dogs, but he had never just pointed the gun into the sky and said *pow, pow.*

Bear led POTUS and Jamaica into the woods, heading for pastures and meadows above the house, keeping to the trees but always watching the fields, on the lookout for groundhogs, which thrived in greater numbers now than before Europeans settled here because it was farmers who cut down forests and created fields where grew the grasses on which groundhogs thrived. Bear loved hunting them, the thrill of seeing brown movement, the agonizingly careful stalk, the aim, the squeeze, the shot, then finally the anticipation of discovering if you'd missed or hit. Although he and the dogs killed a dozen or more each year, there always seemed to be roughly the same number of groundhogs living on the farm. They ate Bear's grass and endangered his cattle because the multiple-entrance burrows were in the woods at the edges of fields and the cattle could easily step in a burrow and break a leg. Bear considered it duty and destiny to keep hunting and killing groundhogs, but it was also his sole recreation.

With his German shepherds snuffling in the woods somewhere behind him, Bear crossed a fence into a pasture of hillocks gently rolling like grass-covered sand dunes with each hill's crest about a hundred yards from the next. Bear was thinking about Katie, not groundhogs, when he saw one busily foraging on the next hill over.

Instantly focused now, Bear carefully stepped back down the side of the hill to put its crest between him and the groundhog. He looked around to see where the dogs were—nowhere in sight, though he could hear them behind him, pursuing scents in the dead leaves. Good, he thought, I won't have to make them sit and stay while I get my shot off. The shepherds were rigidly obedient to *sit, stay* but their profound anticipation sometimes distracted him while aiming.

Bear crawled to the top of the hillock and looked across to the next ridge where the groundhog, oblivious, was still eating grass. Groundhogs were voracious this time of year, coming from hibernation and about to start breeding. Bear watched the groundhog at an elevation equal to his own and about a hundred yards away on the next hill. It would be an easy shot with the little scope that Bear's father had mounted on the rifle one summer twenty years ago, telling him, "If you're going to waste time hunting groundhogs, you might as well start actually killing them."

Moving slowly and hoping the dogs didn't choose this moment to come tearing out of the woods and scare the groundhog into its burrow or up a tree, Bear brought the rifle into position and took a moment to settle his target in the scope. Resting the crosshairs just behind the groundhog's front leg, Bear took a breath and, while exhaling, gently squeezed the trigger as his father had taught him.

The groundhog squealed and jumped before tumbling out of sight on the far side of the hilltop. Bear was thrilled but not sure of success because often a groundhog, upon being startled by the sound of a shot, will squeal and leap in surprise even if the shot missed.

He walked down the hill while his two dogs came scrambling out of the forest with their predator eyes looking at him for direction: What'd you shoot, *where*?

He signaled to the next hillock over and the dogs tore off just as Bear heard what sounded like a little girl's anguished voice coming from where the groundhog had been. She was crying, *Mommy, Mommy!*

Bear stopped. Oh my God, I've shot someone.

The same thing had happened to a man when Bear was a teenager. The man had been out hunting groundhogs, had made a shot from one hillcrest to the next, *exactly* what Bear had just done, though at a much greater distance because the man was using a high-powered rifle, a 30.06. For months after, the man stopped people on the street and in stores trying to explain what had happened, that while stalking a groundhog he came to the top of one hill and saw what he thought was the groundhog scurrying along the crest of the next hilltop so he took a shot and blew it apart, except when he got over there he discovered that he'd exploded the skull of a little girl who'd been running on the far side of the hill, just her head showing above the crest, her ponytail tragically imitating the bounce and fluid movement of a groundhog. Anybody looking through a scope at that distance and at that angle would have thought it was a groundhog, the man had insisted to everyone he met, kept insisting it and explaining it until the night he used that same rifle, a length of string, and his big toe to blow out the back of his own skull.

Bear hoped against hope that this had not just happened to him, that he had only imagined hearing a little girl . . . but then he heard her again.

Mommy!

Bear dropped to one knee and struggled for breath to scream at the dogs, "Here, HERE!"

His voice was so anguished that the German shepherds turned in full stride and made for Bear. He's down on both knees now, what's wrong with him? they wondered.

It's that little girl I had a dream about last night, Bear

thought, the one who said she was my daughter waiting to get born. But instead I shot her, that's what the dream was about, why the girl looked so sad, a warning of what was going to happen today.

Bear listened, hearing nothing more from over the hill.

She's dead.

Using the rifle butt to struggle to his feet, Bear thought, if by some godly miracle she's alive, I'll rush her to the hospital, but if she's dead, I won't stick around trying to explain to people what happened, how her hair looked like a groundhog through the scope, I'll shoot myself right out here in the field and drop down dead next to her.

After ordering the dogs, *sit, stay,* Bear began walking up the grassy hill, his heart banging like something dangerously loose in a great machine. The hill was gently sloped, but to Bear it was like climbing Golgotha. And if Christ our Lord can stumble, it's no wonder that Bear did, falling to his knees and thinking to himself or saying it aloud, he was no longer aware of the distinction: *I killed a little girl . . . I killed a little girl.*

13

At Bear's farm, Katherine stood next to a pen where the big white duck was atop the smaller brown one. She hissed at them to *stop it* and kicked at the wire until the white Peking duck tumbled off the other duck's back and waddled away, quacking indignantly. In some species of birds, a male mounting a male wouldn't be overly intrusive because the male doesn't have a penis and fertilizes by holding its cloaca against the female's cloaca and then squirting sperm across the two openings—an act that's called a cloaca kiss, a name more pleasant than the reality since the cloaca, Latin for *sewer,* is the pipeline that carries products from all three of the bird's tracts, intestinal, urinary, and genital. Unfortunately for Bear's brown duck, the male duck does have a penis, folded away in its cloaca, so that the big white duck was giving the little brown one an authentic rogering.

Katherine knew about fowl because one of her first volunteer projects with an animal rights organization, after college but before she went on to what her mother called a real career, involved trying to shut down an egg factory. Since the breed of chicken used for egg production wasn't particularly efficient as a meat producer, the factory's egg hatchery wanted to keep only female chicks and destroy all males. The only way to tell the difference in newly hatched chicks is to thumb open their vents and check for testes. This has to be done shortly after hatching, because when chicks are a few days old, testes are no longer visible in the cloaca and the chick's sex stays unknown until it starts developing secondary sex characteristics such as the rooster's comb. Assigned to collect information from people who worked at the factory, Katherine hung out at a nearby roadhouse and eventually befriended an older man who sexed chickens. She hated him at first. He was a fifty-three-year-old redneck who delighted in telling her sickening details about his job: he'd grab fluffy yellow peeping chicks from a box, turn each little darling upside down under a lamp, spread its vent, and if he saw no testes, he'd put the chick into another box where it would be returned to the hatchery and raised as an egg producer. But if the sexer saw testes, he threw the male chick in a big plastic barrel that would be emptied into an incinerator at the end of the shift or whenever it got full—full of terrified, peeping, smothering baby chicks.

"And you do that all day long?" Katherine had asked him.

"Eight hours a day, forty hours a week."

"Throwing baby chicks away in a barrel like they were used Kleenex."

"The males, that's right."

"In a barrel where they smother each other and suffer and live in terror until they're dumped in an incinerator."

"They're just chicks."

"And it doesn't bother you, a job like that?"

"Nope."

As the man drank and talked to Katherine and drank more, he eventually admitted that the job was spiritually killing him, and he got drunk like this after every shift. People treated it as a joke that he was a *chicken sexer,* but how many baby chicks can you kill before it's not funny anymore?

Standing by the duck pen, Katherine wore a bulky green sweater over her little red dress, glad for the sweater's warmth now that the breeze was kicking up. Whenever she told the story about chicken sexing, people thought it was funny—an old redneck crying in his beer about being a chicken sexer. Katherine wondered what it was about chickens that people found so hilarious. There was nothing humorous about the way those factory egg-layers were kept in cages all their lives, never able to run or flap their wings, scratch or peck for food. They were force-fed an unnaturally rich diet that Frankensteined them into living units of production. You were considered noble if you saved abused horses or dogs or cats, but if you told people you wanted to start a sanctuary for chickens, they'd grin and wait for the punch line.

Maybe it's me, she thought, maybe having a double mastectomy kills your sense of humor. She stepped away from the pen and turned a circle looking for Bear and his dogs. A dozen or so outbuildings were arranged around the farmhouse. It was a sweet spot here at the base of two hills with flat ground running to the county road.

Katherine heard a gunshot and thought: He's killed himself. That's why the universe has been wobbling, anticipating Bear's death.

14

When he finally crested that hill, Bear, breathless, didn't see a little girl, but a groundhog shot in the spine, paralyzed in the back, pulling its body with front legs. The groundhog was calling toward its den for someone named Lonnie. Not *Mommy,* Lonnie.

This isn't funny, Bear thought. Whoever or whatever is in charge of me going insane, if he thinks this is a good joke, it's not. Trying to convince me I shot a little girl calling for her mommy when it's really a groundhog hollering for Lonnie, that isn't funny and whoever arranged it should be ashamed of himself.

When she saw Bear, the groundhog dragged her front quarters around and snarled.

"I'm not going to talk to you," he told her. "So don't even start."

Assassin! she spat.

He apologized.

The groundhog struggled to face her den and told Lonnie, apparently her mate, to stay where he was because that man is here, Death Walking.

"You call me Death Walking?" Bear asked.

She chattered a curse.

Bear leaned toward her. "I could take you to the vet."

It was of course a ludicrous suggestion and when Bear put out a hand to check the wound, the groundhog went for his thumb.

He jerked his hand back.

The groundhog said to Bear that he should go ahead and shoot her in the head, put her out of her misery. *You call it the* humane *thing to do, don't you?*

Bear knew the groundhog was right, whether she said it or he imagined her saying it, he had to end her suffering by putting a bullet in her head. Groaning and chattering, the groundhog was now trying to bite her hindquarters as if to attack the wound itself.

"I'm sorry," Bear apologized again.

Too late for tears, she won't ever eat spring clover again, or breed with Lonnie or have no more babies, never sun herself on a rock ever again. Bear used to enjoy watching groundhogs stretch out like fat sunbathers in fur coats; then he'd shoot them where they lay.

The groundhog was losing strength. She curled up and told Bear that in years past he'd shot her children, one of her parents, both grandparents, various of her grandchildren. *And now me, what a blood-soaked villain you are.*

Just then Jamaica and POTUS, having broken faith with *sit, stay,* came over the hill and made for the wounded groundhog, who with suddenly renewed vigor began screaming, begging Bear not to let those helldogs tear her apart.

He just managed to grab the dogs by their scruffs, shouting at them to *sit,* to *stay.* Seeing their prey on the ground, the smell of its blood a cloud on their brains, the German shepherds barked furiously and strained against Bear's hands, which were weakened by the burns.

Holding the dogs, Bear couldn't reach the rifle to put the groundhog out of her misery, but the issue became moot when POTUS pulled away and rushed to the groundhog, which turned and chattered her teeth, dissuading POTUS not at all as he clamped his massive jaws behind her head and lifted her up in canine triumph. He shook her twice, then got a new hold and bit down so hard that Bear could hear a rib cage crack like green sticks being broken under a blanket.

Jamaica got loose from Bear's grip, too, and she and POTUS took opposite ends of the groundhog and ripped her open, green-veined guts popping out in obscene bulges.

Bear ordered the dogs to put her down, but they kept pulling on the groundhog. Finally, to escape their master's strange behavior (in the past he had always cheered them on when they caught a groundhog and pulled it apart like this), the two shepherds carried the groundhog carcass off into the woods where they could worry it without interference.

The big man felt like he could sense the spin of the earth, and he plunged drunkenly along the crest of the hill. He dropped to his knees, then lay flat on his belly to get his head under the barbwire fence so he could look right down the hole. "Lonnie?" He waited for an answer then called again, "Lonnie!"

"Who's Lonnie?"

This voice coming from behind him so startled Bear that he ripped a gash in the back of his head on the fence as he crabbed out from under it.

"Who's Lonnie?" Katherine asked again, laughing. "I'm hoping to develop a sense of humor."

"What?"

"Who's Lonnie and what's he doing down that hole?"

Bear was unable to answer, too muddled by all that had happened, by the possibility that even this woman standing here over him wasn't real, though she looked extravagantly real wearing a bulky green sweater over a red dress with a dangerously short hemline. Her also-red shoes were off her bare feet and held by red straps in the crook of one finger, her nails as red as everything else, such as her lips, red with abandon they were so red. She stood with her legs slightly apart as if bracing against the gentle breeze blowing across this hilltop, the wind occasionally lifting that red hem for a quick show of white leg.

Bear was as thrilled to see her as he would've been to see his beloved brother Robert coming home for a visit after all these years . . . except if it was Robert standing over him right now, Bear wouldn't be feeling so funny about bare legs and windblown hems.

"Do you know any chicken jokes?" she asked.

"Just the one about crossing the road," Bear said as he struggled to his feet. He touched the back of his head, which was wet with blood. He stared at her earrings, which were silver and gold feathers hanging almost to the shoulder, and thought, Katie must have the world's best collection of dangling earrings.

"That's a groundhog hole, isn't it?" she asked.

He nodded, staring intently at her face, that wide mouth and those white teeth, red hair and green eyes . . . Katie had more color than most of your bird species. And freckles! Like stars spilled . . . don't tell someone like Bear, a born counter, that stars and freckles don't count.

"Groundhogs are also known as woodchucks and whistlepigs," she said brightly—a student's recitation. "They're called whistlepigs because they often whistle shrilly when alarmed."

Bear nodded again. Many times he'd heard them whistle in alarm when he was killing them.

"Is Lonnie a groundhog?" she asked.

Bear knew she was teasing him, but he didn't care, was beyond caring, had gone dirt-eatingly insane.

"I've always wanted to ask one of them a question," Katherine said, holding her hand toward the burrow. "May I?"

Be my guest, he thought.

She got down on all fours right there in the pasture, wearing that short red dress, barefoot and down on all fours as she crawled to the fence and then went even lower on her elbows so she could direct whatever she was going to say into that burrow . . . Bear agitated as he watched that dress blow high. He could see the whites of her thighs.

"Lonnie!" she called. "Can you hear me, Lonnie?"

Bear waited tensely for an answer from inside the burrow.

"Lonnie," Katherine continued in a lighthearted voice, "I got a question for you, okay?" She started laughing. "How much wood could a woodchuck chuck"—laughing harder—"if a woodchuck could chuck wood?"

Finishing the question, Katherine put her forehead near the worn-smooth dirt of the burrow's entrance, then collapsed into a laughing jag that turned uncontrollable as she rolled onto her side in the grass, apparently unconcerned about soiling the red dress, pulling her knees up, showing panties, laughing, eyes tearing, until she was fighting for breath she was laughing so hard.

Bear watched, mouth dry all the way down his throat.

Finally able to sit up and hold her wet face in her hands, Katherine was repeating parts of the woodchuck-chucking-wood question that she'd asked Lonnie, shaking her head, sniffing back the tears, sighing with satisfaction and occasionally shaking with aftershocks of laughter.

Sometimes when Robert still lived on the farm, Bear recalled, he would get him laughing as Katie had laughed—how long's it been since I laughed like that?

Which was exactly what she said, speaking more to herself than to Bear. "Golly, how long has it been since I've laughed like that?"

She looked at him. "Help me up," she asked, extending a hand to Bear and squinting because the sun was behind him.

He pulled with such sudden strength that Katherine was launched into his embrace. Bear hadn't meant this to happen, at least not consciously, but now that she was in his arms, he held her tightly.

She went stiff.

He squeezed.

"What are you doing?" she asked coldly.

He didn't answer, hugging her close and smelling whatever she had put in her bath, her lotions and soap, feeling those dangling earrings, gold and silver feathers. Bear didn't want to stop hugging even as she insisted, "Let go of me."

He wanted to tell her, shush, hold still and let me hold you for a single minute more, I'll count the seconds out loud.

She brought her elbows in to use both arms against Bear's chest but still couldn't push him away. "You're frightening me."

Bear closed his eyes and squeezed harder.

Katherine pulled her right arm free and worked her hand up to Bear's face. She found a closed eye and gouged it as hard as she could with her thumb.

Bear grunted.

"Let go of me," she said.

He staggered back with a hand held over that eye.

"Don't ever do that again," she warned him.

He fell to his knees and told her he was insane.

Katherine's fear and anger shifted. "What did you say?"

"Animals talk to me."

"Which animals?"

"It started with that cow."

Katherine took a moment, then asked, "What did she say?"

He didn't answer.

"Moo?" she suggested.

15

"I raised cows all my life," Bear told Katie, "and ain't ever heard one say *moo.*"

"No? What do cows say?"

"They trumpet and they can sound like a tuba or a trombone. They bellow and go on like bagpipes, they moan and groan and murmur . . . but they don't say moo."

She straightened the little red dress and pulled the sweater more tightly around her. "You're a poet."

He lifted both shoulders.

"How's your eye?"

Bear opened it to show her. The white of the damaged left eye had gone blood-red where she'd gouged him, and both eyes were producing protective tears.

"You shouldn't grab a woman," she told him. "And if a woman tells you to let go, you should let go *immediately.* Haven't you ever heard of unasked-for attention?"

"I didn't ask you to kiss me . . . out there after that Scrudde cow died and you pulled me down to kiss me, that was unasked for."

Katherine hadn't expected this to be thrown back at her and she took a moment to compose a reply. "Did you fear for your life when I gave you that unwanted kiss?"

Bear admitted that he hadn't feared for his life, no.

"That's the difference," she said. "Just now, I did."

He nodded, he could see the difference.

"Look at your hands."

Bear put them out for examination: they were dirty and infected and bleeding in places where the fire had cracked open his skin.

Katie said she would bandage them again, her first aid kit was in her car, which was still parked at Bear's farm. "What're you doing out here anyway, I heard a shot."

"I was hunting groundhogs. I thought I shot a little girl."

"What?"

"I suppose it's part of going crazy, thinking you've done things you ain't."

"You thought you shot a girl?"

"Yeah, but it wasn't a girl, it was that groundhog."

"You killed a groundhog called Lonnie?" she asked, looking back at the burrow.

He shook his head. "I killed . . . I think it was Lonnie's wife, from what she said."

Katie asked him why he killed the groundhog.

"I shoot 'em all the time, my dogs kill 'em, too."

"Why?"

"They're groundhogs."

"So?"

"They eat my grass."

"How much?"

He didn't understand.

"How much grass do they eat a year?" she asked.

"Is that like what you were saying down the hole, how much wood can a woodchuck chuck?"

"No, I'm asking you, how much money a year do you lose through grass eaten by groundhogs?"

Bear didn't know. The groundhogs from this burrow might eat a hillside of grass in one season and if you baled that grass into hay instead of them eating it, it would make a few bales of low-quality hay.

"A hundred dollars worth of grass a year?" Katie asked.

"No, more like ten."

"Ten dollars." She was surprised it was so little. "Ten dollars per groundhog."

"For a whole burrow of 'em, ten dollars a year at the outside."

"And to save that ten dollars a year, you kill them."

"Also, a cow could step in one of their holes and break its leg."

"How many cows have you owned who've stepped in groundhog holes and broken legs?"

"None."

"None?"

"But it could happen."

"How long have you been raising cows?"

"All my life."

"So to save a few dollars a year and guard against the unlikely prospect of a cow stepping in a hole, you kill groundhogs by the dozen. Does that make sense to you?"

He didn't understand what she was getting at.

"You don't have to kill groundhogs for any economic reason, you do it because you enjoy it, isn't that true?"

Bear thought it probably was.

"And don't call it recreational *hunting,*" Katie said, warming to the topic. "It's not a deer *harvest,* either. Not eradication, elimination, reduction in population. Call it what it is—joy killing."

"I can't see out of this eye," Bear said, covering and uncovering it with one of his burned hands.

"No, we're not going to get diverted from the topic here."

Seemed he was crying now, though it was difficult to apportion his tears between eye gouging and mental distress.

Katherine resisted asking him what was wrong. She knew he wasn't crying for groundhogs, but finally said, "Okay, what is it?"

"If I died," Bear told her haltingly, "nobody'd be at the funeral, maybe just Robert if he could get time off from his job and travel here from Chicago—one man sitting there alone in the church. Maybe the vet would come, too, but that would make only two, not counting the funeral director. It seems a person should make a bigger difference than that, living and dying and getting only one or two people at your funeral."

She put a hand on his arm.

"I'm alone in the world," he told her.

"I know how you feel."

He wondered if she really did. "You know how it feels to be alone in the world?"

"I'm governor of that state."

"What?"

"Loneliness. I own all the albums."

He didn't know what that meant, either.

"You ever hear that song," she asked, "about standing knee-deep in the river, dying of thirst?"

He shook his head.

"That's how I felt back in Washington, I had a fiancé and a great job, lots of friends, money was never an issue, I had a whole *river* of good, standing in it knee deep—but then why did I feel like I was dying of thirst?"

Bear didn't know.

"After college I volunteered for animal rights organizations. I had major problems with their philosophies and attitudes, but the *work* we did was inspiring. It made me feel good about myself. Does that sound corny?"

Bear didn't know.

"The vet, Doc Setton, told me about two horses that are being starved to death. Maybe you and I could drive over there and throw them some feed."

"Who they belong to?"

"Well, that's the problem, isn't it? People around here don't want you interfering with their animals even if you're only trying to help."

"Sometimes my mind gets in a muddle."

Katie started to say something flippant but then realized the big man was trembling.

"I don't know what you're saying," he tried to explain. "What is it you want me to do? I'm a lot better if I got rules to follow. My dad had rules."

"It's no big deal, we'll just drive over tomorrow and throw some hay over the fence for those horses. Something good we can do. Then maybe I won't feel like the whole universe is coming apart and—"

"Me, too."

"What?"

"I feel that way, too . . . like I'm dissolving."

"Let's do this one good thing, then. Doc Setton said the farmer is starving a mare and her foal. Apparently the man has never changed the foal's halter and she's gotten so big now that the halter he first put on her is tightening around her head as she grows, cutting into her. He doesn't care, this farmer. When Doc tried to talk to him about it, the farmer ran him off with a gun. So what I was thinking, you and I can go out there tomorrow and cut that halter off, feed the foal and her mother—"

"More than just throwing some hay over the fence."

Katie agreed. "But we'll make a difference to those animals."

"You say he ran Doc off with a gun?"

"Yes."

Bear nodded, considering the implications.

Here's one way of thinking about it, she told him, if the farmer kills us, shoots us dead right out there in the field with his poor horses, then our deaths will mean something, the publicity will get those horses taken care of, animal rights activists will come from all over the country to our funerals, they'll make us martyrs. "That means—"

"I know what a martyr is."

Looking at his face, Katherine worried that she was exploiting this simple man, enticing him to go out on a rescue with her so she could feel better about herself; then she'd go back to D.C. and it was Bear who would continue living here, dealing with the consequences. "Maybe you should take a day or two to think it over."

He said he was ready to go anywhere with her, do anything, face a man with a gun. He wasn't afraid of dying—afraid of lots of things, of never talking to Robert again, of being embarrassed in front of people when his mind gets in a muddle or he doesn't remember to keep his mouth closed or does something inappropriate—but dying, no, dying wasn't scary to him.

16

"Hello, Robert, guess what, it's your brother."

"Who?"

"It's me, Robert . . . *Bear.*"

"Oh, hey." He laughed in that peculiar manner of his, under his breath like a soft cough. "How you doing?"

"Fine." Bear had decided to tell Robert about going crazy, hearing cows and groundhogs talk, and also about Katie and rescuing animals; these were the topics Bear had written on the sheet of notebook paper grasped now in his bandaged hand.

"I'm fine, too," Robert said. "In fact, I'm feeling no pain."

Bear's heart sank because this meant Robert was drunk, and Bear could hear confirmation of this in his brother's voice. Robert became belligerent when drunk, very like their father, though of course you couldn't say that to Robert, he'd get mad at you.

"You feeling no pain, Bear?"

He ran a quick inventory: the stinging gash on the back of his head where he'd caught himself on the barbwire fence, his left eye, which Katie had gouged and which now ached dully; his burned hands, both newly bandaged by Katie but still deep-well sources of pain; his teeth, which always hurt; that puncture wound on his right leg. And he had a headache.

"Bear?" Robert slurred.

"I'm fine. I wanted to ask you something, Robert. I think I'm going crazy." Bear braced himself for the onslaught of Robert's concern—demanding that Bear go see a doctor, maybe insisting Bear come to Chicago and stay with him and his family until the crisis had passed. But Robert said nothing until Bear repeated, "I'm going crazy."

"We're all going somewhere," Robert said. "I'm going broke."

"I'm sorry, Robert."

"Yeah, I'm sorry, too—the wife, the queen of consumerism, wouldn't listen to me, didn't believe my lectures about how we were spending ourselves into bankruptcy."

He didn't know what to say to that, not since their father's funeral had Bear heard his brother so bitter.

"I was thinking of sending the boys down to stay with you for a while," Robert said. "Until the wife and I settle this between us."

Bear went wide-eyed with excitement. "Oh Robert, that would be the greatest thing ever, I'd teach them all about the farm and show them the animals and keep a close eye on them so they never came to harm and—"

"Just considering it, not saying I will, the wife didn't exactly jump with joy when I mentioned the possibility of sending them to the farm for a week or two—"

"Two weeks! You betcha, Robert, it'd be the best thing in the world for the little guys."

"Not so little now."

"No, I bet they're big and tough like their Uncle Bear, I bet they can take more megahurts than I ever could."

"What did you just say?"

"What?"

"About megahurts, you think you're going to give my boys megahurts?"

"No, Robert, I was just . . . I would never hurt them boys—"

So quickly that it took Bear's breath away, Robert was shouting at him, saying if Bear ever did meet those two boys, his nephews, he better not even dream of giving them megahurts or Dutch rubs or Indian burns. Robert hollering drunkenly into the phone, "Don't you realize the only relationship you had with the old man was *pain!*"

Bear didn't reply. Robert's anger had shocked him mute.

"All those damn games he played with you—the old man

doing it because he was a perverse, sadistic bastard, you accepting it because that's the only way you ever got any attention from him. Don't you remember?"

Bear remembered.

"The old man tried to pull that crap on me," Robert shouted into the phone, "but I didn't go along with it, not like you, Jesus Christ, I think it must have something to do with IQ, maybe if a person is smarter, things hurt more."

Bear thought, Robert doesn't even know how much a dumb old retard like me can hurt.

❦

Outside under a night of such stars you'd wish for poetry, the brown duck climbed a hill by the pump house. Once on top, he turned and paused, then came running downhill, wings flapping, trying to get airborne. But the fat little brown duck had been bred for meat, too breast-heavy for flight. *Nevertheless* he climbed back up that hill, turned around at the top, and came running and flapping back down. Did this over and over and over until the downhill duck met an uphill gust that caught just right, lifted him a few feet off the ground and set him soaring twenty yards or so before he crashed in a rolling heap, brown feathers flying. After collecting himself he stretched to full height, beat his wings in triumph, and quacked so loud he woke up the dogs—and also the big white Peking duck, who came waddling over to rape him in the vent.

On the porch, POTUS, the massive German shepherd, struggled up to the sitting position and watched the ducks with disdain. He was full of pain, cancer, and when the female shepherd came to lick his muzzle, POTUS accepted her attention, closing his eyes and elevating his head and squeezing his eyes shut from the pain.

❦

Robert was still berating Bear, warning him he'd never see his nephews, saying that he had never laid a hand on his sons because the cycle of violence had to be broken, violence that had been handed down in their family by cuff and blow over the years. "Why do you think that happened to Mom? The old man was always knocking her around." Robert had broken the cycle with his sons, he said, had never struck them, though obviously the cycle continued undiminished with Bear, who wanted to put megahurts on his nephews. No, that wasn't going to happen, never.

"I wouldn't hurt them boys," Bear quietly pledged after a gap of silence while Robert sucked at whatever he was drinking. "Somebody could say to me, 'Bear, you better hurt Robert's sons or we'll cut your arms off with a chain saw,' and I'd tell them, well, go ahead and pull-start your chain saw, mister, because I would never—"

"Do you hear yourself," Robert asked, breathless from the drink. "Talking about cutting off arms with a chain saw, Jesus."

Bear was horrified that Robert had misunderstood him. "Not them boys' arms, *mine.*"

"For chrissakes."

Bear was shouting. "Not them boys' arms, *mine!*"

"Bear, calm down."

"I'm sorry!"

"Bear—"

"I'M SORRY!"

Robert waited, then said, "I should've sold the farm after the old man died . . . put you somewhere you could be looked after."

Bear pleaded, "Oh, Robert, don't even say that."

"He left the farm to me, that conniving rat bastard."

After their father's burial, Robert and Bear had met with a lawyer who showed them the will: the younger son, Joseph, known as Bear, was bequeathed boxes of clothing that their father had acquired through some maneuver never made clear, payment of a debt or purchase of stolen goods, box after box of dress clothes for large men, slacks and jackets and yellowing white shirts kept in the attic, Bear never allowed to wear any of this clothing while his father was alive. *Everything else,* the farm and animals and equipment, was left to the older brother, Robert, even though he had quit the farm at age eighteen and since then returned only rarely. Bear worked that farm all his life, full-time since age sixteen, and got nothing but those boxes of clothes. Oddly, the will delighted Bear, who was under the impression that because Robert now owned the farm he would move back and Bear would have company, Robert and his wife and the two little boys Bear had never met. They could all live together like one of those happy families you read about. It was Robert who'd been outraged by the will, who saw it as their father's attempt to reach back from the grave to force Robert to come home even at the expense of Bear's rightful inheritance. Robert put it right, wouldn't leave the lawyer's office until papers had been drawn transferring ownership of everything to Bear, who was disappointed almost to tears, knowing that since Robert wouldn't be owning the farm, he wouldn't be coming home, either.

Bear was in a panic on the phone to his brother. "Dad left the farm to you, Robert, and I've always told you you could have it back anytime you want, but don't be talking about sending me off to—"

"Sell that place and keep myself out of bankruptcy," Robert mumbled as if talking in his sleep. "How much it'd bring—"

"Sell what . . . the farm?"

Robert muttered.

"Robert, I can't hear you."

Although the connection sounded as if it stayed open, Bear couldn't get any response from his brother and eventually hung up.

He threw away his notes, what he had intended to talk to Robert about, and went downstairs to the bathroom but decided not to wash because he didn't want to get the new bandages wet, and then he didn't brush his teeth either because they were sensitive to touch and to cold water. He returned to his bedroom to look out the window at where the barn used to be and to say his prayer, *Dear Lord, I'm ready to put this load down anytime You say.*

17

The next morning, while Bear drove, Katie told him about the animal rights organizations where she volunteered after college. Bear didn't always understand what she was talking about, as when Katie said she didn't play "gotcha," which so many people outside the movement used against animal activists (you don't eat meat but you wear leather shoes—*gotcha*) but she didn't go in for holier-than-thou, either, which so many people *within* the movement used against each other.

"There was a guy we knew who wouldn't give up eating meat. The other volunteers and I considered him a friend and he worked with us on certain projects but he just wouldn't give up meat. Then finally he decided at least to stop eating veal," she told Bear, "but people in the movement still considered this guy a killer for eating other kinds of meat, and they eventually hounded him out. I argued we should've congratulated the guy for abandoning veal, should've encouraged him to evolve even further, encouraged each step he took, giving up all meat, no fowl and no fish, no factory eggs, no production milk."

"What would he eat, then?" Bear asked, feeling sorry for the poor guy.

"Vegetables."

Bear tried to imagine life without steaks, without pork chops.

Katie looked across the truck's cab and thought Bear was dressed nattily for an animal rescue—dark green slacks, a muted yellow vest, dull white shirt, and sporty checked coat. His long black hair was pulled back and tied with a string and his all-red left eye lent him an air of malice.

"You look pretty," he told her.

She didn't feel pretty, wearing jeans and a big navy-blue sweatshirt, no makeup, though green eyes and red hair still gave her color.

Driving now along the Briars River, Bear said, "If you were that river, I'd go swimming today."

Katie wondered about him, how much more there was to Bear than met the eye. She said, "It's a cold river."

"I'd go swimming all the same, like that river you talked about yesterday, standing knee deep in it and still dying for a drink, but if you were that river and I was in it, I wouldn't be thirsty the rest of my life."

Katie worried she might have to fend him off again today. "You know, Bear, I wouldn't patronize you for the world, but—" She stopped when she saw him shaking his head. "What's wrong?"

"Don't know that word."

"Patronize?"

"Yeah."

"It means—"

"No, just give me the spelling, I got all kinds of dictionaries at home and I pretty well know a word after I look it up."

She spelled it for him and told Bear he was a poet at heart, the way he spoke of the river, but, "I have a fiancé and—"

"I know what that word means."

They drove then in silence until Katie asked him, "Tell me about yourself, what—"

"I am Joseph David Long, known as Bear, thirty-two years old, schooled to age sixteen, a devout reader. I own along with my brother Robert a farm, three hundred and twenty acres well watered but not much flat. I raise beef cows for money and lots of other animals for fun."

She laughed.

He looked at her sidelong.

"I'm sorry, but it was funny the way you said that, like a canned response."

He didn't know what a canned response was, but told her

that Robert had taught him to speak up when he was asked a question about himself.

"And you say your brother owns the farm with you?"

"Dad left it to Robert and Robert gave it to me."

"So actually you own the farm."

"You mean actually like legally?"

"Yes."

"I don't know about that part but if Robert showed up tomorrow and said, Bear, give me the farm, I would."

"And Robert is older—"

"Four years older but not nearly my size."

"You like Robert."

A big grin cracked his face.

"I gather from your expression," Katie said, "that the answer is yes."

"Oh gracious, I love him to pieces."

"And Robert feels the same way about you."

"He's always watched out for me." When they were boys, if Robert caught Bear eating clay, he would spit on a corner of his handkerchief and wipe Bear's face and clean his fingernails, tsk-ing as he told his little brother that if he got caught eating clay again the old man would beat him senseless. Although he didn't mean to make trouble, Bear had to admit he loved being cleaned up and fussed over by Robert.

Bear told Katie, "Robert had more girlfriends than you could shake a stick at."

"I see."

There followed another road stretch of silence, then they were at their destination. Katie, turning to Bear, was surprised to see how nervous he looked. She put a hand on his arm. "The Hopi Indians have a word they use when it seems the world is wobbling, life has gone out of balance . . . *koyaanisqatsi.* Can you say that?"

He couldn't but knowing that Indians had a name for it was calming.

"Shhh, shhh," she said, patting his arm—which also had an effect like oil on water.

❦

With Bear's old truck stopped by the side of the road, Katie went over with him the information that Doc Setton had given her about having noticed last month that the farmer's two horses, mother and daughter, were starving and the yearling wore a too-small halter tightening around its skull. But when Doc stopped at the farmhouse and asked about the horses, the farmer—his name was Noyles—ran him off with a gun. Noyles apparently lived alone, Doc told Katie, and had a big black dog that looked like a biter, its name was Mitchell.

"Not much to go on," Katie admitted as she looked out at the pasture, wondering where the horses were, where Noyles and the biting black dog Mitchell might be. "Doc took the information to the county, but by the time the legal process goes back and forth, those horses'll be dead and the most Noyles gets is a fine, probably not even that. As far as our plan of action . . . what do you think?"

"Find the horses," Bear said. "Feed 'em, cut the halter off, treat the wounds, leave."

Katie agreed it was a good plan.

They got out of the truck. Bear took a five-gallon bucket of sweetfeed from the back along with a kit of horse medicine, a length of rope, and a currycomb. Also in the pickup were bales of hay, which they'd leave here and return for when the horses were found. Once they crossed a fence and entered the farmer's stony pasture, Bear told Katie solemnly, "Now we're trespassing."

She touched his elbow. "We're not going to deal with the owner, it's not going to be like that cow with Scrudde and Coote. We'll just treat and feed the horses, then leave."

Bear wasn't convinced.

The mare and her yearling filly were down in a swale, standing in the creek trying to eat water plants, actually scraping moss off rocks with their teeth. Seeing them, Katie was caught between anger and tears. Who could let their animals get in such a condition, was it ignorance or cruelty or stupid indifference?

The mother, still trying to nurse her filly, was in the worse shape: rib cage plainly visible, hip bones tenting, skin draping from bone to bone like rotting old material; she was swaybacked and even her neck looked decrepit like the remains of a suspension bridge. The filly was in a similarly poor condition, but the horror for her was the nylon halter. Because nylon won't tear or break free or rot, most horse people will use leather halters on horses turned out to pasture or at the very least will put a leather top strap on a nylon halter so that if the horse gets hung up it can probably break the leather and go free. The all-nylon halter had been put on this filly some time ago and then never replaced with a bigger size, the halter straps embedding themselves in the filly's head and face as she grew, the way a wire fence will embed in a growing tree. Even this early in April, flies covered the filly's head, attracted by suppurating sores where skin had been rubbed raw to the bone against bowstring-tight nylon.

"I didn't realize it would be so bad," she said.

He nodded. It was bad. Bear had started raising horses after the old man died, but horses are notorious for illness and injury. The old story said the reason cowboys got so mean and drunk in saloons was, they had to deal with horses all day. If you wanted to have a horse to ride on any given day, you'd better keep two more as spares. For Bear, they got too expensive and he had to sell himself out of the horse business . . . maybe that's what happened to Noyles who owned these two horses, he ran out of money and patience for them.

"They're Thoroughbreds," Bear told Katie. "Racehorses."

"They don't even look like horses, they look like something . . . I don't know, something pathetic."

"I don't think they're going to live," he said.

She said *oh* quietly and asked Bear if he could try, please try to save their lives.

He'd seen a lot of death on his farm and could tell if an animal was going to die, not by measurement or test but by the look in its eye, the hobbled hopelessness with which it walked, as these horses now walked, gaunt with a life force that flickered.

"Bear?"

"Not worth the effort."

She asked him again to try, *please.*

He would've preferred to turn around and leave. The aura of death around these horses unsettled him. Bear had seen animals react with repugnance or even rage toward death. One time he accidentally ran over a little black dog he'd adopted from a stray and as the little dog flopped around in death throes, Bear's two German shepherds, who had previously treated the stray with affection, attacked it viciously, as if to kill death itself, as strange as that sounds. Another time Bear found a hen that had been nearly killed by a fox, and although Bear didn't think the hen would live he placed it over in the chicken coop anyway. The roosters ran to the dying hen and repeatedly mounted it, not in the usual gleeful manner of roosters but with fury, as if raping the dying hen. Then the rest of the flock joined in, pecking and spurring the pathetic creature that to the flock represented death. Bear felt a similar distaste for these poor dying horses and turned to leave.

She grabbed his jacket and asked a third time. "Please."

Okay, he thought, but it'll end in tears. "Go down there slow," Bear said.

Steep banks flanked the creek to form a natural corral with escape routes upstream and down. He positioned Katie in the water downstream and then approached the pair of horses from upstream. Bear talked softly and had a natural comforting manner beyond anything Katie had witnessed in all her previous work with animals. With their nickers and soft snorts, the two horses seemed to be telling Bear they were dying, pleading as Katie had done for their lives, please try to save us. Is this what he meant about talking with animals? she wondered. Even when he was cutting the nylon halter off the filly and then medicating her sores, painful procedures both, the young horse would shy away but keep returning to Bear time after time.

While he continued treating the filly, Katie said she'd go back to the truck for a bale of hay. Climbing the bank, she saw someone, presumably the owner, Noyles, approach from across the pasture. With him was a large black dog. Noyles carried a gun.

Katie went stumbling back down to the creek, spooking the horses as she told Bear what she'd seen: a man with a gun and a dog. Bear nodded, told Katie to gather up the horses and keep feeding them but don't come back up that hill until he says it's okay.

"I think we should just leave," she said. "I don't want you to get into any more trouble with the locals."

Locals. Is that what I am to her, Bear wondered, a local? He told her, "Do as I say."

She was put off by that but did as he said. Fifteen, twenty minutes passed. The sweetfeed was gone and she had groomed both horses with a currycomb. Then she started up the hill—and met Bear coming down with a big bale of hay in each bandaged hand.

"What happened?" she asked. "I was worried you'd get shot, I kept waiting to hear it."

"Two bales might be too much for 'em but it's only orchard grass, not too rich, and we'll—"

"Bear, what did that man say to you?"

"Told us to get off his property."

"Did he threaten to shoot you?"

"Yes."

"Did the dog try to attack you?"

"No, but I had the advantage there."

Katie waited to hear what that advantage was, but Bear said, "Come on, let's feed this hay out and go."

When they finished with the horses and climbed up from the creek, Noyles and the dog, Mitchell, were gone.

On the ride back to the farm, Katie was thrilled from the excitement of the rescue and again asked Bear to tell her everything the farmer said and did.

"Just told us to get off his land," Bear replied.

"Do you think the horses will make it?"

"There's a chance." But someone would have to drive over

every day, nearly an hour each way from his farm, to feed the horses and treat the filly's sores. Bear knew from a lifetime of work what the responsibility of animals entailed and wondered if Katie realized what they were getting into. "I hope that farmer doesn't resent us stepping in to care for his animals," she said.

Oh, he resents it all right, Bear thought.

"We saved those horses, didn't we?" she asked.

I didn't, he thought, you did . . . Katie did. Bear laughed.

"What?" she asked.

"Katydid."

18

"What the hell you doing on my property?" Noyles had called when Bear first came up over the hill from the creek.

The man and his dog were about fifty yards away. Bear held up one bandaged hand to indicate he would answer Noyles's question when he got close enough that he didn't have to shout.

But the farmer warned him off: "You come any closer, this dog'll tear you apart!"

Not if his name is Mitchell, Bear thought. Never in his life had he feared a dog whose name he knew.

When Bear was within a few yards and it seemed that the dog was about to attack, Bear said, "*Mitchell,* stay out of this, you hear me *Mitchell*?"

This confused the dog, to hear a stranger call him so confidently by name, and it infuriated Noyles. "How'd you know his name? And who the hell are you, what're you doing here? Who's down that hill with you?"

"Them horses down there—" Bear started.

Which angered the farmer even more. "Oh geez, it's with them damn horses again!" He was about sixty, thin-limbed but bellied like a woman eight months pregnant . . . like he was carrying a huge basketball tumor that sucked nutrients out of everywhere else in the body to keep itself fat. Noyles wore overalls and kept one hand on the big black dog's collar, holding a .22 varmint rifle in the other hand. "They's racing horses, meant to be skinny, like greyhounds."

"You know better, Mr. Noyles."

"Don't tell me what I know, who the hell are you anyway?"

"They call me Bear."

"Jesus, I heard of you. Lost your barn, didn't you."

Bear nodded.

"Was it sticking your nose in other people's business, crossing fences to trespass on their land, fooling with their livestock, is that what got your barn burned down?"

Although he was being sarcastic, Noyles had it exactly right on each count.

"If I shot you right now where you stand, wouldn't be a court in the state convict me." Noyles hadn't shaved in a couple days and his whiskered face pinched up as he ranted. "Whatever happened to minding your own damn business— Hey, hold it, don't come no closer, I'll let slip this dog."

But Bear crossed the last few feet that separated them, telling Mitchell three times to stay out of it. When he realized Mitchell had been compromised, Noyles raised up the rifle. Then Bear did an astonishing thing, he grabbed the muzzle and held it right against his own forehead. "Go ahead and shoot me, Mr. Noyles, make a martyr . . . you know what they are?"

"'Course I do," he said angrily, trying to pull the rifle away from Bear. "Are you crazy?"

Bear admitted he was.

"What I do with my animals—"

"We're going to drive by every day and check, throw some grain and hay over the fence. You leave a halter off that filly, we'll continue treating her sores." All this Bear said while still holding the rifle muzzle firmly against his forehead.

"If you think I'm paying for—"

Bear said there wouldn't be any charge. Only then did he let go of the muzzle, which left a round red dent in the middle of his forehead.

"You don't know nothing about me," the farmer told him.

"No sir," Bear agreed, though in fact he knew that Noyles was shamed on account of the horses, ashamed he'd let the situation go on so long. Somewhere along the line he had become defensive and refused to take care of his horses just to spite those who kept insisting he make it right . . . Bear knew that much.

"Damn horses." The man's face was pinched so tight his features looked tied in a knot.

"I used to raise 'em myself," Bear said. "They was good for burning hay."

Noyles laughed but then caught himself. "Get the hell off my land."

19

That night Robert called Bear. It was almost always the other way around, Bear calling his brother, so this conversation felt odd from the outset.

"Hey Bear . . . I *think* we talked last night."

"We did, Robert."

"Not that I remember much of it, I was feeling no pain."

"That's what you said last night."

"What else did I say?"

Bear didn't answer.

"Nothing to hurt your feelings, I hope."

"No, Robert," Bear lied.

"So what's been happening in your life?"

Bear shrugged, which of course Robert couldn't see.

"Bear?"

"I'm here."

"You okay?"

"Yes."

"Have you started to build a new barn yet?"

"No."

"How come?"

"Dad said stay out of debt."

"Jesus I wish I'd learned *that* lesson from the old man. But if you're not going to rebuild the barn, where do you put hay this summer?"

"I might get out of the cattle business, Robert."

"Really?"

"My heart's not in it."

"Bear, you love cattle."

"I know."

"If your heart's not in cattle, where is it—with that woman you were telling me about?"

"We went out today."

"See a movie, go to lunch?"

"Took care of a couple horses."

Robert asked what this woman was like.

Bear said she was wonderful. "And guess what, Robert."

"What?"

"She doesn't patronize me."

❦

"Hello, Katherine?"

"William! It's nice hearing your voice."

"Well, you certainly sound chipper, that's a welcome change."

"I feel great, actually I do."

"Then maybe you're ready to give up small-town living and return to your life here, hmm?"

"Yes, I think you're right."

"That's great news, Katherine. We all miss you. What have you been up to?"

"I told you about meeting that old veterinarian, Doc Setton, the one who sent some animals that I'm caring for until they can be adopted."

"The dogs and two parrots, yes. But I thought you were keeping them just overnight—don't tell me they're still all there, two parrots and how many dogs did you say, four?"

"Eight."

"*Eight?* You have to be joking. What are they doing to the gardens, the grass? Kath-er-ine, how long have you had them in that little cottage and—"

"The dogs stay outside."

"And how much longer do you intend to keep them, and what about the parrots, aren't they notorious for chewing on furniture, shitting everywhere? Really, Katherine, I didn't exactly visualize you running an animal sanctuary in that little cottage."

"William, what I started to tell you, the vet told me about a pair of horses that were starving to death, one of them needed medical help for a halter that had—"

"What's this got to do with— Oh God, don't tell me you brought *horses* to the cottage!"

She laughed. "No, William, listen to me. I went out today and helped save those horses. There's this guy I met and we—"

"Oh, so now you've met *a guy.* Some local macho type?"

"William, he's like a retarded farmer." Katie stiffened with shame. She'd said it to placate William, but it was a betrayal of Bear and she wished she could take it back.

"So you and your retard—"

"William, don't say that!"

"Darling, I'm quoting *you.*"

"I know. But don't."

"What's wrong? You're not being logical. Do you have a soft spot for this *special* farmer friend of yours?"

"No, of course not," Katie said, lying to her fiancé.

ల

Also that evening Phil Scrudde stopped at the Noyles farm and introduced himself. He asked Noyles if it was true what Scrudde had heard, two people trespassing and interfering with Noyles's stock, one of these trespassers a big dumb retard and the other a freckled fruitcake from Washington, D.C.

Noyles, who didn't invite Scrudde to step out of his Cadillac, said it was true.

"They did the same to me," Scrudde said. "Throat-slit one of my cows and then nearly killed me and one of my hired hands. The retard's name is Joe Long, they call him Bear 'cause he walks like one and has about the same intelligence. The redhead is Katherine Renault, she's living in Briars, taking a long vacation, people say, but I think maybe she's with some animal rights organization—you know, *infiltrating.*"

"What the two of them did here," Noyles said, "was feed my horses and take care of some sores on one of them. That Bear claims they're going to keep coming back and feeding them horses, no charge to me." He paused, spat, used the toe of his boot to cover the spit with dust, then went on. "Hell, I say let 'em, damn fools for feeding another man's stock but I won't stop 'em . . . don't know nothing about no infiltrating."

"We have to take action, Mr. Noyles, or there'll be bunny-huggers all over and you won't be able to raise your voice to an animal, you'll have to air-condition your barns and serve heated meals in winter."

Noyles said he didn't know anything about that, either, but if two crazy people wanted to feed his horses for free, so be it. "I never talked to the woman but that man they call Bear sure was crazy, he held my rifle to his forehead and told me to go on and make him a martyr."

"It may yet come to that," Scrudde said. "But it's the woman who's the troublemaker, not Bear, he's just being led around by his nose . . . if not other parts. We're thinking of putting a group together to go over and pay her a visit, was wondering if you were interested."

Noyles said he wasn't, then repeated his opinion that if two people wanted to feed and treat his horses for free, so be it.

Scrudde told him he was missing the point, didn't see the bigger picture.

Noyles didn't like the insinuation, didn't care for the man's tone of voice or his choice of a cowboy hat for headgear, either. "Get the hell off my land."

Scrudde turned the Cadillac around and took off in a spray of gravel that made Mitchell bark. On the way out Noyles's lane, Scrudde decided to drive over and see if Carl Coote still had plans for the Renault woman.

20

The next morning at Doc Setton's veterinary clinic, Katherine was introduced to a deputy sheriff everyone called by his last name, Miller.

"Miller was Robert's best friend in high school," Doc explained. "Robert being Bear's older brother."

"Ah," Katherine said. "Best friend to the famous Robert."

"Famous?" Miller asked cautiously.

"Bear talks about him all the time."

Miller nodded. He was short, five-six or so, and looked like a banty rooster because of the large, puffy, military-style nylon jacket he wore. The wide-brimmed trooper hat and heavy leather belt with cuffs and gun and spray also lent Miller an air of being all puffed up and armed with no place to go. Unlike his dress, however, Miller's manner and voice and face were soft and friendly. He took off his big hat and put it on the counter. The Cub Scout haircut and pug nose added to his look of a little boy playing deputy sheriff.

The doc had gone in the back to check on a dog, leaving Katie and Miller here in the reception area, which was empty, no patients waiting and no receptionist, either; the vet couldn't afford one now that he'd gone softhearted for animals and his clientele had dwindled to people of a like mind, animal-lovers, a decided minority around here.

Miller told Katie, "Sometimes Bear doesn't handle himself very well in tense situations. In the past there's been some misunderstandings. One time he tried to 'borrow' a couple boys from the Lutheran Home."

"Doc told me."

The deputy was disappointed he didn't get to tell the story. "I took care of it because I like Bear and I know him. If he was to get involved in a tense situation involving an animal rescue, especially one where the animal's owner wasn't cooperating, I'm not sure if Bear could be trusted."

"Trusted?"

"Trusted to keep his cool and not have a breakdown or run away or even, if he felt threatened or cornered, to turn violent."

"You're referring to Scrudde and Coote, the way Bear stopped them from torturing that cow?"

"Yeah."

"I'm sorry that happened, I didn't mean to provoke anything of that nature. Someone told me a cow was being tortured and—"

"That would be Barbara, the bus driver."

"I keep forgetting, everyone knows everything."

"Scrudde talked to me about what happened that morning. He wanted to know his options."

"Options? I guess one option was burning Bear's barn to the ground."

Miller asked if she had any evidence to back up that accusation.

Katie held up a hand. "Forget I said anything, I'm not getting involved in this."

"You're already involved."

"No I'm not," she insisted.

Which is when Doc Setton returned, saw their faces, and asked what was wrong.

"I was just telling her," Miller said, "and I've warned you about this, too, Doc, when you start interfering with another man's animals, somebody's going to get hurt."

"You're right, Miller," the vet said, smiling.

"Then will the two of you please just back off? And don't get Bear involved. I'd hate to have to call Robert and tell him that two people are messing with Bear, endangering him by—"

"Endangering him?" Katie asked.

Doc Setton said, "We don't want Miller to go tattling to Robert. Miller thinks Robert walks on water, isn't that right, deputy?"

"We were best friends in high school," he said defensively as he put his wide-brimmed hat back on. "His father left the farm to Robert but Robert immediately signed it over to Bear because that was the right thing to do; now, if you call that walking on water, I don't know, but all the more power to him. In high school most guys didn't want their younger brothers hanging around no matter what, but Robert took Bear everywhere. Bear acted funny at times, weird, embarrassing, but Robert was never embarrassed, he always stood up for Bear." The deputy turned to look at Katie. "Trespassing onto other people's property and deciding for them when one of their animals needs to be put down, it's not lawsuits you need to be worrying about like you might back in Washington—here, it's getting shot. And on a personal level I wish you'd leave Bear out of it." Smiling thinly, the deputy tapped the brim of his hat and left.

Which is when Doc told Katie, "I got another rescue for you."

"What about the deputy's warning?"

"This one's not a case of cruelty, just an unfortunate situation. An elderly woman living by herself, maybe has Alzheimer's, though I think she's just old and confused. Her cat population has gotten out of hand, no longer healthy for her or the cats. I was hoping you and Bear could stop by and take a look, see what needs to be done."

Katie said they would but not just yet, there was a more pressing rescue on the agenda for tonight.

Doc asked about it, but Katie said she didn't want to go into details with him. "For your own protection."

"Sounds mysterious."

"I contacted some people I used to know."

"And you're involving Bear?"

"Maybe, if he chooses to. He's not the dummy that people take him for."

Doc nodded. "I've always liked Bear, you know that. But let's face it, hon, he's strange. The fact that he never talks, don't you find that uncomfortable?"

"He talks. The only thing I find uncomfortable is the reaction we get from people in town who see me and Bear together. I feel like I'm in the South fifty or sixty years ago and Bear is a black man and people disapprove of me driving around with him in his truck."

"I told you before, Bear and all his eccentricities are accepted because he's always been gentle. A violent Bear will frighten people and make them mad, put him in danger, like Miller said."

"He's not violent. And he's not retarded, either. I feel safe with him."

Setton said he wasn't going to argue with her about Bear.

"I enjoy his company, too—it's not like I regard him as a big dumb bodyguard."

"Good."

"He keeps his mouth closed almost all the time now."

"Really?"

"I think he's magnificent."

"That's great, hon. As long as the two of you don't take any stupid risks and end up getting shot. Meanwhile, the fact that you and Bear get along so well is wonderful. I mean, it's not like you're falling in love with him."

"Of course not, I have a fiancé."

"I know you do. I haven't ever seen him around, but I know he exists."

"I've asked him not to visit, I needed time alone."

"Of course."

"Doc, believe me when I tell you this, I'm not in love with that man."

Setton got a sly smile and asked, "Which one are we talking about, Bear or your fiancé?"

Katie started to answer, then didn't.

21

All day while doing his chores, Bear had that Indian-word feeling that the world wasn't right. He worried about Katie's crazy idea for tonight, that it would end in tears, as his mother always used to say.

Bear and his entourage of dogs, cats, ducks, and chickens walked out to the new shed, where Bear asked Red Cow for some words of wisdom. She stood there chewing her cud. He tried supplying her part of the conversation out of the side of his mouth but grew weary of it.

Bear turned Red Cow out into the pasture with the rest of his herd, penned his dogs, then walked up to the meadow where he'd shot that groundhog. Crawling under the fence he called down the hole to Lonnie, the mate of that groundhog he had killed, but Lonnie either wasn't home or still refused to answer, so Bear went back downhill, unpenned the German shepherds, resumed his chores.

Most of the afternoon he worked repairing fence: tightening wire, splicing broken strands, stapling everything back to posts and trees, replacing posts that had rotted. The burns on his hands were healing but were still so tender that each grip of the pliers and swing of the hammer hurt exquisitely. Bear figured it took him four hours to complete what he normally would've done in one.

Back at the house he kicked the white duck off the brown duck and then sat on the steps leading up to the side porch. When POTUS came over, Bear put his arms around the dog's massive neck and told him he was a good ol' dog. Jamaica came by, wagging her tail and nosing in, and the big male moved off because he didn't like competing for affection. Bear wasn't as emotionally close to the female but he patted her head and told her she was lovely.

In the kitchen, checking the pantry for something to eat, Bear discovered that mice had got into a bag of rice and also left droppings on the shelf. He set out traps and smeared one with bacon grease, which mice were supposed to find irresistible. After lunch (Bear fixed a big sandwich but took only two bites and fed the rest to the dogs, his appetite having left him since Katie told him about tonight), Bear went to one of the sheds and worked on a water pump, cutting homemade gaskets from an inner tube and fashioning a diaphragm from leather. The pump was old, parts probably weren't available even if Bear could afford them.

Richard Parkland, president of Briars Savings and Loan, had called and said he would lend money to rebuild the barn but Bear feared a loan, his operation was marginal and he survived primarily because he carried no debt. When times got lean, Bear could cut costs by not buying coffee and other luxuries, and never driving his truck into town, saving on gas, tax, and license. But when you take out a loan they don't let you cut back on payments in the tough times.

After he had the old pump back together, Bear took apart his chain saw to see what parts needed replacing; he was considering cutting timber to make enough money for building a new barn. Bear didn't want to have a timber-cutter come in because the loggers around here were notorious for tearing up your property and leaving limbs and tops all over so you couldn't even walk through your woods and then within a few years everything grew up in briars. He figured he could cut selectively on his own, use the tractor and truck to skid logs to the county road, have the sawmill come over and pick them up. You get a better price that way, no middleman, and your forest land isn't trashed. The question was, could Bear cut enough logs to pay for a new barn by the time he needed that barn to store this summer's hay . . . how much wood could a woodchuck chuck?

As he did chores, Bear thought of Katie in ways that were inappropriate considering she had a fiancé. He'd been infatuated with two women in his life, one was that tall gal who worked at the library and always treated Bear nicely when he came in looking for books, and the other was the woman who used to deliver mail and flirted with Bear to the point he'd find excuses for being around the mailbox come mail time. One morning she got out of her truck to hand Bear a package and he hugged her with both arms. At first she hugged him back just to be friendly but then she said that's enough now and when Bear kept hugging her she started crying until Bear finally let go. The tall gal from the library moved away and the mail lady stopped flirting with Bear, then lost her contract to another carrier. Neither the librarian nor the mail carrier, however, had fired Bear's imagination and dominated his thoughts as Katie did. Katydid.

Bear figured he must be in love. What else do you call it when you think about the person all the time, get excited about seeing her, feel dopey in her presence, and wonder what she looks like without any clothes on? If that's not love, Bear thought, then I'll have to ask Robert what is.

An hour before Katie was due to arrive, Bear showered, slicked his hair back, brushed his teeth even though it hurt to do so, and trimmed his goatee. It was Robert who had suggested Bear cut off his bushy beard in favor of a neat little goatee, Robert always the one with great ideas. Bear dressed in dark red slacks, a clashing red jacket, white shirt that had yellowed at the collar and cuffs, and a burgundy red vest with big black buttons. He went out on the porch to wait. That gash in the back of his head was healed and his left eye, though still red from the gouging, was clear-sighted and tearless. His other wounds and scratches and injuries were tolerable.

Here comes Katydid.

She drove up in that old Nova, hugged the German shepherds, hollered to the white duck to get off the brown duck, clucked at the chickens who came running, scratched at the ears of cats, making her way toward Bear like a woman coming home to Papa. He thought about hauling her upstairs to a bedroom and chaining her to a wall where he'd keep her like a pet monkey.

"Hi Bear!" she called brightly. Katie was dressed like a commando in black slacks that buttoned up the side and an oversized black sweatshirt. Except unlike a commando she was wearing makeup, red lipstick and green eye shadow—no earrings, though. Her red hair was freshly shampooed; Bear admired how clean and shiny it looked and he could smell its soapy freshness. "You're Mr. Red tonight," she said, indicating his ensemble.

"Red's hard to see in the dark," he told her. "It's the first color to drop out in low light."

She raised her brows while the corners of her little mouth pulled down, showing she was impressed. "Are you ready?"

He asked her to tell him again why they had to do this at Scrudde's place, pointing out to Katie, "There's plenty of farmers around here in the dairy business, raise veal calves."

"But Scrudde's the one who burned your barn down."

The plan was to let all of Scrudde's veal calves loose for the night—"freeing" them was what Katie called it, as if she and Bear were on old John Brown's team.

"If we're not careful, we'll end up being them martyrs you were talking about," Bear said. "Shot and killed. Scrudde wouldn't hesitate."

"It won't come to that," Katie assured him. "Scrudde is out of town, his tenants have gone visiting their relatives."

"How do you know?"

"Women at the library told me."

"And we're just going to let them calves out for one night of freedom, right? Let 'em romp, then Scrudde can collect 'em tomorrow, am I right?"

Katie said, "Let's go in, we'll have some coffee and wait for dark."

Over coffee, Bear got the impression she was trying to have an official conversation with him, asking leading questions about books he's read and movies he's seen, and does he think travel broadens, what's his favorite season, if he were to live at water's edge would he prefer river or ocean? Bear had been on the receiving end of these efforts before. When he was at church, ladies came over to engage Bear officially in conversation . . . or at least they'd try, Bear usually clammed up when there was a big push to make him talk. To avoid Katie's current efforts, he would pretend he didn't understand a question she had asked or the point she was trying to make. But this old act didn't always work with Katie who would smile and look him in the eye and seem to know better.

After dark, leaving the dogs in the house, Bear and Katie began the walk to Scrudde's farm, up the road a mile or so. Moon and stars provided light enough that Bear and Katie didn't need the flashlights they carried. Night sounds came from the forest to their right, and on their left a sweet creek flowed like a continuous sigh after a hard day, crickets and frogs and the occasional screech of an owl adding to the symphony of this surprisingly warm evening. Katie talked veal.

Animals are heir to such pain and calamity at the hands of man and in the natural world too, she told Bear, that it's a sure way to go insane if you try to get your mind around the whole of it: dolphins herded into shallow water and clubbed to death by Japanese fishermen, scientists performing unnecessary experiments on caged monkeys, rednecks who torture cats for fun. Katie said that when she volunteered at those animal rights organizations, she didn't try to embrace everything that needed to be done, every animal that needed to be saved. Instead, she focused her thoughts and energy on those very few situations where she could save at least one animal. Similarly, thinking about the meat industry as a whole was overwhelming, and to give yourself any hope you had to concentrate on a specific aspect—like *veal.* "It's horrible the way farmers keep those calves locked tight from when they're a couple days old until they're slaughtered four or five months later, it's torture for them twenty-four hours a day. Their little heads locked in stanchions or tethered with a two-foot chain so they can't turn and lick themselves or lie down in a tight curl the way they would in a pasture. Fed a low-iron milk replacer that keeps them anemic."

Bear liked veal cutlets fried up just like a pork chop except you didn't cook the veal quite as long.

"That's why the meat stays white instead of being red," Katie continued. "The poor creature is kept anemic on a diet that also produces chronic diarrhea. Imagine that existence every hour of the day, week in and week out, locked so you can't even turn around, suffering constant diarrhea, never running or jumping, never feeling the sun on your back or eating a blade of grass or nursing from your mother or being groomed by her or playing with others of your kind."

One time Robert took Bear to a restaurant where they ordered something called veal parmigiana, a name Bear would never forget. It came covered in a red sauce with lots of cheese. The meat had been cooked so it was crispy around the edges but tender and juicy in the middle. It was maybe the best meal Bear had ever had . . . and the last one with Robert because after that he went off to college and then got a big job in Chicago.

"When calves are born to milk cows," Katie explained, "if the calf is a *feminine* female, that is, resembles the characteristics of its mother, then that calf is kept and used as a milk cow, a grim existence in itself. If the female calf has masculine characteristics or if it's a male calf with a full complement of masculine characteristics, it'll probably be kept for a couple years, then slaughtered as beef. It's the male calves with feminine qualities that end up in boxes as milk-fed veal, see if you can't figure out the sublimated bigotry in that. At least the calves raised as beef get one or two glorious summers before they're shipped off to the feed lots. You know this better than I do, Bear—how exuberant baby calves are, how they adore life, chase each other and play silly buggers with the adult animals. But veal calves are restrained on a chain or kept in a box a couple feet wide, just long enough for the animal to fit, can't even take a step. What happens to *their* exuberance, can you imagine the torture of a being in a box from when you're born to the day you're slaughtered for your anemic flesh?"

Bear had tried to fix that veal parmigiana at home but it

didn't come out as good as it was at the restaurant. He had better luck with something the local butcher told him about, you either flattened a veal cutlet or sliced the meat real thin, made a coating with flour and spices, cooked it lightly, and served it with no sauce at all. That veal was so tender and juicy you could cut it with a fork. Bear wished he hadn't given his sandwich to the dogs this afternoon, he was hungry.

When they got to Scrudde's farm, Katie's intelligence from the library ladies proved correct: no one home. Bear collected the dogs—Scrudde's tenants had half a dozen but Bear knew all their names—and put them in an outbuilding. Then he and Katie went to the milking barn.

Inside along one wall were twenty tiny stalls made of rusting one-inch pipe, each stall less than two feet wide and about five feet long, the floor concrete. The front of each stall was equipped with a pair of vertical pipe stanchions that could be closed behind a calf's head. Over these stanchions, racks had been fitted to hold buckets with rubber nipples from which the calves would suck their anemic gruel. The backs of the stalls were open to allow access for shoveling out the manure, though this task had obviously not been performed with any regularity.

Twelve of the twenty stalls had calves in them, standing as they did every hour of their existence, Scrudde having broken even the pitiful regulations that required restraints to be fixed in a way that allowed veal calves at least the opportunity to kneel. No sounds came from the twelve little captives who looked at Bear and Katie with blank hopelessness.

Producing a small camera from the back pocket of her slacks, Katie went around taking flash pictures of the calves' faces, of the way the calves were restrained in those stanchions, of the size and filthy condition of their tiny stalls. Each flash startled the calves, but none of them struggled to get loose.

Bear asked her why she was taking pictures.

"Proof of how they're being kept."

"Proof?"

"Come on, let's set them free."

With Bear's help, Katie loosened the stanchions and then went around to pull the calves out from the back of the stalls. They tried to return, bleating now from fear of the unknown, preferring the familiarity of imprisonment. Some of them could barely walk, and once forced away from the stalls, they all acted bewildered, up on their hooves as if wearing high heels for the first time. Katie could maneuver the stronger calves out of the barn by herding and guiding them from behind, but Bear had to carry three of the weaker ones. They took all twelve through a gate and into a hay field just starting to green up this time of year and full of early dandelions. The calves stood where they were put, showing no desire or ability to move; some of them bleated like sheep. Katie wanted to encourage their movement by pushing them along through the grass but Bear told her it would come naturally or not at all.

Sitting in the grass, Katie looked up and found constellations she knew and told Bear their names. Back on earth, the great Bear pointed to a corner of the field where a down of rabbits had come out to feed on new grass.

The black-and-white calves eventually began exploring, raising their heads, walking gingerly, smelling the ground. After a while longer, they chanced a quick run and buck. They investigated one another. They sniffed and jumped sideways and ran unsure sprints that occasionally ended in spills, these babies still not steady on their pegs. But quickly their instincts for play, for life, kicked in and soon they were butting one another and fleeing imaginary predators. One of them found the rabbits at the far end of the field: *Look, RABBITS, they run!* Rabbits and calves formed an immediate alliance, chasing one another. Unaccustomed to exercise, the calves tired quickly, but they had enough energy for extended bouts of grooming, flipping their heads around to lick their backs, licking each other, going into that grooming trance that offers one definition of bliss. Exhausted, they pushed themselves for one more buck, another sideways jump, a quick ten-foot race . . . all the more endearing because they were so obviously earnest about this new thing, freedom of movement, and so obviously weak.

Seeing headlights on the county road, Bear touched Katie's arm.

Incredibly, she turned toward the road and flashed her camera right at the headlights . . . then did it again and again. Bear was mystified why she would want to give away their position.

It was a ton truck with dual wheels and an enclosed back like you'd use to haul furniture. When the truck came to a gate, someone got out to open it, and the truck pulled into the pasture.

Katie greeted the driver. After a moment's discussion, the two of them and the woman with the driver chased down the veal calves. Bear didn't join in, Katie didn't ask him. Because the babies were weak, it was easy enough to catch them, but lifting the calves into the high back of the truck was difficult for the three of them. Still, Bear didn't offer to help. Finally all the calves were loaded. Katie had a long talk with the two people, then opened the gate for them and closed it after the truck was gone.

"I didn't tell you," she said to Bear after joining him where he had waited in the pasture, "because I knew you'd disapprove."

He did. "You're stealing 'em."

"Liberating them."

He shook his head. "You're good with words but taking what don't belong to you is stealing, I don't need a dictionary for that."

"At one time slaves were considered personal property, an opinion validated by the highest court in the land."

Bear said it wasn't the same.

She wanted him to understand. "Right now, tonight, there are one million veal calves suffering. We can't save them all, chained in stalls, but we saved twelve of them, didn't we, Bear?"

"You should've told me."

Hearing that and seeing his open, hurt face in moonlight, Katie knew Bear was right, she *should've* told him. "I won't ever keep anything from you again," she promised.

"What's it matter, you're going back to Washington and get married."

That was also true. Katie hadn't thought this through, the consequences. Witnessing the incident with the dying cow and then saving those two starving horses, she had been swept up with a sense of righteousness, with the drama of it all, figuring she'd cap off her stay here with a bold liberation of veal calves and then leave—leave Bear holding the bag, as it now appeared.

"Where they going, them calves?" he asked.

"A sanctuary."

"Somebody's going to keep 'em and feed 'em for however long they live, twenty years or more?"

"The movement has places that do that, yes."

He shook his head, it struck him as nonsense. "When Scrudde finds out it's me, what's he going to burn down this time? My house, I guess."

"No, the publicity will be too intense. I'll send the pictures I took tonight to newspapers."

Bear shook his head again. "That'll just make it worse."

She was sorry. If it were possible to call back that truck, Katie would have returned each of those calves to its stall. "I was trying to get revenge for you," she said weakly. "For Scrudde and Coote having burned your barn down."

"I call him Cootie and revenge ain't ours to get."

"I'm sorry."

He shook his head. "It'll end in tears."

"What?"

Right before she left, Bear's mother started applying that judgment to everything. She'd be washing the dishes and looking out the window and saying over and over to herself, it'll end in tears, it'll end in tears.

When Bear didn't answer Katie, she took his arm and tried again to express her regret. "Is there anything I can do to make it up to you?"

Bear nodded as if he'd been waiting for the offer. "Come home with me."

She considered what he meant by that, then agreed.

22

In his living room, Bear asked Katie to tell him the rules.

"What do you mean?"

"I do good with rules, tell me what they are and I'll follow 'em."

She still didn't know what he meant. "Rules for what?"

"Loving you . . . for how you and me can fall in love."

Katie smiled thinly and wondered how the hell she was going to get out of this without hurting his feelings. "I'm not aware of any rules for how people fall in love. Part of it is just the chemistry between them."

"You got the formula?"

"Bear, be serious."

"I am. I am serious as a tree."

"People fall in love at first sight—"

"Yep."

"Or after spending a lot of time together. They tell each other stories."

"You go first," he said.

"Pardon me?"

"You tell a story, then I'll tell you one."

"Bear . . ."

"Come on, I bet you know a story. It's a good rule, spend time together and tell each other stories. I'll write it down. You tell your story first."

"I don't know any."

"Go on," he encouraged her.

"Okay, give me a second."

"I'll give you ten thousand."

On the spot, seeing his intense stare, she said, "I'm trying to think of one."

Bear said he would wait, he had all the time in the world, closing his eyes and counting to himself.

❦

Katie's story was about an emperor who engaged a poet to compose poetry, then recite his verses to the emperor and his sons and courtiers of an evening when nothing important was on the agendum. This the poet did to the satisfaction of all. When the poet's tenure was over and he was presented for payment, the emperor, feeling peevish that day, pondered aloud what an appropriate payment might be for something as intangible as a poem, the product of the poet's imagination, something without substance, unlabored and unresearched, just something a poet thinks up the way any of us might if we had the time. The poet said that whatever payment the emperor chose would of course be entirely satisfactory. (This was a wise thing for the poet to say as the emperor had been known to behead those who questioned his payments.) The emperor finally decreed he would pay for poems with something from the emperor's own imagination: a gold mine deep in the mountains, an imaginary gold mine, but all the same it's yours, he told the poet to laughter in the court. How clever, our emperor, how droll. Oddly the poet didn't seem offended, he thanked the emperor profusely and immediately traveled to a town known as Gateway to the Mountains. There the poet outfitted thirty imaginary mules and engaged the services of fifty imaginary miners for an imaginary trek to find the imaginary gold mine. The emperor was kept informed. After a month and a season, the poet returned to court and announced that his imaginary troop had indeed located the imaginary mine and had loaded twenty imaginary mules (ten of the mules had been eaten during an imaginary famine that plagued the imaginary miners). The imaginary gold, brought now to court, was of such purity as to make it more valuable than any gold ever mined in the empire. The poet was hereby turning over all this fine gold to the emperor, asking in exchange one favor: the hand of the emperor's daughter in marriage. Everyone watched to see the emperor's reaction. Amused by the poet's bold cleverness, he granted the favor. The emperor had only sons and was therefore giving the poet an imaginary wife. Again the poet was profuse with his thanks, retiring to a seaside village from where he sent the emperor regular reports, in the form of poetry, of course, on the life that the poet was living with the emperor's imaginary daughter. The poet wrote to tell the emperor: Your daughter, my wife, sings with a voice of such beauty that fish swim near shore to listen and villagers walk the beaches to collect those poor fish who lingered too long listening on the ebb tide. The emperor, accustomed to the rough voices of his sons and living without a woman's company ever since his beloved wife died many years ago, wondered what it might've been like to have a daughter who could sing so beautifully as to charm fish ashore. The poet sent poems celebrating the birth of imaginary children, all girls. As the emperor's sons in turn gave him only grandsons, news of these imaginary granddaughters, their antics and manner of dress and their pet names for him, intrigued their grandfather. Years passed and the emperor's sons struggled against one another for power, the grandsons grew old enough to embarrass the court with their drunken sprees, and the emperor grew ever fonder of reports from the poet living at the sea with the emperor's imaginary daughter and those sweet, kind, sensitive imaginary granddaughters. Has the poet sent me anything today? the emperor would ask eagerly each morning. He was delighted when the latest poem was delivered, grumpy when there was no news. The imaginary granddaughters, six in all, were artists: singers and poets, painters and potters; one of them embroidered with such skill that people would, unbidden, put on gloves before touching her embroideries. In his late years, the emperor finally abdicated in favor of his third son, who turned out to be the most ruthless of all: sons and grandsons had been crippled and slain in the struggle for power. To escape this bloodshed, the very product of his blood, the emperor decided to retire to the seaside village and spend the rest of his days reading the poet's poems about his gentle, talented, loving imaginary granddaughters. The emperor would require at least one poem a day, three on those days he felt moody, and for this he would pay the poet real, not imaginary, gold. Upon arriving in the seaside village, the emperor found a poem waiting for him. It told of a tragedy: an imaginary fire had swept through the villa, killing the emperor's imaginary daughter and all six of his imaginary granddaughters. The one who did the beautiful embroidery had survived for a few days after the fire, horribly disfigured and in enormous pain before she finally expired. Unfortunately all her imaginary embroideries were destroyed in the imaginary fire. The poet, in imaginary distress, had left the empire for real. Upon reading this, the emperor dropped to his knees and wept as a child. He would live the remainder of his life in real grief, not imaginary. This is the fate of anyone, even an emperor, foolish enough to abuse a poet.

❦

Bear said he had no idea poets were so powerful.

"They are," she assured him.

Still sitting on a couch in his living room, unused in the years since his father died, they had moved close to each other as she told her story in the quietly awed voice you might use on children. Katie's version ran more than an hour and was embroidered with fanciful detail about the size and color of the imaginary fish that came to shore to hear the imaginary woman sing, for example, and the subtle differences in the texture of hair of the six imaginary granddaughters.

Bear said he knew of no story as grand as the one Katie had just told.

"I bet you do," she said.

"Cazador and Rubia were the lovers," Bear said, speaking so abruptly that Katie laughed.

"What's wrong?"

"Nothing. This is a story about a Spanish couple," she said confidently.

"They were horses I used to own, Robert helped me with the Spanish."

"Of course . . . so this is a true story."

Bear said he didn't know any of the other kind. "This is back in the days when I owned horses." Cazador, Bear told Katie, was a big seventeen-hand black Thoroughbred gelding raised to be a hunter-jumper, while Rubia was a little fifteen-hand quarter horse, a roan filly considered flashy because she had a blond tail and mane and four white stockings. Old Doc Setton used to look at Rubia and tell Bear that his horse had a lot of chrome.

"Cazador and Rubia were in love," Bear told Katie. Then he said you have to understand about horses in general and geldings in particular, they can form deep attachments with each other and, because the gelding's attraction isn't influenced by sex, his love for another horse can be powerfully pure. Cazador's favorite thing in life was putting his big head over Rubia's small neck and then just standing there, gently leaning. He went crazy when she was out of his sight. Rubia liked to torment him by running to the back of the loafing shed where he couldn't see her. When Cazador came around to find her, she ran to the front. Rubia was the most important creature alive to him and Cazador chased her around that loafing shed with the stamina of a Thoroughbred. She was spry and quick and could maneuver the corners way ahead of Cazador; in fact Rubia would lap him and come up from behind. This freaked the big gelding because one moment his lady love was somewhere in front of him and the next moment here she is behind him, the filly must be magic. Also she'd outdistance him running around the loafing shed and then turn to meet him head on. Cazador got the biggest kick out of that; he would skid to a four-hoof stop and if horses laughed he did. When the flies were bad, the couple stood head-to-tail so that one's flicking tail kept the flies off the other's face. Cazador would do anything to maintain contact with Rubia; sometimes he just pressed his forehead to her flank and stood like that in the sun, and you could tell he preferred this to those chasing games around the loafing shed.

Bear told Katie that the love affair between Rubia and Cazador rendered them useless as riding horses because if you took Rubia out, Cazador would injure himself getting through fences to follow her, and if you took Cazador out by himself, he would fight the bit and whinny in distress and take every opportunity to turn around and get back to his blond-tailed, blond-maned, white-stockinged love.

"So I sold Rubia," Bear said.

Katie made a soft sound.

"When the new owner came with his trailer, I put Cazador in the barn and shut all the doors so he couldn't see what was happening."

"How sad," Katie said.

Bear agreed it was. After Rubia was loaded and the trailer left the farm, Bear released Cazador. The big horse ran to the loafing shed but of course Rubia wasn't there. He ran up and down the fences calling her. He hung his massive head over gates to search all the fields he could see. No Rubia. Working himself into a foaming sweat, Cazador ran around and around the loafing shed hoping to summon Rubia by playing her favorite game—maybe she would come up behind him unexpectedly or suddenly appear running back toward him, that wily Rubia was famous for such tricks. Around and around counterclockwise he ran for an hour at the gallop, an hour at the trot. Bear knew that Thoroughbreds were capable of running themselves to death, that's the kind of heart they had, and he worried this was happening to Cazador.

"So I finally went in there and got him," Bear told Katie. "I was going to put him up in the barn for the night. When we were walking out where the trailer had been parked to load Rubia, we came to a big load of manure that she got rid of during when she was being loaded." Bear explained that horses will evacuate their bowels when stressed, an instinct from when they were prey animals, when getting rid of a load of manure as you were about to flee predators might make the difference between being caught or not—and this is also where the expression *having the shit scared out of you* came from.

Katie laughed, then bid Bear to continue.

"When that Cazador came to those fresh manure piles from Rubia," he told her, "that big old gelding put on the brakes and leaned his nose so close it was almost touching." Bear said the horse stood there shaking as he took in that aroma, the very essence of Rubia. Then all of a sudden Cazador relaxed. The horse looked up and nickered. Maybe nothing in this world sounds sweeter than a nicker, Bear told Katie. If humans could nicker we'd do it to babies in their cribs and to people we love who've come back after a long time away. Bear was thinking Robert.

"So here's the poem," Bear said.

Katie was charmed. "There's a poem too?"

He admitted there was.

"You old slyboots."

Bear grinned. "You want to hear it?"

"Of course."

"*If I cannot see your gentle prancing . . .* this is Cazador talking about Rubia."

"Okay."

"In poems, horses can talk."

"Of course. Go on."

He put a burned hand to his chest and lifted his chin in theatrical pose. *"If I cannot see your gentle prancing . . . or hear that sweet nicker . . . if I'm never allowed to hang my neck across your flank . . . or chase you around the shed . . . at least I have this . . . from you to me . . . at least I can smell your shit."*

Katie busted out laughing and that got Bear laughing, too. She made him say it again and he did, becoming abruptly sober to bespeak the lines as if they were Shakespeare. Soon they were both laughing again, laughing extravagantly, red-faced and gasping.

“Did you make that up?” she finally asked him. “Or is it something from the famous brother, Robert.”

“I made it up all on my own,” Bear announced, suddenly standing to pirouette around the living room, lifting his arms and watching his feet, dancing in a manner both mad and ecstatic and thoroughly wonderful.

“What are you doing?” she finally asked.

“Dancing,” he said dreamily.

“Let’s go upstairs.”

“Upstairs?”

“To your bedroom.”

He went all *koyaanisqatsi.*

23

Upstairs in his bedroom, on the bed he once shared with Robert, Bear and Katie had their shoes off but were otherwise still clothed.

She told him, "I said before that I wasn't aware of any rules about loving someone, but actually, now that I think of it, at least in my case . . . I guess there are a few rules."

He showed her a tablet he'd written on while she was in the bathroom. *Rules for Loving Katydid* was at the top of the page, and beneath it, *Number 1. Spend time together and tell each other stories.*

"Again with the Katydid, huh?"

Bear nodded. "I name things," he told her. "Count things, too. Ever set of stairs I climb, I count 'em. I could tell you the number of steps I take between the porch and ever building on the property." Bear indicated his tablet and pen. "So tell me them rules that apply in your case."

This is going to be tough, she thought, telling him softly, "You don't have to take notes."

"I do too, otherwise I get muddled."

"I know, but—"

"I got three problems."

"Really?" She wondered if he was about to announce sexual ailments.

"My mind gets muddled sometimes . . . and also I engage in inappropriate behavior . . . then sometimes I forget and let my mouth hang open."

"You've been doing real well lately on keeping your mouth closed."

"Thanks." He readied his pen and paper.

"Okay. I feel silly making them sound like official rules, but . . . okay, I'm going to keep my top on and you mustn't try to remove it. Don't even try to touch my breasts."

He wrote both rules, then looked at her, waiting for more.

"That's it."

He was amazed. He thought rules for loving Katie would take up a whole tablet.

In truth she could think of other rules for loving her: A man should turn off that male mania for logic when what I'm doing or saying doesn't make sense and what I need is understanding, not logic. To love me, you should have an inexhaustible supply of patience. She looked at Bear looking at her and thought: You should look at me like you are now. Putting her hands on his cheeks, holding his face, which Katie loved for its guilelessness, she said, "Your turn."

He didn't understand.

"Do you have any rules for me?"

He shook his head.

"Nothing?"

He shrugged. "I ain't had much experience in this line. I never even done the deed, which is what Robert used to call it, doing the deed."

"You've never . . . had sex?"

"Nope."

"How far have you gone with a woman?"

"Zero distance," he assured her.

Katie was intrigued. "I'm not trying to embarrass you or be dense about it but I want to make sure I understand." She bit back a smile. "You have to admit it's kind of unusual, a man—How old are you?"

"Thirty-two."

"A man of thirty-two who's never had sex, it's—"

"Never even seen a woman naked."

Now Katie was incredulous. "You've never seen a naked woman?"

"Nope."

"Just pictures?"

"None of them, either. Robert's friends had some once except Robert wouldn't let me look."

She laughed.

Bear looked horrified and Katie quickly assured him she wasn't laughing at him, it was just so unusual to be with a man who's never had sex. Then she stopped being amused, thinking Bear's first time shouldn't be with her. "Maybe this isn't such a good idea."

"Yeah," he replied, "it's a real good idea."

"I don't want to mislead you or—"

"I know you got one of them fiancés and I know you're here right now 'cause you feel so bad about lying to me on stealing those calves, so you're like condescending to go to bed with me, that's a word I wrote down when I was looking up patronizing."

"You are a perceptive man."

Patronizing, he thought . . . but didn't say it. Instead he told her, "I love you, Katydid."

She shook her head. "Let's think of this as sex, not love."

"You can but I won't."

"Bear . . ."

"I got my reasons for loving you."

"Like what?"

"Well, I hope you got about a million years to listen, 'cause I got reasons to love you like the night sky has stars."

That should be another rule, Katie thought. A man should say things like that on a regular basis.

Bear went over and turned off the light, returning to the bed where Katie told him softly, "Women generally don't have rules about not trying to touch their breasts, that's just *my* rule. I don't want to mess up your concept of what sex should be."

"I've raised animals all my life, I know what sex and breeding is, I know how it works, what you do, seen it done between animals a thousand times, it's just I never done it myself, never had the occasion."

She pulled on his ear. “The occasion?”

“That’s right,” he said defensively.

“So this is a *big* occasion for you.”

“I reckon.”

“Then go back over and turn the light on. I might have to keep my top on but I’ll let you see everything else.”

“Really?”

“If you want to.”

“I reckon I do.”

“Well then, I reckon you better stroll back over there and put some lights on.”

Bear got off the bed, flicked the light on, then turned, watching with the eyes of a mongoose at cobra’s approach as Katie worked the buttons of her pants while he silently revised his nightly prayer: *Not yet, Lord, not yet.*

24

Katie and Bear were awakened in the predawn hour by a sharp snap from somewhere distant in the old farmhouse, Katie asking sleepily, "Whazzat?" Before answering, Bear required a moment's acclimation to her presence here abed, naked from the waist down, with all her limbs wrapped around him like a monkey holding tightly to a tree. "Hmm?" she asked, her eyes already closed again.

"I think I just caught a mouse," he told her, untangling and then getting out of bed. He dressed and went down to the kitchen pantry where he had last placed a trap. Upon opening the door, he saw the mouse caught belly-down with the snapping bar across both back legs. Bear had seen dozens of mice caught in traps, but this morning he saw this one differently and thought, I'm an assassin.

"But I ain't talking to no mouse," Bear told him. Bear did offer to lift the bar and let the mouse go free.

But the back legs were broken and that meant the mouse wouldn't live, there would be no going free. All he had left were a few moments, dying in a trap. When Bear tried to free the mouse, it bit him.

It was Bear who apologized.

The mouse didn't tell him to go to hell but Bear thought it just the same.

"You were getting into my rice," Bear said.

The mouse had a life expectancy of two years at the most and Bear had robbed him of what was left of that tiny portion. Using superior brain power, Bear had cleverly smeared the trap with bacon grease and now the mouse was dying. Over a few grains of rice and some droppings. Bear had done this to a creature who possessed so little when Bear had so much, bags of rice the mouse couldn't eat in two dozen lifetimes and a woman upstairs in bed. I got everything, Bear thought, yet I take this little guy's wee ration of life because he ate a few grains of my rice, dropped a couple dry turds on my shelf space. What a blood-soaked piece of work am I.

He apologized again.

Go to hell.

He told the mouse he was going to change his ways. For one thing, no more traps and, for another, no more veal. "And now that Katie is with me, I'm going to help *rescue* animals, not kill them."

Go to hell.

"I swear. I'm not going to kill anything anymore."

Go to hell.

"You're the last one, you've become like a martyr to the cause."

The mouse used its front legs to crawl, pulling the trap, hiding partway behind a bag of rice. Bear gingerly reached around and grasped the trap's wooden base and pulled the mouse out, those shiny black eyes already gone dull dry.

Bear went outside where even the air seemed tinted pink-red by the approaching dawn, birds singing because they'd made it through another night, the air bracing but not cold enough to show breath, though he shivered hard while peeing on the stone wall. How many mice had he killed over the years? Of all the things he'd counted he hadn't counted mice. Dozens at least, maybe hundreds.

Over in the grass by the side of a red shed that would see first sun, the male German shepherd lay with ducks tucked in right next to him, chickens too, two cats curled on his back, guinea hens scattered here and there like sentries. Some Christians believe that the reward of heaven is spiritual proximity to the light of God (hell's punishment is distance from that light), and if that concept were applied here on Bear's farm, all these animals close to POTUS were in heaven. On a more corporeal level, the big shepherd was also their protection. Whenever Bear brought a new animal to the farm—and it didn't matter if it was a calf, a cat, or a chick—POTUS would sniff the creature all over and nip at it and nudge it as if entering its statistics into his memory bank and then, ever after, that creature was under the dog's protection and woe be to the predator who threatened any of his charges. Bear had seen him attack four stray dogs that were after a calf, wading into the pack and immediately killing one dog by breaking its back, so injuring another that Bear had to shoot it, and running the last two off . . . yet this same POTUS would hold a baby chick in his mouth for Bear's inspection, would carry a cat around the yard in his jaws just for fun.

Bear went over to pet POTUS's massive head, telling him, "If there was one animal in the world I wish I could talk to, it'd be you." The German shepherd looked away, too elegant for speech.

After instructing POTUS and Jamaica to *stay,* Bear set off up the hill, enjoying this day's dawn even as it brought further evidence of insanity—*talking to a mouse, Jesus help me.*

He crossed the meadow, climbed a hill, crawled under the fence, and shouted down the burrow. "Lonnie! Lonnie! Hey, are you down there, Lonnie? It's Bear. I own this farm."

No answer.

"I've been here a couple times trying to get you to talk to me, trying to apologize for shooting your wife. Maybe you moved out after that but if you're down there I got something important to tell you."

Bear cocked his head to listen, heard nothing, then turned again to speak down the hole. "It's over." He thought how he wanted to say it. "*Never again.* Lonnie?"

Nothing.

"I will never again shoot a groundhog. I realize I've shot dozens of them, of you, but never again. You hear me, Lonnie, it's a sacred promise I'm making, *never again* to shoot a groundhog."

Bear thought he heard a soft voice from deep in the burrow. "Lonnie? Is that you, Lonnie?"

No answer.

Bear wondered where he should start apologizing. Five years ago he had run a hose down a groundhog hole and let exhaust from his tractor fill the borrow. He never did it a second time because the gassing seemed a sneaky way to get rid of groundhogs, when you can't see them or even know for sure if anything is being killed.

Bear called down the hole and said he hoped it wasn't any of Lonnie's kin that got gassed.

The burrow remained silent.

"Lonnie? I know I've done some rotten things to groundhogs."

Bear remembered seeing a mother groundhog with a brand-new set of babies. They were out in his alfalfa. Bear killed the mother first, then as the four babies stood up on their hind legs, rigid and waiting because their mother wasn't alive to tell them they should run for home, Bear shot the babies one by one. He even had to stop and reload, but the final baby waited its turn anyway.

"Lonnie?"

Maybe the worst thing he ever did to groundhogs was that time he dug up a den of them. They were still hibernating. Bear rolled them out on the ground. They were in a stupor and didn't try to get away. He cut them each in half with his shovel.

"Lonnie, I really am sorry. But all that's in the past now. You can spread the news to all your friends and family, whatever groundhogs live on my farm are now protected, you got free rein from now on to come and go." Except what about the dogs? Bear called down the burrow, he couldn't promise that the dogs wouldn't keep hunting groundhogs, it was their nature.

A sound of contempt came topside.

"Lonnie? Is that you, old son? Lonnie, answer me. Lonnie!"

One question.

"A question? I can barely hear you. You got a question for me? Okay, shoot."

What did you say?

"Nothing. Sorry. Ask your question."

It was something regarding Katie, a few days ago, shouting down the hole about a woodchuck chucking wood, then laughing her fool head off, what was that about?

Bear had to admit he wasn't sure what she meant.

Chucking wood like throwing it?

"It's just a saying."

Groundhogs don't throw wood.

"I know they don't."

Weird.

"Lonnie?"

No answer.

Bear waited by the hole another twenty minutes in case Lonnie wanted to say something more or had another question. Then Bear got up and left. Since everything was talking to him this morning, Bear decided to give Red Cow another chance. He walked down to her pasture, where she was lying by the creek. The old cow rose stiffly at his approach.

"You didn't need to stand up for me, Mother," he told her. "I just came by to see how you're doing."

Mornings are tough on these old soup bones.

Bear knew how she felt.

The cow stretched her neck.

"I'm crazier than a bedbug," Bear told her. "Magic things are happening to me left and right." Last night in bed, for example. It was spectacular, the details stranger than a visit to Morocco. Bear said, "There's so much I don't know about women."

The cow gave him some advice, that when Bear returns to Katie this morning he should tell her she's beautiful, sensuous, and lovely to behold.

"I don't know if I could ever say something like that."

Try a little tenderness.

He thanked her and headed back for the house.

In the kitchen, he sat at the table, stood, walked to the bottom of the steps and listened for Katie, returned to the kitchen, sat, stood, sat. If it wasn't so early he'd call Robert and try to get some advice on how to charm a woman. For godssake don't mention marriage, Bear told himself, because that ain't in the cards and you'll just make a fool of yourself. He knew this wasn't going to last, this thing with Katie, sex with her, being happy with her, telling each other stories, laughing, waking up with Katie holding on to him with both arms and legs like a monkey. Bear knew none of it would last, she was getting ready to go off and marry some fiancé.

He pressed the fingertip where the mouse bit him but it didn't hurt much, though enough to get Bear vibrating as he grabbed the puncture wound on his leg and squeezed the tender flesh with both hands. "One megahurt," he said and squeezed harder. "Two megahurts." He squeezed harder, his hands powerful in spite of the burns. "*Three* megahurts." Harder yet, quivering with the pressure he was applying, the pain he was producing. "*FOUR* megahurts." You blood-soaked retard, he silently cursed himself, can't you press any *harder*? *"FIVE MEGAHURTS . . ."*

"Bear?"

He released his grip and turned to see Katie standing in the doorway. Dressed in one of his white shirts with a sweater over it but bare-legged and still sleepy-eyed, she was so cute and rumpled, he had to steel himself not to rush there and sweep her up in his arms.

Instead, Katie came to him. Padding over on bare feet she sat on his lap lightly as a cat and wiggled her shoulders until he put his arms around her.

Remembering the cow's advice, he told her, "You're sensuous and beautiful and lovely to behold."

"What?" she asked in a voice that suggested it was too early for that kind of talk.

"I love you," he said.

She leaned away from his chest to see his face. "Why are you crying?"

"It hurts."

25

After breakfast, Bear went to feed the Noyles horses. Mother and filly were waiting in the pasture. Bear brought them sweet-feed, hay, and various supplements Katie had gotten from the vet. When the horses started nickering, Bear thought back to the Cazador-Rubia love story he'd told last night, the way his horse-shit poem made Katie laugh.

While the horses ate, Bear treated the filly's head where it had been scraped raw by that tightening nylon halter, he used a pick to clean their hooves, and with a trailing hand, checked all over their bodies, under manes and tails and in ears and mouths, for wounds and signs of parasites. He'd worm them next week. The horses were no longer starving to death but, in their weakened condition, the slightest thing going wrong—a cold, a cut—could kill them, and Bear still didn't put their chances above fifty-fifty.

When he gathered up his things and headed for the fence, the horses stayed so close that he had to keep stopping, going around them. Bear said, "I'll be back tomorrow." Then he thought to ask them, "Did either one of you want to say anything to me?" They didn't.

As Bear was crossing the fence he saw Noyles and Mitchell come out of a shed. Bear raised his arm to acknowledge them. Noyles refused to wave back, Mitchell barked.

❦

When she got out of her car at the cottage, Katie laughed at how happy all the dogs were, they jumped and spun in circles and ran the fence and barked excitedly. They hadn't missed a meal (Katie had fed them last night before she went to Bear's and it wasn't time yet for their morning feed) and there was plenty of water and they had one another for company: the dogs were just happy to see her. Katie entered the yard and knelt to hug and pet and get kissed, offering special attention to the blind Jack Russell before making her way to a bench where she took each dog up on her lap for an exclusive cuddle. The ones waiting their turns were yapping *hurry up hurry up.* As soon as one of those barking dogs got lifted to Katie's lap, he became regally quiet, looking aloof and spoiled, gloating to his pack mates, Look at me, I'm on her lap, I'm in her arms, oh, you poor rabble, look at me.

At a retreat sponsored by one of the animal rights groups where she volunteered, Katie had heard an Indian shaman tell a story of creation, the Great Creator having made a representative of each animal that was to populate the earth. These representative animals mingled together while the Great Creator watched. Soon it was apparent that although each animal had unique talents, Man's talent for thought and speech was dominant and troublesome. So the Great Creator decided that Man could never again be permitted to mingle with animals on the same spiritual level, Man must be set apart. After separating Man from the other animals, the Great Creator caused a seam to open between them, the crack widening, the spiritual distance between Man and animals growing greater and greater until it would be forever uncrossable. But just before that happened, one animal, Dog, ran from the others and jumped the widening chasm to come and sit by Man. So be it, the Great Creator told Dog, you have cast your lot.

With the back of her fingernails Katie was scratching under the jaw of a beagle-basset cross that had been let out of a car along a highway. The person who brought the dog to Doc Setton had actually seen the abandonment. Apparently the people in the car just opened a door, took the dog by its scruff, and dropped it from the rolling vehicle. Once the dog righted himself, he gave chase on stumpy basset legs but with a beagle's full voice, the dog in a wild panic, heedless of traffic: don't leave me,

I love you. Now, as Katie continued stroking the dog, it closed its eyes and raised its snout, ignoring the barking all around, soaking up this human attention. It was clear the dog had forgiven everything, even abandonment: just don't leave me, I love you. Katie thought that Bear loved her as these dogs did.

In the cottage, the two parrots were also happy to see Katie and went into wild dances that had them bouncing on one leg, then the other, screeching and fluttering, calling to her. One was an African gray parrot that adored being held by Katie and would even spread its wings and try to hug her. The other, a huge blue-and-yellow macaw, was thought to be sixty years old, and while he obviously enjoyed Katie's presence, he didn't like being touched and would bite if you tried to stroke him. The African gray had the unique talent of answering back with antonyms to words you shouted at him. If he didn't know the word or if it didn't have an obvious opposite, the bird would screech *"Next!"* Katie said "Cold" and the parrot answered *"Hot!"* It had been given to Doc Setton after its elderly owner died.

The old macaw had been rescued from a household where little boys had used it as a target for those arrows with suction cups on the ends. When this parrot first came to Doc Setton, it was completely bare of feathers as far as its beak could reach, looking like a chicken that had been plucked for butchering but managing, horribly, to stay alive.

I should call Doc, Katie thought. He said something about another rescue, an old lady with too many cats. But first Katie had to send off the film of those veal calves. Then call William. She was just returning the gray parrot to its perch when the phone rang.

"Kate?"

"Doc. I was about to call you."

"Kate, honey, Deputy Miller is trying to find you, he said he went to your place around dawn but you weren't home."

Knowing this was about the raid on Scrudde's veal operation, Katie felt the fear rise in her throat. "What does he want?"

"Last night, livestock got stolen from Phil Scrudde's barn."

"What's that got to do with me?"

"Listen, hon, I don't want to play games and I certainly don't want you to tell me anything that I'm going to have to lie for you about later on. The stock taken from Scrudde's farm was veal calves and Scrudde is saying that it was the work of an animal rights group, which is why Miller wants to talk to you. Where were you at dawn?"

Katie wondered if she should say.

"Hon?"

"I spent the night with Bear."

Doc didn't comment.

"He's not the person you or anyone else around here thinks he is," Katie insisted.

After a long pause, the vet said, "So you and Bear are each other's alibis."

Katie hadn't thought about it that way, but *yes.*

"Hon?"

"I don't know what we're being accused of," Katie said, her voice rising, "but if anyone wants to know where we were last night then the answer is, we were together, yes."

"I'm on your side."

"I'm sorry, I didn't get much sleep."

"I'm not even going to ask about that. Did you still want to take a look at that elderly woman with the cats?"

"I'm meeting Bear back at his farm around noon. Give me the information and we'll check it out."

❦

At Bear's house, Katie had tomato soup and toast for lunch while Bear wondered what kind of sandwich he could make that didn't involve the dead flesh of animals—did baloney count? He was going to ask Katie, but he could tell she was in no mood for hilarity.

After a quiet lunch, they loaded cages into the truck. Following Doc Setton's directions, they drove to the outskirts of Briars where in an isolated hollow at the end of a dirt road they found a small white house where the cat lady lived. For some reason, the setting seemed spooky even though the house looked normal from the outside, not an overabundance of trash and no broken windows, no bodies hanging from oak trees.

"This is a friendly rescue," Katie reminded Bear. "We're just going to find out if we can give any help to the woman who lives here, she's apparently very old and frequently confused and has way too many cats."

"Does she know we're coming?"

"Doc told her but the woman forgets things."

"How many cats?" Bear asked, and Katie said she didn't know. The vet had lent them fifteen cages, now stacked in the bed of Bear's truck.

Waiting on the porch after knocking on the door, Bear and Katie could hear the cats and, through windows, could see them moving everywhere. Bear said they were going to need more cages and Katie reminded him they weren't here to remove cats against the woman's wishes but would take away only those she couldn't properly care for, and only with the woman's permission.

"You already told me all this," Bear pointed out.

"I know."

"You think I forget things like this old woman does?"

"No."

"I'm not dumb," he said, crossing his arms.

"I know you're not." She reached forward to knock again just as the door opened. Katie said *Oh!* and turned away, covering her mouth and nose with both hands.

26

When he drove up and saw Coote's truck, Scrudde said, "Praise Jesus."

In the week since Bear choked them, Coote hadn't shown up at Scrudde's farm to work. Scrudde had driven out here to Coote's trailer several times to check on him, but this was the first time he'd caught him at home.

Scrudde knocked on the door and waited. Coote's truck was here, where was he? Scrudde walked around, cigarette butts and beer bottles everywhere. The old mint-green trailer was out here all by itself in the woods, power lines coming in from above and, under the trailer, plastic pipes leading into the ground. Walking now at the back of the trailer near an open window, Scrudde heard the unmistakable grunt-push-bedsqueak of sex.

He stood listening, short and dumpy and mid-fifty. A thoroughly unscrupulous man, Scrudde was a regular churchgoer, a member of the church's board, and a surprisingly generous giver when it came to what he called brick-and-mortar projects, adding an activities room to the church building, for example—Scrudde Hall. But ask him for a few dollars to fund a food drive and he'd throw you out of his house with a parting lecture on self-reliance, Scrudde begrudging the poor their holiday turkeys as if those Butterballs were pounds of his own flesh.

Inside the trailer, *doing it in the middle of the day,* Coote and his sexual partner continued without commentary their sweaty stomp. Scrudde, standing closer to the window now, wished they'd start talking about what they were doing to each other, it would help him visualize. He was a sexual sneak, positioning himself outside the women's toilet to get a look when the door opened, working the state fair crowds, women in their shorts and their sleeveless summer blouses. And now, standing under a window listening to the couple having sex, Scrudde let his mouth hang open.

Suddenly they were finished, leaving Scrudde disappointed that neither Coote nor the woman had spoken. They simply stopped and then, presumably, disengaged. And then one of them, with a loud squeak of the bedsprings, got up and left the room. Scrudde heard the click of a lighter as the other began to smoke.

He waited, then slunk around to the front.

Sleepy-eyed and beer in hand, Coote finally answered his door. "Scrudde," he said, one of the few people to pronounce *Scrudde* to rhyme with *Hud,* because of course Coote had name-pronunciation issues himself. "What's up?"

"We got a crisis on our hands," Scrudde said, stepping into the trailer, its interior a filthier mess than what was outside. The floor was littered with trash, pizza boxes and hamburger wrappers, beer cans and full ashtrays. Expensive or at least loud stereo equipment was stacked to the ceiling and rock posters papered every available wall.

"Yeah, what crisis would that be?" Coote asked, unimpressed. Usually Scrudde's idea of a crisis was a tractor tire that needed to be changed or a fence that was down, some piddle-ass job he couldn't find anyone else to do because of the way he paid his help, the way he treated people.

"They raided the farm last night," Scrudde said dramatically, taking off the cowboy hat to wipe his face. It was hot in the trailer, you could smell what they'd been eating. Scrudde wondered if the woman might come out of that back bedroom and, if she did, what might she be wearing, *nothing*?

Coote opened the refrigerator, scratching under his arms. "Hey, you want a beer?"

"I don't drink alcohol."

"Yeah, churchman." Coote returned to the couch.

"Christian."

Coote nodded and leaned back to suck at the freshly opened bottle. Eyelids at half mast, his hair a tangled mess, he could've been modeling for a painting, *Insolence on a Couch.*

"Last night I had a dozen veal calves stolen right out of my barn. You know who's behind it, don't you?"

Coote smiled dreamily. "Katherine *Reee-no.*"

"You said you were going to take care of her, remember when we were talking in the car after Bear nearly killed us?"

"I burned his barn down, is what I did— Oh, there you are, sweet thing." Coote looked past Scrudde and toward the far end of the trailer.

The older man spun around expecting Coote's sexual partner to be some pretty young woman, maybe half dressed, cotton-candy blond hair and perky breasts . . . but Scrudde saw she was that gum-cracking waitress from Briars Café, overweight and henna-haired and only a decade or so younger than Scrudde himself, maybe forty-three to his fifty-six. Even more scandalous to Scrudde, she went to his church on occasion.

"Hey Phil," she said to Scrudde.

He opened his mouth but nothing came out as he continued staring, the woman was wearing a big tee shirt that barely covered her private parts. The material was thin and Scrudde could see the outlines of huge dark nipples. He finally said, "Hey Diane."

She got a drink of water at the sink, then asked Coote if they were going out to eat.

He said there was still pizza in a few of these boxes, she should heat some up.

She said it was her day off, she wasn't going to heat up his pizza, he could heat it up his own damn self or better yet he could take her out for dinner.

Coote told her to get her fat ass back in the bedroom. "Scrudde and me got things to talk about here."

Wearily compliant, she turned and walked away, Scrudde watching her ass jiggle.

"You want some of that?" Coote asked him.

"Pardon me?"

"Take me five minutes to convince her to do you," Coote said. As he waited for an answer, the tip of his tongue peeked out from his lips.

Scrudde was shaking his head, reaching for a chair when something scurried from under the couch, scrambling across pizza boxes, heading for Coote's legs.

"Rat," Scrudde murmured, standing.

Coote laughed and scooped up the little rodent, telling Scrudde, "It's a chipmunk. Since when you think rats got bushy tails?"

Scrudde sat back down. "How'd it get in?"

"Get in?" Coote lifted the creature to his face, the ground squirrel putting two little paws on Coote's cheek, then looking crossly at Scrudde. "This is Henry and he's my pet—ain't you, Henry? He lives inside."

Squirming in the aluminum-tube chair, Scrudde told Coote they had to deal with Bear and his new girlfriend and deal with them *right now* or no farmer in this area would be safe from their assaults.

"First off," Coote said, draining the beer and offering it upended to the ground squirrel, which put both paws on the bottle's mouth to lick furiously at the last drop, "I could give a rat's ass about the farmers in this area, and second, I burned the man's barn down, which makes us square, Bear and me."

"You should've waited until it was full of hay—"

"Yeah, well, I did it when I did it but at least I did it."

"Remember what you said you were going to do to that woman?" Scrudde asked, lowering his voice and leaning toward Coote.

"I burned the barn down, why don't *you* take care of the woman."

"I'm a Christian, it's not in my nature—"

"Oh yeah it is, just catch her home alone and step right up, no discussion, and bust her in the nose. The pain and blood makes 'em meek as a mouse. Then do whatever you want. A high-tone woman like that, she'll be outta town in about one day."

Scrudde, nodding and grinning, told Coote *he* should do it because obviously he had experience in this area.

"I don't hold nothing particular against that woman, it was Bear choked me." Coote lifted the ground squirrel on a flat palm and then suddenly turned the palm over, but Henry was quick, scrambling around to the knuckle side of Coote's hand. Shaking his bushy tail, he chattered angrily at Coote, who laughed and offered a finger for the squirrel to hold, then told Scrudde, "I burned Bear's barn, Bear and me are square."

"You don't get it, *she's* the troublemaker."

"Then *you* take care of her."

Scrudde leaned even closer. "I'd come along with you."

Coote smirked, though he was still looking at the ground squirrel, not Scrudde. "Yeah, I remember . . . you like watching, don't you."

Uncharacteristically, Scrudde admitted to it.

But Coote said, "I think I'll pass."

Scrudde leaned back and looked down into his upturned hat. "She's been telling everyone in town how you were so scared of Bear you wet your pants."

"What?"

"That's right, the boys in the café got a big laugh out of it."

"She said—"

"She said you wet your pants outta pure fright, Bear got you so scared you was begging him to let go, crying like a girl, then you wet yourself, that's what that Renault woman, that's what she's going around town saying about you."

Coote placed the ground squirrel on the back of the couch and picked up his empty beer bottle. "Wonder if she'd repeat it to my face."

"Why don't you find out."

"I just might."

Scooting the aluminum chair quickly across the floor until he was close enough they could smell each other's breath, Scrudde nudged Coote. "Yeah, come on, let's find out."

27

The cat lady's white hair stood in electric wisps all over a balding pink skull, her rheumy eyes wide in confused astonishment, dried snot around her nose and some kind of food smear on her left cheek, oatmeal or peanut butter or both. She was wrinkled and turkey-necked and everywhere sagging. Her thin pink dressing gown was filthy, as were her bare feet, and you don't even want to know the condition of her toenails. Some aspects of this woman, Irene Bayt, age eighty-eight, were caused by age and neglect, but it was cat piss that was responsible for the odor that attended her like an invisible shroud and exhaled from the house worse than rotting breath.

"Hello, Granny," Bear said to the woman in such a sweet unpatronizing voice that Katie felt ashamed for having covered her mouth when the old woman first opened the door.

Bear gingerly grasped the confused woman's hand and introduced himself. "My name is Joey Long, they call me Bear, and this here's Katie Renault, I named her Katydid. We're here to help you with your cats."

"There got to be too many," the woman said.

"Yes, ma'am."

"How many are there?" Katie asked.

The old woman gave her a fierce look; she didn't like the way Katie had reacted when the door was opened.

"Doesn't matter," Bear said. "Granny, if you don't mind we'll come in and clean up, let you keep as many cats as you want, then we'll take the rest where they can find new homes."

Only five feet or so in humped height, Mrs. Bayt was both

terrified and angry, looking up at them as if they were giants intent upon her bones. "You from church?"

Bear said, "We're just going to come in and clean up, Granny. After we're finished you can keep as many cats as you want."

"Too many of them," she said, stepping aside to let the giants in.

Inside—this is the bad part—the inside of that house, though not evil through intent, was nonetheless a construction of hell by stench and filth and the lurid condition of cats everywhere crying for attention, from pain, out of hunger, screeching because they were hurt, getting screwed or wanting to screw. The smell of cat piss overwhelmed the air, making Katie's eyes water, and even Bear, ever suffering, had to squint from the stench that seemed wet on the face. Cat hair of various colors littered and sprinkled all available surfaces and in a shaft of light from the window you could see cat hairs floating thickly like asbestos fibers. The place was crawling and tailing with cats of all ages and sizes and conditions, many of them injured, squinted-shut eyes a commonality here along with fresh wounds and old wounds and tumors right out there in the open where you had to look at them. A tail-hooked tom came through on his way to some privacy, carrying a dead kitten in his mouth.

Cats were everywhere around the old woman as she shuffled her feet across the living room. Katie and Bear shuffled as they walked, too; otherwise they'd end up stepping on paws. When Mrs. Bayt sat in a chair, the cats swarmed her in a way that seemed to the observer less affectionate than alarming, especially when a slack-gutted yellow cat found the food on the old woman's left cheek and commenced a fit of aggressive licking, both paws bracing the woman's face.

"Let's take a look," Bear said to Katie, then to Mrs. Bayt: "Granny, we're going to take a look around, see what's needed."

She didn't reply.

Touring the one-story, one-bath frame house, Bear listed aloud everything that would be needed, the tools and bleach and plywood and extra cages. Twenty-seven cats in all, it would turn out, with a dozen of them males, nobody neutered. Along with their widespread territorial spraying, many of the toms had claimed corners of rooms as their personal toilets, these areas so thoroughly saturated that the carpet and pad were ruined. Poking with his big pocketknife, Bear discovered that in places the wooden floorboards had been turned to brown mush, the result of being continually soaked with tomcat piss. Bear suspected the plywood subfloor might be contaminated, too. No use trying to clean it, the wood would have to be replaced along with the carpet. (When Bear lifted carpet to inspect the floor, the smell blossomed so sickeningly that Katie had to wait out in the hallway.)

Inspection completed, Bear and Katie found the old woman in her kitchen making coffee and putting out some cookies "I just baked yesterday." A dozen cats were up on the counter, drinking out of the creamer and pulling cookies from plates and meowing aggressively and scrapping with each other. Mrs. Bayt absently pushed the cats out of the way and put the partially eaten cookies back on the plates, the cats returning to steal the cookies, Mrs. Bayt grabbing a tail or leg, this tug and pull being performed so handily you could tell it was a constant feature of her kitchen counterwork.

When the old woman opened the refrigerator, cats actually jumped up onto the shelves, and Katie saw that the back of Mrs. Bayt's dressing gown was stained in ways to break your heart.

"I'm taking her home to the farm," Katie said quietly to Bear, who marveled at her use of *home* when referring to his farm. "I'll clean her up, put on fresh clothes, you start caging the cats."

Bear nodded, it was a good idea for the woman to be out of the house because her cats weren't going to like this part.

Katie asked Bear to come out to the truck with her, and Bear asked Mrs. Bayt if they could take their coffee and cookies with them, the old woman saying that would be fine—she was brushing cats away from the cups and plates right up until the moment she handed everything to Bear.

Once they were at the truck, Bear and Katie quickly disposed of the coffee and cookies, both contaminated with cat hair. With

Bear's help, Katie began writing a list of everything needed to start the repairs. It was agreed she'd assemble the material and bring it back in the truck after she'd finished bathing Mrs. Bayt at the farm, *at home.* Bear said he'd start ripping out the carpeting and pile it in the yard for burning.

They stood there by the truck for a long time without speaking, neither of them ready to start their assigned tasks or willing to return to that house.

"We could just drive away," Bear said quietly.

It was exactly what Katie had been thinking.

❦

She had never bathed another human being, Katie having no children or nieces or nephews, being an only child with both of her parents still young enough not to need care. As she stood in Bear's bathroom with Mrs. Bayt, Katie wished that her first experience bathing someone could've been with a fat baby. Her second choice would've been a young man. Before the illness and operation she had suggested to William that they bathe together but he always replied archly that bathtub frolics were clumsy for sex and inadequate for hygiene.

When she removed Mrs. Bayt's clothing, Katie teared up, not from the odor this time (although the smell of cat urine was *of* the woman, like an aura), but from sadness that we end up this way, *ruined.* Katie thought that if given a choice, either to live a healthy full life until some appropriate age, seventy or seventy-five or whatever, and then immediately die, *or* to live another twenty years beyond that but suffer such indignities as to bugger the imagination, most people would *say* give me a healthy life and then immediate death. But when the time comes, when we're told it's a terrible operation or death, we change our minds, mortality making cowards of us all as we meekly opt for mutilation and fogged minds, anything for another year, another month—give me one more hour—life worshiped even as it makes wrecks of us.

She helped the old woman into the tub of warm sudsy water

and began gathering supplies and tools to clean her. Katie was surprised that Bear kept his house so orderly and scrubbed, everything properly arranged on shelves lined with pristine white paper. He had a dozen containers of baby powder.

She returned to the tub with a basketful of toiletries.

"Ladies from the church use to come and do my hair sometimes," Mrs. Bayt said.

But ladies from the church don't come and wash your butt, do they? Katie thought. She knelt there next to the tub, hesitating to touch the old woman, and wondering why she could readily bathe a mangy stray dog but found a fellow human so uninviting.

"Ready?" Katie asked.

"I need a bath, it's been a while."

Katie nodded at the truth of that and then bent to the task.

He spent more than an hour catching cats, getting his hands and arms and face scratched and bitten, there's nothing quite as unholdable as a cat that doesn't want to be held, and though Bear was very nearly fearless when it came to animals, he found himself intimidated more than once, reaching under a bed or couch to bring out a spitting, screaming cat, all claws and needle-toothed. Catching them however was the easy part.

Bear had performed hundreds of unpleasant tasks in his years of farming, he had reached into cow's rectums, castrated calves and lanced boils, squeezed pus from suppurating wounds, and once enucleated a cow's cancerous eyeball. But nothing he'd done was quite as nasty as pulling up the carpeting soaked with years of tomcat urine. Bear tied a handkerchief around his face, covering his nose, but it didn't help.

Working with tools he'd kept back from the truck, crowbar and hammer, mainly, Bear pulled up dripping carpet and soaked padding, rolled them, dragged them outside, and piled them for burning, which would require gallons of diesel fuel. Then he began prying loose the tongue-and-groove floorboards, the wood fibers mushy, and carried them out to the yard and adding them to carpet pile . . . maybe a whole barrel of fuel would be needed.

In some of the corners, the subfloor looked dry. Bear leaned down to smell if it was okay but realized he could no longer detect what stank and what didn't, the whole world now smelled like cat piss to him.

Bear found various litter boxes that had been used beyond capacity and he carried these outside, too. Then from under furniture he began collecting empty cans of cat food. In the little house's utility room, he made a discovery so unsettling he spoke aloud. "Sweet Jesus."

Trying to reach some empty cat-food cans, Bear had moved the washing machine. Next to it, behind the dryer, was a basketball-size hole in the plasterboard wall, near the floor, between the studs. Pushing both the washer and dryer out of the way, he knelt and looked into this hole and discovered upon a bed of broken drywall a mother cat and five newborn babies, dead so long they were desiccated. The mother was lying on her side with head up, looking out eyelessly at Bear, while the kittens were tucked in nursing positions, each with its tiny paws flanking a dried teat.

Bear imagined what might have happened. The mother cat used that hole as her den because it would be warm there behind the dryer and out of the way of the other cats, especially the toms who were known to kill kittens, to eat them. But then Mrs. Bayt or someone who was helping her with the laundry pushed the washer and dryer tightly against the wall, trapping the mother in there with her five babies. The mother cat must've called out incessantly, but in this household of constant screech and yowl, who would've heard? The kittens stayed hungry, of course, the mother cat resigned to nursing them until she died, her babies still sucking at that lifeless body, the milkless teats, until they too died in place. Maybe the warmth of the dryer accelerated the desiccation, because it was so complete that when Bear reached in to remove the horrible tableau he was astonished at how light it was, as if made of wasp paper.

Although the cat and kittens initially stayed together as a unit, they were so crumbly that by the time he made it to a wastebasket Bear was mothering a pile of fragments in his cupped hands.

He decided not to tell Katie.

She returned in late afternoon with supplies and another fifteen cages. Katie said that Mrs. Bayt was taking a nap at the farm. The old woman had gone with Katie to the hardware store to pick out colors for new carpeting, though Mrs. Bayt didn't have any cash. "I'm willing to pay for it," Katie told Bear. "I just have to transfer some money from another account." He said they had plenty of time because once all the contaminated material was removed and everything had been bleach-cleaned, it would be a good idea to let the house air out before installing new flooring.

"Will it ever be clean?" Katie asked. She meant, would the house ever be free of the odor of cats?

Bear didn't know.

Although they were outside by the truck they could still hear the cats screeching. Katie had brought coffee and a cheese sandwich for Bear but he said he couldn't eat because every time he raised his hands toward his face he could smell the cat piss even though he'd washed his hands about a dozen times.

Katie said she felt the same way. "I asked Mrs. Bayt how many cats she wanted to keep for herself if we could find homes for all the others and I was worried she'd say eight or nine, too many for her to care for, but she surprised me."

"She wants just one or two," Bear guessed.

"No," Katie said. "She doesn't want *any.*"

"What'll we do with 'em all?"

"Doc Setton will help us arrange adoptions for some, but the others—"

"Yeah, it's a shame but it has to be done."

"What has to be done?"

Bear looked at her like she was being dense.

"Oh," Katie said. "You mean kill them."

"Some of them, yeah . . . cats that won't nobody adopt."

"We could convert one of your sheds into a cattery."

"A what?"

"A place for cats to live, lots of warm nesty areas, limbs to climb, scratching posts, a large toilet area. They could live out their lives in peace and contentment."

"You saying I should start a place for homeless cats?"

"And maybe other animals, too, strays and abused animals."

Bear looked away. "I ain't even done nothing about my barn yet and already I got the Noyles horses to look after every day, then we have to finish Granny's house here because you can't start something like this without finishing it, now you're talking about taking on even more, converting sheds for stray cats and who knows what else."

Using his goatee as a pull, Katie turned his face her way and asked sweetly, "Was there a question in there?"

"Yes. Am I doing this all on my own?"

She let go and didn't answer.

They worked together the rest of the day cleaning Mrs. Bayt's house, then Bear caged the remaining cats. By the time they delivered the cats to the vet clinic and returned to the farm, Bear had to complete his chores in the dark. When he came in, Mrs. Bayt, looking fresh and clean like a real granny with fluffy white hair and wearing a pretty print dress, sat at the kitchen table while Katie stood at a counter cutting vegetables. Bear marveled that in one week's time his life could come to this: women in the kitchen.

The three of them shared a simple supper of soup and bread. The old woman's eating habits were atrocious from living alone so long and competing at the table with cats. Katie would reach over occasionally and clean Mrs. Bayt's face. The woman always thanked her.

After fixing a bed for Mrs. Bayt in the room where Bear's father once slept (Bear figured the old woman wouldn't even notice the lingering smell of his father's Lucky Strikes), Katie said to Bear, "I assume you and I are sleeping together."

It was like hearing her say, I assume you and I traveling to the moon tonight.

28

For the next two weeks, Bear and Katie worked hard every day. He was accustomed to it but Katie would collapse into bed each night in exhaustion, sometimes she wouldn't even eat supper. She ached all over. Before her arms built up strength and endurance, they were so weak she couldn't lift them high enough to shampoo her hair and had to lean over in the shower, until her head was nearly at her waist. She got cuts and bruises, and sometimes a whole day would go by without Katie ever checking in a mirror. The physical labor wore away her anxieties until she no longer worried about the universe.

She and Bear did the chores at his farm, they converted one of Bear's sheds into a sanctuary for cats, they continued caring for Noyles's horses, and they installed new flooring and carpeting in Mrs. Bayt's house. On the first of May, beautiful May, they walked the cows up to summer pasture. Bear tried to get Red Cow to say something, to amuse and mystify Katie, but the cow remained mute. When he saw groundhogs scurrying through the grass, Bear called greetings. After they returned to the farmyard, Bear said, "Watch this!" He stepped behind the old pickup and lifted its back bumper, one hand in the tire well, until he went red-faced and the truck was one tire off the ground. Katie told him, for godssake put that truck down.

While she was staying on the farm with Bear, someone broke into her fiancé's cottage and trashed the place. When Deputy Miller drove out to report this, Katie was less concerned about William's property than with the condition of eight dogs and two parrots.

"You know what brought this about," Miller told Katie and

Bear. "It started with the cow that Bear put out of its misery, then the barn burning, then those calves being stolen off Scrudde's farm, and now someone shows up at the house where you were staying," he said, nodding at Katie, "and trashes the place, and what do you think would've happened if they'd caught you at home?"

"You should go talk to them," she suggested. "You know it's Coote and Scrudde, one or both of them."

Miller shook his head. "I did talk to them. They gave each other alibis for where they were when your house was vandalized, just like you and Bear give each other alibis for where you were when Scrudde's livestock was rustled. So where's this all going to end?"

In tears, Bear thought.

"Even cleaning out Mrs. Bayt's house," the deputy continued, "which you might think was a generous act that nobody could argue with, but her daughter and granddaughter were fit to be tied that you took the old woman here without their permission—"

"To *bathe* her," Katie quietly insisted.

"Just the same, her relatives are all upset you've embarrassed them by stepping in and taking care of Mrs. Bayt. So what I'm saying is no matter how kind you think you're being, how selfless, when it involves another person's property, stepping in when you're not asked, it's going to have repercussions. Now I'll ask you again, what do you think might've happened to you if you'd been to home when they broke into your house?"

She said she didn't know.

"I think you do."

After Miller left, Katie told Bear that she thought the deputy was right. "This might end badly for both of us, for you especially because this is your home."

"Ain't it yours too?"

"I haven't talked to William in a couple weeks, I'm going to have to call him now . . . tell him what happened to his cottage. We should go over there and look, see how bad it is before I call."

It was bad. Someone had driven a truck across the yard, pulling down the picket fence. The dogs got out. Windows had been broken. Inside, furniture was tipped over, pictures knocked from the wall.

"William will be devastated," Katie said.

"You don't have to tell him nothing was broke," Bear assured her. "I can put it all right again, reglaze the windows, reset the fence outside, we'll just add this to the chores we do."

"I still have to call him," she said. "About us."

"Okay."

"It wouldn't be fair otherwise."

"I know it."

"Even though he hasn't called *me* for two weeks, either."

"Probably just busy with that good job he's got," Bear told her, seemingly without guile.

Eventually six of the eight dogs were recovered and one of the parrots. Bear and Katie came by the cottage every day to continue the cleanup. Bear was as good as his word, the restoration nearly perfect, house and garden both. "I'm still worried about those dogs," Katie told him. "They were the two most vulnerable ones, that little blind Jack Russell and that beagle mix." Bear promised the dogs would be found.

One afternoon when Katie and Bear got to Noyles's farm to feed the mare and her filly, the horses were nowhere to be found. Bear went up to the house, talked with Noyles for a few minutes, and returned to the truck with bad news: Noyles had sent both horses off to slaughter.

Katie was astonished. She and Bear had offered to take the horses, to buy them. "Why would he do something like that?"

"For the money," Bear said.

"But he knew we would've bought them, didn't he?"

"Yes."

She couldn't get over what Noyles had done. "Then *why*?"

"He didn't want to sell to us, he did it for spite."

Katie didn't speak for a long time on the drive back to Bear's farm, then she said that one word, "Spite."

"Yep," Bear told her. "Mr. Noyles came right out and said he was just waiting for us to get them horses to put on weight, get strong enough they could be loaded and make the trip to the slaughterhouse."

Katie cursed and instructed Bear not to call him Mr. Noyles, call him Devil Noyles.

But next day she was at it again, never yielding. She went to the cottage and looked for the missing parrot, volunteered at Doc Setton's clinic, labored hard on the farm without complaint. Bear admired her. He thought he was pretty good at taking pain and misfortune and whatever else life threw his way, but pound for pound Katie was more of a fighter than he'd ever be.

Katie returned from the clinic one afternoon with information on another rescue. Bear asked if she'd like to wait awhile before taking on any new responsibilities, he didn't want her getting downhearted by things not working out as she'd hoped. Noyles selling those horses, for example, and Mrs. Bayt's family being mad at the way Bear and Katie had tried to help out there.

"Discouragement is what gets people out of this work," Katie told him. "Discouragement was what made me quit the animal rights organizations I belonged to. You can't give in to it."

Today's rescue, Katie explained on the way there, was of an old dog kept on a short chain attached to a post in the yard—no shelter, no shade from the sun, no place to get warm in the winter or get out of the rain. It was threatening to rain on this particular day, sweet early May.

The house was a modest frame bungalow right in the town of Briars. The dog looked like a thick-coated retriever mix, black, its muzzle gray. The animal was well fed, fat even, and its water bowl was full, but you had to wonder what peculiar kind of torture it was for a retriever to spend its life, day and night, on a six-foot tether.

"The owner must take him for walks, huh?" Bear asked hopefully as they parked in front of the house.

Katie was shaking her head. "The information I have is that the dog is never let loose, never off that chain, never taken for walks. The man feeds and waters him, picks up the poop, but never lets him in the house or gives him any exercise. For a start, what I'd like to do is offer the man a free doghouse, which we'll drop off, then at least the dog can get out of the elements. We'll try to convince the man to let us come around and walk the dog every day."

Another chore added to the list, Bear thought.

"You talk to him first," Katie said. "These men resent a woman trying to tell them anything."

She got out of the truck and went to pet the dog, which immediately performed a repertoire of submission. Bear was at the door. He hated this part. Even though he knew in his heart that Katie was right, that these rescues were morally right, on another level, Bear believed it wasn't any of his business how a man treated his animals.

The door was answered by a friendly old guy in his seventies, thin and bent, white hair, wearing jeans and a checked shirt. A clear plastic tube carrying oxygen was fixed under his nostrils, held there by a strap that ran around his head, the oxygen tube leading to a four-foot tank that the man maneuvered on a dolly.

"What can I do for you?"

"My name's Joe Long, they call me Bear."

"Oh, I know about you, I knew your family."

He came out on the porch, holding the door open behind him so his oxygen line wouldn't get crimped, and shook hands with Bear. "My name's Eddie Lancor, I lived in this house all my life. Who's that out there with Old Bob?"

"That's Katie Renault," Bear said. "Your dog's what I come to see you about . . . Old Bob, huh?"

"Used to be just Bob but when he turned gray around the mouth like that, I took to calling him Old Bob."

"How long's he been chained?"

"What do you mean?"

"I mean, he gets let off sometimes?"

Eddie Lancor kept his friendly expression as he explained. "He ran away once when he was about six months old, I said that's the last time you'll do that, son, and put the chain on him that day and it ain't come off since."

"And he's how old?"

Lancor's brow furrowed. "What's this about? Old Bob is ten this year."

"Nine and a half years on a six-foot chain for running away one time is kind of hard punishment, ain't it?"

"Ain't punishing him, just keeping him chained so he don't run away . . . my dog, my call."

"Yessir." Bear turned toward the dog. "See how he's looking over here at you, I bet he spends all day watching the door, waiting for you to step out."

"Used to be, he spent all day waiting for me to come home from work, but since I retired and got this lung thing, I stay pretty much in the house. You selling something?"

"No sir, I'm not, but I'd like to *give* you a doghouse, we'll deliver it and—"

Lancor got a disgusted look. "You *are* selling something." He started backing up into the house.

Bear used a foot to keep the door open. "I swear to you, Mr. Lancor, we're giving you a doghouse just to keep Old Bob out of the weather. We'd also like to come by and walk him—it's nothing that costs you anything, it's what me and that woman have started doing around here, rescuing animals."

"Rescue?" He was genuinely confused. "Old Bob don't need rescued. Rescued from what? *Me?*" You could tell the old man's feelings were hurt.

"He could use a free doghouse, couldn't he?"

"That thick coat he's got, weather don't bother him."

"Just the same—"

"What's she doing?"

Bear looked over in time to see Katie unchaining Old Bob and bringing him over by the collar. No, Bear thought, don't do that.

Lancor was suddenly livid, his gray pallor going dangerously purple. "That ain't your dog, lady!"

When Katie reached them, Old Bob was wagging his tail so

vigorously that his whole body swayed back and forth and he nearly tore loose from Katie's grip trying to get close to Lancor, the dog grinning at his man and straining forward to lick him and generally acting as if this skinny old oxygen-tubed dying specimen was a star and Old Bob his most fervent satellite.

"This dog loves you, Mr. Lancor," Bear said.

"Put him back!"

"Can't you let him in the house with you?" Katie asked.

"Put him back or I'm calling the cops!"

As she pulled Old Bob back to his post, Bear told the man, "I bet if you could open up that old dog's head and see what he was thinking, you'd see a picture of you coming out of this door, that's what he has on his mind all day, you coming out the door, it's what he lives for, ain't it?"

Lancor adjusted his oxygen tube and spoke hopelessly. "He's happy to see me 'cause I bring his food, is all."

"Naw, that ain't it. I bet he ignores the food until you get back in the house, doesn't he? Ignores the food and concentrates on looking at you, sending you mind rays to make you pet him, ain't I right?"

Lancor shrugged. "I'm dying."

Bear said, "What?"

"The doc said I won't see another Christmas. You should leave me alone."

Bear felt poleaxed by this declaration but kept talking in an inappropriately chirpy voice, like a salesman who'd lost his mind. "We'll still drop off that free doghouse and we're more than willing to walk Old Bob for you, free of charge, but it'd be better if you were the one who walked that dog, Old Bob will think he's done died and gone to dog heaven."

"Mister, you're crazy."

"You ain't supposed to walk?"

"The doc said exercise or don't exercise, it won't matter much to the timetable." The old man turned thoughtful. "Let me ask you something."

"Okay."

"You ever see those movies where the dying patient says, 'Doc, don't sugarcoat it for me, I want the truth'?"

"No."

"Well, I'm sitting in my doctor's office and he's telling me the truth like it's today's weather report and I'm thinking, 'Hey, Doc, put some sugar on that why don't you.'"

"Might be good for you and Old Bob both, taking walks."

Lancor shook his head to indicate Bear wasn't getting it. "Not your call to tell me what's good for me or my dog, now get the hell out of here and keep your free doghouse, too."

"Mr. Lancor, that woman there in your yard needs a victory real bad."

"A victory? What's that supposed mean?"

"She needs something to go her way for once. If you was to take Old Bob off that chain—"

Lancor stepped back and pushed the door shut.

Katie and Bear left the yard and reached the truck just as the skies opened, Old Bob getting soaked as he stood there with his ears down and his expression resigned, staring at the door to the house, until finally he lay down with grizzled muzzle on his front paws and eyes closed against the rain.

❦

That night in bed, Katie told Bear she had something she wanted to talk to him about. He thought it was going to be Old Bob, but instead she asked, "You know why I'm having such a hard time calling William? I have to tell him about us and that means breaking off the engagement. What I want to say to you is, my breaking off the engagement in no way obligates you to stick with me or think of us in terms of a couple or anything like that. I have sort of *imposed* all this on you: me, the rescues, everything. So when you've had enough just say uncle."

"I don't know exactly what you mean," he said.

"I'm your first . . . girlfriend," she said, embarrassed to be using an adolescent term, but how else was she going to phrase it, that she was his first lay, first lover, first woman?

"First and last," he told her.

"No, not last. You'll meet someone less . . . damaged than I am. You deserve an interesting sex life, not the limited version I can give you."

"I don't even know what that means."

"One of these days, you're going to wonder what it would be like with another woman who doesn't have . . . the restrictions I do. Who doesn't go to bed every night wearing a top, won't let you touch—"

"You're perfect."

"No."

"Yes."

"Do you want to try some sex games?"

Bear's breathing became shallow.

"Some role-playing?" she asked.

"I don't even know what that is."

"It's acting. Let's try this. You come in and push me around while I pretend to protest, but if it gets to where I can't handle it, I'll use a safe word—you know what that is?"

He admitted he didn't know what that was, either.

"A safe word is something I say that tells you the role-playing should end. For example, if you're holding me down and I insist you let me up but I'm just playing the role of the helpless damsel, then you should keep holding me down. But if I say the safe word, you have to let me up right away, the game's over."

"I don't think we should be doing this."

"It'll spice up our sex life."

Bear thought their sex life was plenty spicy.

"The safe word can be . . . *giraffe.*"

"I don't want to, Katie."

"Don't be silly. If the role-playing gets out of hand I'll say *giraffe* and you'll stop immediately."

"No, I really don't—"

"You get naked, I'll take off my underpants."

"Okay."

Katie pretended to be asleep—sprawled naked from the

waist down on the bed without covers—and Bear was supposed to pretend he was a mean old drunk husband just come home from the tavern and wanting romance. He waited out in the hallway trying to find motivation and then entered the room and without preamble straddled her on the bed.

"What the hell are you doing!" she shouted angrily.

Bear got off. "I thought I was supposed to be the mean old drunk husband."

Katie smiled. "You are, sweetie, and I was playing the wife who was just awakened and wanted to know what the hell her mean old drunk husband was up to. See, I didn't say *giraffe,* so you should've continued."

"Okay."

"Are you enjoying this?"

"No."

"Except for the naked part?" she asked, touching him.

He grinned and went back out of the bedroom to make his entrance again.

"What the hell you doing!" she shouted as Bear straddled her.

"I want some pussy!"

"Bear, don't you *dare* talk to me like that."

He hesitated, but Katie nodded encouragement so he grabbed her wrists.

"Let me go," she said.

He put one hand down between her legs.

She screamed at him, "Stop *manhandling* me, you bastard!"

He apologized and got off the bed.

Katie was trying not to laugh as she explained, "It's still part of the role-playing, hon. Remember, I didn't say *giraffe.*"

"I don't like this game."

"You want to make love the regular way?"

"Yes."

Afterward, as they lay in each other's arms, Bear apologized for not being a very good pervert. Katie said it was okay.

"You do that sort of thing with William?" Bear asked.

They did, William and Katherine enjoying, at least until last year, a varied, even kinky, sex life, but she gently lied to Bear and said no.

He nodded.

"You never try to touch my chest or even ask why I always wear a top."

"That was the rule you gave me."

"I know." She thought how to broach it. "I have scars."

"Me too," Bear said, getting out of bed and turning on the light, pointing to a purple puncture wound on his leg. "That's where Scrudde stabbed me with a pitchfork." He showed Katie his forearms. "And those scratches are from Mrs. Bayt's cats, when I was putting them in cages. See here?" He put his foot up on the bed and pointed to an ugly horizontal scar across his left shin. "I was trimming branches from a log when the ax slipped, it went all the way down to white bone."

"I bet that hurt."

He opened both eyes wide to indicate how much. "Dad said when you die and your soul goes to heaven, God takes a look at the body you left behind and if there ain't any scars or marks on it, God isn't very happy because He gave you this wonderful gift and you didn't do anything with it all your life, never gave your body much use, never banged it up, what was the point of God giving you such a great gift if you just kept it safe and sound? Look there at my knee, a chain saw did that."

"Bear?"

He flicked the thumbnail of his left hand against three fingers, the little, the ring, the middle. "These three fingers got no feeling in the tips, none at all. Come from using a gas-powered posthole digger all one summer."

"Bear, I want to show you something."

He indicated dead white skin in the web between thumb and forefinger. "Snakebit."

She pulled off her top.

Bear looked hard at her puckered scars.

She asked him if he thought God would be pleased with her for not keeping her body all brand-new and untouched.

A few days later a doghouse for Old Bob arrived at the clinic and Katie paid for it, still intending to make the delivery even though Bear had told her that Lancor didn't want it.

"What's he going to do once we drop it off?" she asked. "It's free to him, he'll leave it right where we put it, and then at least that dog'll have shelter."

When they got to Lancor's house, the post and chain were still there . . . but no dog.

"He put that poor animal to sleep," Katie said quietly. "Just so he wouldn't have to deal with us."

"We don't know that," Bear told her.

She thought of the horses Noyles had sent off to slaughter . . . and now this. "I wonder sometimes if we're not doing more harm than good."

Just then the door opened and Eddie Lancor came out on the porch and waved at them, Old Bob next to him.

Bear nudged her. "Katydid, look!"

Lancor, who wasn't wearing his oxygen tube, beamed a bright good mood as Old Bob kept pressing against his leg in an effort to stay close, the dog's head turned up to stare into the man's face.

"Ain't that a picture," Bear said. He and Katie got out of the truck and came over.

"That dog adores you," she told the man.

Lancor didn't deny it.

"And it looks like someone's had a bath," Bear noted as he bent down to pet Old Bob, who pretty much ignored Bear to keep his concentration on the one he worshiped.

Lancor was grinning like a kid. "I had to clean him up if I was going to keep him in the house."

"He lives in the house now?" Katie asked.

"Yes, sleeps on the floor in my bedroom—my father would turn over in his grave if he knew I had a dog in the house. On days when my chest is feeling okay, Old Bob and me take walks.

He minds good and I see people in the neighborhood I ain't talked to in years. I want to thank the both of you."

Bear looked over to Katie, whose face was like a spotlight.

"At first I was mad for you sticking your nose in my business, but then after you left that day I looked at Old Bob out in that rain and I thought to myself, he's going to die of old age soon enough and me too and here we are both chained up, Old Bob to a post and me to that air tank—what's the point? I don't know why I didn't unchain him before this, force of habit, I guess. When I grew up, dogs weren't allowed in the house. Anyway, taking care of Old Bob, being with him in the house, having him around, I guess it's lowered my pressure. I don't need air half as much as I used to. I doubt any of it's going to keep me from croaking before Christmas, but at least Old Bob gives me things to do, walking him and brushing him and— You'll think this is crazy but I talk to him, too, *how you feeling today, Old Bob, do your bones ache like mine do?* That sort of thing. I was waiting for you two to drop by, got something for you . . . here." Lancor pulled a check out of his shirt pocket and handed it to Bear.

Five hundred dollars made out to cash. Bear said, "No we couldn't accept—"

But before he could finish or give the check back, Katie took it and thanked Mr. Lancor.

"See, I was thinking," Lancor said, smiling, "that if I go before Old Bob, maybe he could come out and live at your farm."

Katie and Bear both said Old Bob would be welcomed.

Lancor nodded, tears in his eyes the way old men get overly emotional. "I used to be such a hard case, then somewhere along the line turned soft." He looked down at his dog. "We got to go watch a program on the Animal Channel," Lancor said, stepping back toward the door. "Come on, Old Bob."

The fat shaggy dog heeled immediately while keeping both eyes laser-locked on Lancor to see what else might be expected of him, determined to do nothing that might jeopardize this beautiful turn of fate, allowed to live in the house with the man.

Just before closing the door, Lancor said to Bear, "Tell your wife there she got her victory."

In the truck Katie asked what that meant.

"When we were here the first time I told him you needed a victory," Bear said. "You needed someone to break down and do right by their animal for once."

"Well, he did, didn't he?"

They drove home happy. That night in bed, Katie asked, "How'd it make you feel when Lancor referred to me as your wife?"

"Syrupy."

❦

Across town in Lancor's bedroom, Old Bob got up off the floor and put a paw on the man's bed. "I knew it would come to this," Lancor said. They had already crossed other barriers: Lancor fed Old Bob at the table, sometimes let him eat off his fork. The dog whined softly, the man sighed dramatically. "Come on then, you big baby, get up here." That's all it took, Old Bob was next to the man and immediately curling into a you-won't-even-know-I'm-here tight ball, unable to believe his ever greater fortune—first I get to live in the house, then I eat at his table, now I get to sleep next to him—the dog determined not to cause any trouble . . . except—I just got to do this one thing, can't help myself—Old Bob reaching out with his gray muzzle to kiss the man's cheek. "Enough of that," Lancor told him, throwing an arm around the old dog's neck.

29

May was a month, if you were planning to kill yourself, you'd wait to June. At the farm, work continued on converting sheds and outbuildings into places where cats and dogs and other animals could be kept while awaiting adoption or stay permanently if it came to that. The big German shepherd didn't understand why he wasn't allowed to sniff and nip at the new animals to enter them in his memory banks and bring them under his protection, didn't understand why some of the animals showed up one day and left the next. Women from the library were always coming and going. POTUS would sit on the porch by himself, mystified at these new arrangements.

Bear didn't quite understand what was going on, either. Would he be putting up hay this year, rebuilding his barn, selling off the calves to market this fall as usual? Was he now in the animal sanctuary business, no longer in the farming business? He knew that some of the people who were adopting animals were also giving Katie checks—did animal sanctuary pay any better than farming, which didn't pay at all? In spite of all his worries and questions, whenever Katie came to hold his face in her hands and ask, "Is everything okay with you?" he'd always reply everything was fine by him.

One night in bed Bear said, "I could show you something."

"What's that?"

"Barely people."

"Who are they?"

"Stay back in the woods, collect forest products, live in caves, eat clay, a kindly but backward tribe."

She smiled at the odd way he phrased things. "I'd like to see them, sure."

"I seen evidence they're roaming close these days."

"Evidence?"

"They make little baskets out of reeds and weeds and sometimes if you surprise a tribe of *barely people* they'll run away and drop their baskets, none of them much bigger than a grapefruit, and in those baskets you'll find hellgrammites and hellbenders—"

"What?"

"Lizards and salamanders for fish bait. They also collect ferns and moss for the florist trade."

"You've seen these things, lizards in little baskets?"

"*Barely people* wander around at night mostly, let's go now."

"Are you serious?"

Bear said he was.

They got up and got dressed and made the dogs stay at home. It was a beautiful night and Bear wouldn't let Katie bring a flashlight, he said *barely people* could spot a light miles away. They walked two hours into the mountains, following game trails; Bear knew the way and Katie got the feeling she was being taken on an elaborate snipe hunt, though it was pretty out and warm and she didn't ask to be taken home.

Explaining that they were now on a ridge overlooking one of the favorite clay deposits visited by *barely people,* Bear positioned Katie under a tree and told her to stay here on this hillside no matter what.

"Where you going?" she asked, concern rising in her voice. She hadn't bargained on being left alone.

"I'll circle around and when the *barely people* hear me they'll back off to keep out of my way, which means they'll drift over here. You watch down there by the creek, there's a clay hole been popular with them for years and years."

"It's too dark."

"Moon'll rise soon, stay put."

He went off more quietly than she thought a big man could

move in these deep woods overhung with ferns and briars, hillsides so thick with rhododendron it was like being walled in. As time passed and she kept watch, Katie felt like Dian Fossey waiting for one of the big primates to show itself in the forest. Nothing happened, though, and Katie was ready to go home, then:

"Kak-kak-kak-KAIeee!"

Hairs raised on her arms, skin puckered at the back of her neck, and she felt chilled all the way through. The call was followed by an eerie forest silence and then a few minutes later Katie started trembling the way Bear did, because she heard something crash in the rhododendron above her, coming this way.

It was Bear.

"Did you hear it?" he asked.

She jumped up and hugged him.

"Did you hear it?" he asked again.

"I heard something."

"It was one of them *barely people* calling to warn the others I was in the woods."

"You sure it wasn't you, trying to scare me?"

"No, honey, that was the cry of the *barely people,* once you hear it you'll never forget."

"Let's go home."

Back in bed Katie said she'd never led such a life as she had these past weeks with Bear . . . a life where you work hard all day taking care of animals, saving their lives, then go out into the forest in the middle of the night looking for *barely people* and don't return home until dawn. "It's magic."

"I guess that means we're in love," Bear said.

"I guess it does."

❦

May was great but lasted only a month. On the first of June the county newspaper published a story about Scrudde's veal calves being "liberated" because they were allegedly kept in inhumane conditions. Scrudde was quoted as saying he treated those calves like pampered pets. An animal rights activist contradicted Scrudde and said that photographs proved he had been keeping his animals in daily torture.

That evening a woman who said she worked in the sheriff's department called for Bear and told him he should come in for some questions, that Deputy Miller wanted to ask about Scrudde's stock being rustled, and Bear should come by himself.

"You sure you don't want me to go with you?" Katie asked.

"She said just me."

"Okay. I'll wait dinner."

"Bring POTUS in the house with you."

"Why?"

"He's good company."

After Bear left, Katie was just going outside to find POTUS and Jamaica when the phone rang again. A woman (Katie had no way of knowing it was the same one who'd just called Bear) asked, "Do you know anything about a little white dog that's blind?"

"Yes!"

"And another one, looks kind of like a beagle."

"*Yes,* where are they?"

"At that little house where you used to live, them two dogs are setting up a racket barking and howling. Someone's going to go down there and shoot 'em if you don't come pick them up right now." The woman clicked off.

Katie figured it would take her fifteen minutes to run over there, pick up the dogs, bring them back here, start dinner, then wait for that man to come home.

30

When Scrudde and Coote emerged from the little cottage later that evening, their clothing was marked on shirtsleeve and pants knee by her blood.

They wouldn't even look at each other, this repressed fifty-six-year-old self-professed Christian and the sleepy-eyed twenty-five-year-old self-proclaimed ladies' man. Neither did they speak. Drained of their previous sexual glee, the men felt not remorse but anxiety—they'd gone too far into foreign territory.

Coote walked to his car and drove to the trailer in the woods, where he immediately showered. He ordered Diane, the waitress from Briars Café, to wash his clothes. "If you ever tell anybody," he warned, referring to the calls she'd made on his behalf, getting Bear to go the sheriff's office and then luring Katherine Renault with the story about the dogs, "I'll kill you." When Diane saw the marks on his clothing and realized what they were, she believed Coote's threat heart and soul.

Back at his big house in town, Scrudde also showered, laundered his clothes, and then went down on his knees and prayed, not out of repentance but out of fear, please God don't let me get arrested over this. How such a prayer might be received is a matter of conjecture. The Bible says Jesus loves you no matter what, but the Irish claim God hates a coward.

31

When Bear arrived home and saw that Katie's car was gone, he called Doc Setton, who said he hadn't seen or heard from her. Bear told the vet something strange was going on—he'd been summoned to the sheriff's office, but Miller wasn't there and no one knew anything about a questioning, they put it off as some kind of mistake. Doc said he'd call Deputy Miller at home. Then it occurred to Bear that Katie might've gone again to look for those two little dogs.

He got into his truck and drove to the cottage, which was dark.

The night was dark, too, without wind. Clouds covered the moon and there were no countable stars.

Bear brought a flashlight from the truck and called, "Katydid?" before going inside.

He saw her lying in the middle of the living room. She was naked. Even before checking for a pulse, Bear found her top, a knit wool sweater, and put it on her—he knew how sensitive she was. As he lifted her into his arms, she felt too light to be alive. Bear didn't vibrate or tremble, but he felt something deep inside uncouple, unplug.

He carried her to his truck and rushed to a hospital nearly forty-five minutes away, where she was taken from him, Bear left to himself in the dull horror show called Hospital at Midnight. Doc Setton and then Deputy Miller showed up. What happened? they asked. He didn't know. How is she? No one's told me. Miller and Setton went off to get some answers while Bear sat and waited with a stomach full of gravel.

Deputy Miller and Doc Setton were still gone when a doctor,

tall and handsome with what they call a shock of gray hair, like a maestro, came out and asked Bear if he was the husband. Bear marveled that a man in real life could look so handsome and heroic, like in the movies; Katie was in good hands.

Not getting an answer from Bear and not caring, the doctor said, "The choice is going to be scars or reconstructive surgery on her face."

As if Bear had to decide right now.

"Although maybe, all considered, she doesn't worry about scars anymore."

Bear knew what the doctor was referring to and was ashamed for him.

"We administered the rape kit. Good news there, no penetration."

Bear wondered if this man had been hired to come out posing as a handsome doctor and torture Bear with talk of reconstructive surgery and rape kits and the good news of no penetration. Wouldn't you think that the first thing a real doctor, a healer, would say is: Guess what, she's going to make it, your wife is going to live!

Toward morning, Miller and Setton were allowed to see Katie, but Bear had been acting squirrelly and the hospital staff, discovering he wasn't Katie's husband, made him wait outside in his truck. After a pep talk from Doc Setton about staying calm, and with a change of personnel for the day shift, Bear went back in. Katie was swathed and sedated. He sat bedside and held her hand, they didn't talk.

When morning visiting hours were over, Bear drove to the farm and did the chores, went back to the hospital in the afternoon, returned to the farm for evening chores and then to the hospital for evening visiting hours. This was the routine he followed for the week Katie was in the hospital. That tall, handsome imposter-doctor who'd been so cruel to Bear and who'd never been informed Bear wasn't really her husband, stopped him in the corridor one evening and said, "Your wife should be home. There's nothing we can do for her here that can't be done for her at home. She's been through a terrible trauma but now she's malingering."

Bear wondered how many years a man had to practice to get that mean.

When the time came to check Katie out of the hospital, Bear and Doc Setton had a strained conversation. The vet said he had the medical training to care for Katie, Bear said the farm was her home. Like two boys deciding to let Mother arbitrate, they asked Katie what she wanted to do. She responded as she had during the entire week, with single words rolled up like hedgehogs and short sentences prickly as sea urchins: *I don't care . . . whatever . . . it's up to you.*

Bear won the argument by leaning real close to the dapper little vet and saying, "I'm taking her *home.*"

❦

At the farm, Katie stayed in Bear's bedroom while he slept on a mattress in the hall outside her door.

Bear never knew what a visit to that bedroom might bring. One morning she asked him to get a bucket of sand and put it by her bed. When he wanted to know what it was for, Katie told him, just bring the goddamn sand. He was surprised to hear her curse.

Injecting medications and changing dressings he could handle—a lifetime of farming had worked all the squeamishness out of him—but Bear feared he was too blunt and inexperienced to deal sensitively with Katie's emotional trauma. He was always relieved when Doc Setton came over.

Doc explained that Bear would have to become large with patience, deep with understanding. Bear asked what that meant. Katie, Doc said, was likely to tell him he was wrong whatever he did. If he was very careful, she might complain that he was treating her like fragile glass that's going to break apart in his hands, but if he tried to cheer her up by making a joke, she might yell at him for acting like this whole thing was funny. Absorb and dilute her anger like you were the Pacific Ocean, Doc said, that's what I meant about becoming large and deep.

"It's one of them rules, ain't it?" Bear asked.

"Rules?"

"About how to love her—hold up a second." Bear got out his notebook and wrote it down before he forgot. *Number 4. Have patience and understanding like the Pacific Ocean's got water, be large and deep for her.*

Katie spent all her time in bed: sleeping, reading, curled in a fetal position or lying on her back staring up at the ceiling or on her side staring out the window at where the barn used to be. "Now that that ol' barn is gone," Bear told her one night, "you can see the moon real clear."

She didn't reply.

"I could tell you a poem I wrote about the moon."

She didn't reply.

He brought her cups of soup and glasses of water, pitchers of iced tea, of lemonade. She seemed perpetually dehydrated. And she was desperate to read. He went around retrieving books from various shelves, and though you wouldn't think that Katie would be particularly interested in *Principles of Farming Grass,* she was often absorbed in these texts and wouldn't even look at Bear when he brought in something new for her to drink, as if to say, don't bother me, I want to see how this intensive grazing part turns out.

Deputy Miller visited several times, but the interviews never went well. Katie said it was Coote who hit her but Scrudde was there, too, she saw him standing behind the younger man. We could nail Coote, Miller said, because he's got a record, but convincing a grand jury that a man like Scrudde was part of this would be difficult. Do you want me to lie, Katie asked him, and say that Scrudde *wasn't* there?

One afternoon, when Bear was in the yard and Miller was questioning Katie up in the bedroom, their voices became so loud Bear had to go up and referee.

"I want you to throw this *deputy* out of the house," Katie said as soon as Bear came in. Her facial bandages had been removed the previous day and much of the swelling was down, leaving

Katie with deep bruises, yellow and black, that made her look old, sleep-deprived, jaundiced.

Miller, in his puffy jacket and holding his big hat in hand, looked sheepish as he tried to explain to Bear: "If we could go after Coote and Coote alone, we'd arrest him today. But Scrudde has no record, no arrests, not even a speeding ticket that I could find, he's a prominent church member—"

"Which I guess qualifies him for one free assault," Katie said bitterly.

Miller was shaking his head, still talking to Bear. "I didn't say that either . . . but on a purely practical level, being realistic, if Katie isn't believed in court when she says Scrudde was in the house that night, it's going to get Coote off the hook, too."

"So I'm supposed to change my story," Katie said.

"We arrest Coote and cut a deal, he testifies against Scrudde—"

"For a reduced sentence," Katie added.

"Yeah, but this way, we get them both, case closed."

Katie said the case would never be closed for her. Is this the kind of justice you dispense here in the mountains, Coote set free on probation for cutting a deal, and then what about first-time offender Scrudde, does he get community service, picking up trash along the highway on weekends? Such bullshit, she said. The victim is disparaged, the criminals go free. Fine. As soon as I can, Katie declared, I'm getting a gun and killing both of those bastards, because then, as victims, they will finally get raked over the coals, while I, as the criminal, will get some sympathy.

Miller turned to Bear. "Saying things like that will get her in trouble."

Wincing, Katie sat up in bed and requested that she not be discussed in the third person, and then she again told Bear to throw Miller out of the house.

❦

For dinner he brought her brown rice and salad. Katie told him to take it away, the sight of food made her sick to her stomach.

When he checked on her an hour later she asked if there was any ice cream, he said no but he'd go to town and get some. Katie said it wasn't necessary. Bear went anyway, but when he brought her a bowl of the ice cream he saw that she had fixed herself some cold cereal. Now she said she wasn't hungry, that Bear could put the ice cream in the freezer or he could throw it out for all she cared, she had told him not to go to town for ice cream in the first place.

As Bear was leaving the room, Katie thought she saw him make a put-upon face and told him, "If you're getting tired of this and wondering when am I going to be better, I got news for you, the answer is *never.* I'm tired of getting better. I'm staying exactly the way I am, so don't go around rolling your eyes and wondering why I'm not better yet."

He denied rolling his eyes.

"I come from a gentle, reasonable family," she told him. "All my friends are gentle and reasonable people. I've never been struck in my life. This isn't a good place, these mountains, and what happened to me wasn't fair. Not on top of what I've been through the past year, it isn't fair. I don't plan on getting better."

He said okay and left the room.

Katie made her way to the top of the stairs and hollered down, "Don't be looking at that kitchen calendar marking off the weeks, I've already done that, marked off weeks for the past year, it doesn't help, *I'm not going to get any better.*"

32

Katie got better. She had surgery on her face and came home to the farm stitched like Frankenstein's monster, but by the time the surface sutures were removed and the ones you couldn't see had dissolved, Katie got better despite her promise-prediction never to. So went terrible June. It was normally such a benevolent month, pregnant with summer, the month when windows get unstuck from winter to let in night air that's finally warm, June-moon and all that. But not this June.

It rained and went damp cold and stayed that way. One morning doing chores, Bear thought it actually might snow. Storms would scream in and blow out so quickly that you could rush for home but get caught by rain; then, when you were at the house, safe, sunshine came out to mock you. Once it happened with hail. Bear was working on a fence when suddenly like in a movie the wind was upon him. As he ran for a shed, he got hit hard by falling ice, but as soon as he was under cover, the hail stopped, leaving the ground scattered with the oddest hail he'd ever seen, clear like from a factory. When the sudden sun came, it looked like you could walk anywhere you wanted on diamonds. Bear tried to show Katie, but the ice melted before he could rouse her to go outside.

At night there were unfamiliar noises. Katie and Bear would awaken (she from the bed, he from the mattress, still on the floor, but moved from the hallway into the bedroom). "What's that?" one of them would ask. Sometimes the noise was caused by a sudden wind rattling walls to be let in, but most often the question never got answered and they returned to sleep unsure of what they'd heard versus what they'd dreamed.

One night a tiny bat flew in the window and Katie awoke with it here and there above her battered face as if examining the effects of reconstructive surgery. She pulled the covers over her head and shouted for Bear, who immediately stood, the bat fluttering to him like a scrap of crepe paper caught by a crazy wind, Bear swinging and missing with an open hand as the bat flew around the room, while from under the covers Katie screamed, "Get it out of here! Get it out of here!" Bear finally caught the bat in a blanket. He carried the blanket outside and he shook it—well away from POTUS, sleeping surrounded by ducks and chickens and cats. The night was moonless, and Bear didn't see the little bat fly away.

At the kitchen sink getting a drink of water, he felt something on his leg, behind the left knee, a tickling of the hairs, nothing more. Bear looked down and saw the bat, the black creature smaller than a dollar bill folded in half, making its way from around the back of his knee, maneuvering by reaching out with a tiny hand to grab hairs and move another inch sideways. Bear could've swatted the bat like a big bug, but instead, he stiff-legged himself back outside and, in the yard, tried to pull the bat off with his fingertips, but the little menace held on with its claws. Finally he used a stick to pry, the bat gripping as tightly to the stick as it had to his leg. Bear brought it to a lighted window where he could get a good look. The bat resembled some hellish, winged version of the mouse killed in the pantry trap. Bear threw the stick in the air, thinking the bat would leap off midair and fly away, but the bat stayed on the stick, riding it to the ground for a hard hit. Bear picked up the stick and said, "Fly away." In answer, the little creature flared its black skin wings and hissed. Bear wedged the stick on a tree branch, hoping the bat would be gone come morning.

Unsettling things like that kept happening all through June. The psychologist will say we become predisposed to find signs, good or bad. But how was it Bear's predisposition to cut open a tomato and discover he'd sliced a fat black worm in half, its green guts leaking onto red tomato flesh and both halves writhing with such unwormlike vigor that Bear expected the worm to cry out in pain?

One night in the dark bedroom, with a window screen now protecting against bats, Bear was on the mattress on the floor when Katie, up in bed, asked him if he still wanted to know why she kept that bucket of sand nearby.

Bear said yes.

She began a story about tribes and warriors and women. Bear loved stories about Indians, so he listened closely, feeling entertained, as if this was one of their storytelling sessions . . . until Katie said, "Whenever the women of the tribe heard enemy warriors approaching, the women packed their vaginas with sand to make rape difficult."

Bear required a moment to understand it.

"That's why I keep this bucket of sand by the bed. When I hear Scrudde and Cootie coming up those stairs—"

Bear assured her she didn't have to worry about that.

Katie ridiculed his naïveté.

He said, "They'd have to go through POTUS outside and then me in here—"

"When I hear them coming up the steps," she insisted, "I'm going to start packing myself with sand."

"They won't ever hurt you again."

"You're worse than ignorant," she told him.

Which hurt Bear like hot copper wire.

"When the warriors of the tribe returned," Katie said, her voice back in storytelling mode, "to discover that their women had been violated, they revenged this atrocity by sodomizing the enemy. Do you know what that means?"

Still stung from being called worse than ignorant, Bear didn't answer.

"Sometimes, in preparation for this avenging raid, the warriors dressed themselves in women's clothes and marked their faces for war. Contemporary accounts indicate that even the most battle-hardened among the enemy were terrified of being attacked by warriors dressed as women."

Bear thought, even if I'm worse than ignorant, I can figure out what she wants me to do.

❦

June continued, it got worse. People scurried around without casting shadows. One evening, storm clouds squatted down on the farm to obliterate the natural space between sky and earth; black and yellow, the color of Katie's bruises, the clouds descended into the trees like it was the end of the world. The image was so eerie that Bear, returning from town with supplies, drove into the farmyard looking at the clouds, not watching where he was going.

POTUS crossed in front of the truck.

Bear hit the brakes while turning the wheel hard in the opposite direction, missing the big German shepherd but not the fat white duck who'd been following him.

Bear jumped out and ran around to where the duck was flopping in unmistakable death throes even though the pristine white feathers were unmarked by blood. For once in its life the big white duck was not quacking.

The small brown duck, however, made a huge racket as it waddled in to mount its companion, using its beak to hold on to feathers at the back of the white duck's head. With wings and feet, it maneuvered the white duck's twitching body into position and then, while the white duck died, the brown duck raped its vent.

"Stop that," Bear said, intending to kick the brown duck off as he'd so often forced the white duck to dismount the brown.

But Bear stopped when he got close enough to hear what the brown duck was squawking, that payback was a bitch.

Measure, the duck grumbled, closing his eyes to coordinate words with the slow deep thrusts of his body, *for measure . . . an eye . . . for an eye . . . a taste . . . of your own . . . medicine . . . two can play . . . that game.*

Repulsed, Bear turned for the house when, incredibly, the brown duck came flying off the white duck to attack Bear, looking up at him with hate in his beady eyes, screaming, *Tit for tat! Tit for tat! Tit for tat!*

"Get away!" Bear shouted, kicking and shooing as the duck pecked at his hands. It was like being in a horror movie where the world's gentle creatures turn suddenly murderous.

POTUS put an end to the nonsense by neatly grabbing the brown duck in mighty jaws and trotting off as the duck called to Bear, *Quid pro quo!*

"Don't hurt him!" Bear shouted, but POTUS looked back with disdain: of course he knew not to hurt the duck . . . the duck was one of his.

Shaken by all this, Bear came into the kitchen to see Katie in the kitchen, posing in her white nightgown like a saint or an angel or insane woman, smiling at him in a way that seemed demented rather than welcoming . . . is she about to attack me, too?

"Do you have binoculars?" Katie asked.

"What!"

"From the bedroom window . . . I think I saw those people you were talking about, they were wandering around in the woods, those *barely people.*"

"No!"

"Why are you shouting?"

"They don't come close to the house," he said, trying to modulate his voice.

"But I saw them clearly out there—"

"No!"

"What's wrong?"

"Enough of this foolishness," he told her.

"Foolishness? I saw some people in the woods, is all I'm saying. About a dozen of them, including children. The children were never put down on the ground, they were carried on the adult's backs or clasped to their chests, the children holding on like monkeys."

Bear slumped.

"Did you get the groceries?" Katie asked pleasantly.

He nodded.

"I'll go out and bring them in," she said, putting on a pair of slippers that lived by the door. "I want to see that sky anyway, it's been looking very strange."

"Watch out for the ducks."

"What do you mean?"

Bear meant watch out for the white duck's corpse—he didn't want Katie to be traumatized by it—and also watch out for the brown duck because it might attack.

"Bear?"

His mind was in too much of a muddle to answer.

Katie's smile came unpasted as she told him, "I don't have enough room inside me to deal with whatever it is you're going through." Then she went outside.

Bear climbed upstairs to go to bed on his floor mattress. He stayed there in his clothes until past feeding time. Katie had to get dressed and do the chores for him.

That night as they lay in their respective positions in the dark, Katie said she realized why Bear was upset, she saw that he'd run over the white duck, but surely he understood she couldn't deal with anyone else's troubles.

"I know what you want me to do," he said.

"What?"

"Kill Cootie and Scrudde, sodomize 'em."

"Bear—"

"Tell me again about them warriors in dresses getting revenge."

"No," she insisted, "I want to tell you a different story."

33

"As soon as I stepped into the cottage, something exploded. I thought it was the gas stove or water heater. Later I was told that the optic nerves can react to severe facial trauma by producing impulses that the brain interprets as bright flashes of light.

"You've heard that expression, 'at first I didn't feel any pain.' Well, it was true in my case, true but not comforting because the sensation of walking into an explosion, being stunned and knocked senseless, it's worse than pain. Since then I've wondered if it's how hogs and cows feel when they're electrically stunned coming into the killing room at a slaughterhouse or how chickens feel in the slaughter factories when they're dipped in that electrically charged water that's supposed to stun them before the automated knives start working on their throats. If so, we should just skip the stunning part and go right to the pain of slitting throats because, if my experience is any indication, the feeling of being stunned is as bad as any pain I can imagine.

"Hands were on me and, honest to God, at the time I still thought there'd been an explosion and maybe I'd been unconscious for a while and now rescue workers had arrived and that's whose hands were working on me. It was dark, my eyes had finally stopped flashing lights to my brain. I didn't know where I was, in an ambulance or already at the hospital . . . I had no feeling in my face beyond a weird kind of neurological buzzing.

"Somebody's taking my pants off, must be a nurses at the hospital, except they weren't being easy with me. My nose felt broken, teeth knocked loose, it was awful the way these nurses—I was still thinking they were nurses—how they were manhandling me.

"As feeling returned to my face, I also started getting my mental faculties back. Somebody was working his hands between my legs.

"When I told him to stop I got punched in the face again, this second blow, arriving on top of the damage from the first one, caused more pain, immediate pain."

Bear got off the mattress on the floor and came up on the bed to lie with Katie, though he stayed on top of the covers.

"Someone was hollering at me, it was Coote. He was hollering, 'Repeat it to my face, how Bear got me crying like a girl.' I had no idea what he was talking about. Scrudde was there, too. I wasn't able to stop them from taking off my pants, but when Coote started pulling up my sweater, I fought him. He slapped me a couple times, then got it off. Suddenly he's shining a flashlight on me. Coote just stood there; he was blocking Scrudde, who stayed behind him. Coote kept the light on me. Scrudde was saying, 'Let me see, let me see.' But Coote turned the light off and said they were leaving. Scrudde asked him, 'Ain't you going to do her?' Cootie told him to shut up. They left. I wasn't raped . . . but they'll be back."

Bear knew enough now not to promise Katie she'd always be safe with him. Instead, he made his offer again. "I'll kill 'em for you . . . like you said about those warriors getting their revenge."

She didn't answer.

"Katie?"

"Do you know why he didn't rape me?"

Bear figured he did.

"How am I supposed to feel about that? Relieved?"

Bear didn't try to answer such a question.

34

The next morning after breakfast, after changing the oil in his truck, Bear began the trek up into the hills where his cows were finishing the grass on their first summer pasture. POTUS and Jamaica accompanied him. When the dogs saw a groundhog and tore off after it, Bear hollered for them to stop and *come.* Upon their return he gave them a stern lecture about no more groundhog killing, at least not in his presence, not under his auspices. POTUS took the dressing-down with his usual dignity, then headed for the house—this was crazy, this no-killing-groundhogs rule, it didn't make any sense.

Bear asked Jamaica, "How about you, you going home with him or coming with me?"

She raised her right paw to shake hands and told Bear that POTUS was dying.

Bear looked at her and shook his head, there was nothing wrong with POTUS. "He's down in the hips a little, happens to any dog his size when they get old."

Jamaica said POTUS wouldn't make it through winter.

"Don't say that! And don't even talk to me."

She said Bear didn't understand, he didn't sleep next to POTUS the way she did. *You don't hear him whimpering the way I do.*

"That dog has never whimpered in his life, not even as a puppy."

Jamaica said something about denial and told Bear she was hoping to have another litter with POTUS, one last litter.

"You're too old to have puppies and I don't have time for

this nonsense, there's too much else going on. I don't have time to talk with no old dog about having one last litter, it's crazy."

Jamaica again held up her right paw to shake hands.

"No . . . git home, go on, *git!*"

She left at a trot.

Bear resumed his uphill trek until he found his cows, checked each one for injuries and infestations, then moved them to a new pasture and brought Red Cow down the mountain with him. He put her in the loafing shed where Rubia and Cazador, the lovers, once played chasing games.

"Sorry I can't give you the new shed to stay in," Bear told the cow, "but it's been taken over as another sanctuary for strays. I'll bring some feed and water, then nail boards across the front to keep you in . . . unless you want to just stay here on your own."

The cow said nothing.

He nailed the boards, fetched her sweetfeed and water and hay, then told the cow he'd be back after supper, there were some things he wanted to talk about. Bear was turning for the house when he saw Jamaica sitting there.

She told Bear he should be talking to a fellow predator, *her,* and not to some old cow.

"Don't even start on it," Bear warned.

But now your woman wants a predator, needs *a killer to get her justice.*

"Shut up!"

Tonight would be a good night for it, Saturday night, Cootie'll be drunk, you show up in war paint and white dress—

"No! I'm not discussing this with you. Git back to the house."

She whoofed and left.

After chores and then a polite though oddly strained dinner with Katie, Bear said he was going for a walk, had some things to think about, did Katie want to come with him? He was relieved when she said no.

The night was black. As soon as Bear got outside he heard the strange muttering of an old man somewhere in the dark complaining in that universal voice of the crank, all spit and crackle. Bear shined his light and saw it was the brown duck ascending pump house hill, muttering with each waddling step about payback and tit for tat and comeuppance.

Bear crossed the hill just as the brown duck reached the top and saw him.

You let that white duck screw me in the vent for two years and didn't do a thing about it.

"I used to always kick him off you."

You should've done more, I was being raped.

Bear shook his head and started again for the loafing shed, then turned when he heard the duck's webbed feet beating the ground and its wings flapping. Bear saw the brown duck go airborne halfway down the hill, three feet off the earth, an ascent glorious though brief. Unable to sustain flight with its meat-heavy breast, the duck lost altitude and hit hard, rolling tail over beak in speaker-blasts of squawks and quacks.

"You weren't bred to fly," Bear told him honestly.

The duck, staggering from the impact, snapped back with an obscenity, and Bear wondered, since he himself didn't cuss, how could he imagine animals being so foul-mouthed.

At the loafing shed, Bear found Red Cow lying down chewing her cud. Upending a bucket to use as a stool, Bear sat there by the entrance, just a few feet from the cow, close enough to smell her sweet fermenting breath.

"I got something big facing me," he told her. "This state don't have capital punishment, I looked in the almanac, but that don't mean I won't be in jail for the rest of my life. Plus, of course, I lose my immortal soul. My question would be, is it worth it?"

She chewed her cud and watched him as he spoke.

"That dog, Jamaica, says I'm a predator . . . and plenty have been telling me how blood-soaked I am," Bear said quietly, "but you know I worked hard to be a good shepherd to all my animals. I doctored them when they got sick, provided shelter, tried to keep you all free of parasites, made sure you had food and water. Even when I did things like castrations or polling horns, I tried to do it the best, least painful way I knew how. I groom coats and trim feet. In blizzards I have carried your babies into barns where there's soft hay. I've put you in green pastures and led you to creeks with sweet water and—"

Bear laughed at himself. "Well, I guess you're going to say that before I get too holy maybe I should remember I wasn't exactly leading your baby calves *through* the valley of the shadow of death, I was hauling them by truck right into it. I sent all your babies to slaughter and I never gave a second thought to a single one, happy for the checks I got, so much carnage paid out by the pound."

He waited for her to comment but she continued chewing that cud.

"Robert told me once that his first nickname for me was Chicken Bone because as a toddler boy I'd go around the house with a chicken bone in hand, using it as a pacifier, like a baby monster so blood-soaked I carried the victims' bones wherever I went.

"I know there are people right here in America who their whole lives ain't killed nothing bigger than a bug. Katie says people who've never killed an animal still support death by eating meat or wearing leather, but I say in comparison to me their souls must be spanking clean. I can't even imagine how that must feel, free of death's mortgage. I've killed so many animals, I have stopped so many hearts . . . from the time I could get up on two legs and use my hands for the killing.

"Was I five years old when I got my first pocketknife? I don't remember, but I used that new knife to cut off the hands and feet of a toad I caught in the garden. You know what it did in reaction to that pain? That poor old fat toad opened and closed its mouth but no sound came out . . . maybe it was trying to talk to me even back then. I buried the toad alive because I was shamed by what I did, buried its severed hands and feet separately and covered everything with dirt and let the old toad die in pain and suffocation. My *first* act against an animal was mutilation."

The cow stopped chewing.

"And with my first gun I began killing birds just to see if I could hit them. One time I picked off a songbird no bigger than my hand and as I held it I could feel its heart still beating, I could see that soft feathered chest go in and out, up and down with actions of heart and lungs . . . then one big breath, one last race of heartbeat, and it was dead, died in my hand, by my hand. I threw its body over the fence and went in for dinner, I think we were having lamb chops that day—I liked 'em and still do.

"I've killed chickens by the score, cut off their heads, wrung their necks, tied their feet to clotheslines and gone among them slitting throats. What must they think? All their lives I come out bearing food and water, except one day I got that knife in my hand, and there I am, Death Walking in the henhouse. One flock of laying hens got too old for eggs and too tough for meat, I went out and killed them all with a bow and arrows just for the sport of it. Ducks and geese and guinea hens . . . crows and owls and hawks and even a few buzzards before my dad told me, leave them alone, they're nature's garbage collectors.

"I've killed so many groundhogs that they've made me a cautionary tale told to their babies. I've shot them and dug them out of hibernation and used a shovel on their slumbering children . . . sicced dogs on them and chopped trees down to get at them . . . used rifles and shotguns and, one summer, a pistol. If groundhogs have any say about who gets in heaven, I'm in trouble.

"Frogs and fish and cats and dogs, I've killed them all and more. I decided some time ago I'd keep two or three cats on the farm, my two or three dogs, and any others that showed up I'd kill as strays rather than let them attack my stock or die of starvation in the woods . . . that was my excuse for killing stray hounds that came to me wagging their tails. I've shot cats and sometimes when I didn't get a good first shot and they screamed and trembled and vibrated, I shot them again. I've drowned kittens by the sackful and I've taken an ax to little puppies. When I perform these executions I blame the people who dropped the dogs off, let the cats loose, abandoned the litters. But it was I who did the actual killing.

"I've stomped on snakes and pinched off their heads and

killed them with hoes. I know how to grab 'em by the tail and snap 'em like whips, my dad taught me that, how to break their spines or, if you're really good at it, snap off their heads.

"I give myself reasons, of course. I'm killing snakes as protection from being bitten. Killing chickens for food, hogs for money, strays for mercy. Killing groundhogs 'cause their holes might break a cow's leg, killing mice for eating my rice.

"I've killed deer and I've killed cows"—he watched for her reaction, Red Cow burping up another cud—"and I've killed pigs. Shot a horse once that impaled itself with a broken board and was suffering.

"Turkeys wild and domesticated, little ol' bobwhites that wouldn't make a meal for a fairy, pheasant, fox, and one time a black bear that was just crossing my property on its way to somewhere else. Coyotes, half a dozen of them over the years. Rabbits to eat and rabbits 'cause they were in the garden. I suspect there's not a species on this farm I ain't killed at least one of its kind.

"I pledged to that mouse in the pantry I'd never kill another animal, but now's come the time to decide about Scrudde and Cootie, they need killing in the worst way, but is it mine to do? What do you think?"

She chewed, paused in her chewing, then resumed.

Bear spoke softly. "I've killed so many." He gave the cow another chance to speak, then got off the bucket and headed back for the house.

After Bear left, Jamaica, who'd been sitting around the corner, came to the front of the loafing shed. She asked the cow what all that was about.

The cow said Bear was upset because he had decided to kill Scrudde and Coote.

Jamaica said, why shed tears over the likes of them?

You know how men are when death comes to their own kind, Red Cow said, like it's the end of the world.

I think the way they cling to life is sick, don't you?

Mmm, the cow agreed.

35

Bear went up to the bedroom, where he told Katie he was ready. He would go tonight and kill Scrudde and Cootie, then get sent to jail for it, lose his soul for it, and the only regret he'd ever have was being away from her.

But she said she had a different quest for brother Bear.

"Okay."

"Love me."

"I would've done that anyway."

"Tell me you have reasons to love me like the night sky has stars."

"I do, I will."

"And know when to stop being logical and instead just . . . I don't know, just . . ."

"Be like the Pacific Ocean?"

"What?"

"Have patience like the Pacific Ocean has water."

"Yes. And show me magic . . . like the *barely people.*"

"I will."

"And tell me love stories like Cazador and Rubia."

"I will, every night if you say."

"And make up poems."

"I'll do that, too."

"The next rule is a tough one."

"Name it."

"Could you stand giving me a bath?"

He went all wide-eyed and told her, "I could stand it like a tree."

Bear scooped her from the bed and carried Katie downstairs

to the bathroom, where he drew a tub of water and they both got in. They washed each other's scars and then lay together in the warm water hugging like monkeys.

"Now, if you're going to do all that for me," she said, "what can I do for you?"

"Say it a million times."

"Say what?"

"I ain't never heard it said to me before there was you," he told her.

"What's that, sweetie?"

"I love you."

She pressed her cheek against his wet broad chest and told this man again what he'd never heard in thirty-two years of life, *I love you.* Bear drank it in like a man knee-deep in a river as Katie said it over and over and over again. *I love you, I love you, I love you.* I'm counting them, he told her, and I'll let you know when you reach a million.

36

His father used to tell Bear he didn't have much going for him, wasn't bright, lacked a devious nature that might've made him a clever cattle trader, didn't have an easy way with people, was nothing at all like his brother Robert. "But you do have one talent that might hold you in good stead," his father would say, dangling faint hope in front of the boy. "You possess a God-awesome talent for work. You can outwork three men and a fat boy, you can outwork a horse. So remember what I'm saying, Joey. You might not be able to outthink your neighbors, outcharm or outtrade them, but by God, you can hold your own against the bastards by outworking them."

Since his father's death, Bear, by working harder than anyone else, had been able to squeeze out a living from nothing more than a small herd of cattle. His land was underlaid and overlaid with limestone that soaked into the soil and made it sweet, encouraging grass so lush that two acres, if properly managed, would keep a cow-calf pair all summer, whereas on the big cattle ranches out west, that cow-calf might need to range ten or twenty acres of scrub to find enough to eat. But now Bear was out of the cattle business—a decision that had evolved between him and Katie—and he directed his indefatigable talent for work toward building an animal sanctuary. In fact, Bear worked harder than ever before in his life. He worked from first sun to last light and then he worked hours more under electric out in one of the sheds.

Volunteers much more serious than those ladies from the library began showing up at the farm, helping with the animals, going out on rescues. Among them were some militants who wanted to launch raids to free veal calves, to steal away starving horses, to unlock chained dogs. These militants organized themselves into a strike force they called the Animal Rescue Militia, and they collected enough money to commission a large sign in the farm's front field. Bear would do it, he had a talent for lettering, but the militants wanted to make sure Bear got it right: a sign constructed of two sheets of plywood, four feet by sixteen feet, nailed to four white-oak posts, facing the county road for all to see, black letters on a white background, the initial letter of each word painted boldly: **A**NIMAL **R**ESCUE **M**ILITIA.

At the unveiling of the sign in July, however, the militants were disappointed. Intimidated by Bear, they groused to Katie: He got it wrong. Bear had painted: **A**NIMAL **R**ESCUE **M**ISSION.

After dinner, when Katie and Bear were in bed, the light still on, she asked him about it. "You knew they wanted *militia,* not *mission,* didn't you?"

"I'll change it if you want me to."

"It's those new volunteers. They felt, since they were paying for it, the sign should read what they wanted."

"I'll change the sign," Bear said again. "I'll paint over *mission,* which means people organized to provide a common good, provide charity and welfare for a target group—which in our case would be animals that need to be rescued. I'll paint that out and put in *militia,* which comes from the Latin word of the same spelling that means warfare, a state of disharmony, an effort to destroy, acts of conflict and killing."

She reached over and grabbed his goatee. "Let's talk a minute about your so-called three problems, getting in a muddle and acting inappropriately and letting your mouth hang open."

He waited.

"They're a smokescreen, aren't they?"

"Smokescreen?"

"Bear," she said, tugging hard.

"Smart people like you and Robert and them new volunteers,

you all keep words in your head. But I have to keep words in a tablet, that's how I come to know about militia and mission, 'cause I looked 'em up and wrote 'em in my tablet."

Still holding on to his goatee, Katie came over on an elbow and stared into his eyes but it was like trying to divine the depth of the Pacific Ocean by looking at blue salt water. When she released his goatee, he rubbed it and complained that she had really hurt him. But then Bear had to turn away so she wouldn't see him smiling.

ꝏ

Thank God hateful June was finally over. Bear borrowed money from the bank to build a new barn and began putting up hay because even rescued animals you don't intend to slaughter need to eat. He refitted sheds and outbuildings as housing for cats and dogs and birds. He and Katie accepted horses that were being starved and potbelly pigs that got too large to be household pets, and they took in litters of puppies and kittens found in cardboard boxes by the side of the road. Although the more militant volunteers eased off after the incident with the sign, other people came out to help, sponsors came by with checks.

Late one morning Bear inadvertently closed POTUS in the new barn and didn't think about the dog as the day progressed. Bear rigged a conveyor belt to carry hay bales up to the loft and changed a tire on his tractor and cut scrap lumber for next winter's firewood. He worked all day and was doing chores for the night before he realized POTUS wasn't around to get his evening meal.

Bear got worried because of what Jamaica had told him about POTUS dying—maybe the old dog walked off into the woods as they often will do when the time comes. Bear and Katie went around the farm buildings calling POTUS's name. Dogs in the sanctuary barked helpfully, but no word from POTUS. "Where were you when you remember seeing him last?" Katie asked. Bear said he was working near the new barn. They hurried out there and opened a door to find POTUS sitting patiently.

Bear got down on his knees and hugged the dog's big neck. "Seven or eight hours locked up, how come you didn't bark or nothing to let me know you were here?"

When Bear finally released him, POTUS got up and walked out of the barn, annoyed that everyone was making such a fuss: You locked me in, I waited, you let me out, end of story.

The next day they let Jamaica and POTUS breed. Mating was the only time in his life when the big faithful POTUS ever lost dignity, all that humping and then being stuck inside Jamaica for half an hour, nothing to do but look chagrined.

❦

Deputy Miller had been to the farm several times with state police and sheriff's-office investigators to continue questioning Katie about the assault. She told over and over again how it happened, Coote striking her in the face, Scrudde standing behind him, how they stripped her but didn't rape her. Scrudde and Coote denied everything and there was no physical evidence to place them at the cottage that night—no fingerprints, no fluids—and the grand jury was disinclined to indict a prominent citizen like Scrudde, which meant that Coote got off the hook, too, just as Deputy Miller had predicted.

Katie and Bear were sleeping together now but not having sex. She told Bear that she didn't know when, if ever, she might have sex again.

He lied and said it didn't matter to him.

Another night in bed, Katie saw Bear's erection before he turned out the light, and she said, "It might be easier for you if we started sleeping apart."

"I got a better idea," he said. "Katie, will you marry me?"

Yes was what she thought, but what she said was, "I've brought so much trouble into your life."

"I'm asking you to marry me."

"Are you sure?"

Bear reached over and turned on the light. "Look at my face."

She did.

"Look at this stupid old face."

"It's not stupid, it's a wonderful face."

"Are you looking at it?"

She said she was.

"Then you must see the answer, you must see the answer plain as my face."

She did and told him, "I love you."

"That settles it, then, we're getting married."

37

Activity on the farm increased as Bear and Katie prepared for their wedding, scheduled for the tenth of August. Katie returned to Washington, packed up her apartment, had everything shipped to the farm, and met with her friends, who thought she looked radiant—smiling brightly, her hair still red and her eyes still green—but *changed.* Part of what made her look different were those healed injuries to her face. In spite of the plastic surgery, Katie's nose had bent a little and she had thin scar lines running through her freckles. But being in love had changed her, too.

When she returned to the farm, Bear asked if she'd seen William, and Katie said no, he was out of town. Bear said, "Good . . . and guess what? I decided what I'm giving you as a wedding present. I'm painting the house."

She said that was a wonderful present but told Bear that not seeing William in Washington didn't end the matter. "I still have to give back his ring, return the keys to the cottage."

"I have three letters for you."

"Letters?"

"U.P.S."

"I was engaged to him for two years, he deserves a face-to-face explanation—"

Bear held up his hand and left the room, he didn't want to hear it.

He didn't want her to go see him, that fancy-worded fiancé, when August turned the page and William came to town.

"I have to," she said.

He shook his head. "I wish you wouldn't."

Like most adults, Katie had experience in breaking up with

one lover, starting anew with another, figuring what should be carried from one affair to the next, what's left behind . . . but not Bear, Katie had been his one and only. When the time came for her to go see William at the little cottage, she told Bear, "I'll be back in an hour."

"Can't take that long to return a ring and a set of keys," he said peevishly.

She explained that William would want her to sit down and have a glass of wine, he would want to talk, to tell her she wasn't being fair to him, get it all off his chest . . . then *she'd* feel better, too. "I'll be back in an hour," she said again.

He gave her a ten-minute head start and followed.

❦

William was a little drunk but compensated by being overcordial to Katherine: *How are you doing, dear . . . so good to see you after all these months . . . did you enjoy the cottage . . . I understand you had injuries to your face but I must say you're as beautiful as ever . . .*

She accepted the wine he offered and, without stating its contents, placed an envelope containing keys and ring on the table.

"I'm sorry it didn't work out between us," she told him. "But I'm very happy here. I told you about my volunteer work with animal rights organizations after college. We've started an animal mission but without the stridency or cant of those—"

"We?" he interrupted.

Katherine waited for what he might say next, William sitting there in casual elegance with his beige slacks and powder-blue shirt, legs crossed at the knees with tanned ankles showing above expensive sandals, blond hair tousled just so. She had forgotten how handsome he was and surprised herself by feeling a twinge of desire for this man she didn't love but had made love to many times.

"I'm not sure how to say this without sounding querulous . . . but, Katherine, really, you haven't acted very honorably at all."

"I know."

"If you wanted to take up with some *farmer,* you should've

broken off the engagement first, should've moved out of this cottage and *then* taken up with your farmer."

"Yes, I—"

"I simply can't win with you. If I had left you and broken our engagement when you got sick, I would've been considered a creep. But I stayed with you through it all, the operation, the recuperation, and I offered this cottage when you simply had to get away from me and your friends. So I wasn't a creep. Instead I get played for a fool. It isn't fair."

She agreed it wasn't and apologized again.

❦

From across the street in the growing darkness, Bear watched the cottage with a brand-new feeling in his gut, because if you've never been in love before, you've never felt jealousy before. He wanted to cross the street, kick down the door, and drag her out. Instead, he turned to the tree behind which he was hiding and started counting ants.

❦

"I can't believe you're asking this," Katherine was telling William.

"I think it's completely understandable . . . and not unreasonable."

"A farewell fuck?"

He winced. "That's not the way I put it."

"I'm sure there any number of women in Washington willing to accommodate you. I'm not so naïve as to think you've been completely faithful to me."

William got up and poured them each another glass of wine, then returned to his chair. "You're trying to turn the tables. I wanted to make love to you as soon as you were ready after the operation. I waited. I was *eager* to make love to you before you moved here, if you recall. You said no. Fine. I was willing to wait. Meanwhile, you're giving it away to the farmer in the dell."

"William, really."

"No I'm serious, I think I have earned a parting gesture from you."

"Gesture? William. You're not owed sex because I broke off the engagement."

"Because of the *way* you broke it off, *after* you already found someone else but *while* you were still living here in my cottage."

"I could pay you back rent, would that satisfy you?"

"Don't be sarcastic. I want what I've asked for, Katherine. I certainly don't intend to force myself on you, but I would feel less *injured* if we could make love one last time. We used to be in love with each other."

"William, we were never in love."

He looked genuinely hurt.

"Not love-love." Not like with Bear, she thought, not crazy love. "Our engagement was more like a merger. We had the right friends, the right jobs, we were on the right career tracks, so we took out separate assets and merged them. But you were never crazy in love with me."

"Like a country-western song?"

"You know what I mean."

"You done me wrong."

"William, we've known each other for five years . . . let's cut through the banter and—"

"I'm trying to do exactly that. No games. No passive-aggressive guilt trips. I've told you what I want, what I'd like to have to make me feel less aggrieved. And, as you say, we've been together for years, we've made love hundreds of times, what's one more, one last time?"

She shook her head more in contemplation than refusal as he got up again and refilled their glasses.

❦

While across the street it had become too much like night for counting ants, so Bear watched the little cottage and counted seconds until the cottage lights went out, which is when he went dark, too.

38

After coffee the next morning, Bear got started painting the house. He walked around it several times writing notes in a tablet. He made mental notes, too. Around and around he walked, squinting, shading his eyes, pointing with a finger to count so many of this, so many of that. Volunteers who saw him thought it must be true, Bear really is retarded, look at the way he's walking around the house mumbling to himself. But when he finished these circumnavigations, Bear had, in mind and on paper, a list of materials, tools, supplies—gallons of paint, running feet of replacement clapboard, ladders, tubes of caulk, how many brushes of what various sizes. The job was so accurately gauged that Bear wouldn't have to make more than a couple trips to town for unplanned items and at job's end would be able to haul away the scrap in a wheelbarrow, such was his talent.

He scraped the entire house by hand and then power-washed away all the chips and stains. He replaced the yellow poplar clapboard where it was damaged and he repaired windows by glazing panes and installing new sills. He caulked holes and cracks. He got up on the roof and scraped the tin by hand and dragged hoses up there to power-wash it clean. He fixed molding. He renailed. He replaced loose gutters and downspouts. And all this he did while completing the usual chores morning and night and going off on private missions.

Bear wouldn't tell Katie or the volunteers where he went, what animals he was rescuing, or how he'd heard about them. One time he came home with an eye blackened and his nose flattened. Katie asked what had happened, Bear said only that he got into a little scrap.

But mainly what he did in those days leading up to the wedding was paint. The house would be white, its trim green, the roof red. Bear started painting as soon as morning chores were over and the dew dried. He didn't quit until it was dark or dew fell again, when he would clean his brushes and equipment and put everything out of the way so no one would trip over ladders or buckets; then he'd do the chores. Next morning he began again. A crew of three might've been able to complete the job in two weeks, Bear did it by himself in the same time. The secret was, he painted. When others might've gone on breaks, Bear painted. When a professional crew might've discussed what aspect of the job should be undertaken next, Bear painted. Others might've walked around the house to admire the work in progress, Bear painted. For those two weeks, visitors and volunteers who drove up and saw him on a ladder eventually no longer took note, it was like seeing the walnut tree or the old stone wall: there they are as they have always been.

When Bear was away on one of his private rescue missions, Katie called his brother to ask if he would come to the wedding. Robert said he wished Katie and Bear well but it was unlikely he could visit, he was in the middle of a divorce and bankruptcy. "I could send you the money for the ticket," she offered. He said thanks, he wanted to but just couldn't. "It would give Bear such joy to see you," Katie tried again, because this was to be her present to Bear, getting Robert to the wedding. Robert said, no can do.

"Your brother's a complicated man," Katie told Robert. "He thinks and worries more than anyone suspects, hurts more, too. And loves more. It's bitter in my mouth to say this but I think I'm second in line to you." Robert said he doubted that very much—tell Bear I'll try my best to get out and see him soon. "No," Katie said, "when I see you coming up to the door, I'll tell Bear his brother is here, but meanwhile I won't give him false hope by saying Robert is trying his best to come visit you."

When Bear finished painting the house, he built and painted an arbor by the creek where he and Katie would be married. He bought more paint and painted the garage. He painted a shed.

On the day before they were to be married Katie came out at noon and, without speaking to him, hammered on the lids of all his paint cans even though Bear was on a ladder still painting. She confiscated his brushes and washed them. She took away his ladders and folded up his tarpaulins.

At the wedding under the arbor by the creek, a liberal minister officiating, Doc Setton gave Katie away and Deputy Miller stood for Bear. Also in attendance were Ronny Ward, the manager of the Briars Café, who buttonholed people to talk about the night Bear's barn burned to the ground; Eddie Lancor, who had received permission to bring Old Bob to the wedding; Mrs. Bayt of cat-house fame, accompanied by her son-in-law; a half dozen animal lovers from town, and another dozen volunteers who'd been working at the Animal Rescue Mission.

As always at a wedding, people out of earshot of the loving couple speculated acidly on what they could possibly see in each other. Bear was being taken advantage of by the smart city girl who wanted her hands on his farm, some said, while others insisted that Katie was doing charity work by marrying Bear, just a big dumb guy she felt sorry for. Doc Setton overheard some of this talk and told the gossipers he knew the real reason Bear and Katie got married.

Why, they all asked.

The dapper little vet smiled as they waited to hear the answer.

Crazy love, he said.

People looked at one another.

Eddie Lancor didn't catch it. "What?"

"Crazy love," one of the volunteers told him.

Lancor nodded. There was a thing or two he knew about crazy love.

Animal guests, along with Old Bob, included POTUS and Jamaica (more than halfway through her pregnancy) and the brown duck, who had put on weight; various cats, which kept to the top boards of nearby fences; chickens; guinea hens; geese; and a Shetland pony rescued a few weeks ago, who roamed the yard following POTUS everywhere, under the delusion either he was a dog or the German shepherd was a Shetland—one way or the other they were simpatico.

On their wedding night, Katie and Bear talked in bed. Bear hadn't told her that he'd followed Katie to the little cottage where she met with William, that Bear watched until the lights went out. He wanted to ask what she and William got up to in the dark, but then again he didn't want to know. Katie asked Bear what was wrong. Nothing, he said. She asked if he was still worried about animals talking to him.

"It ain't like I didn't realize what was happening all along," he told Katie. "I was supplying their voices in my head. But it seemed real enough at the time. I ain't particularly ashamed of it even now. I keep trying to get them to talk to me, especially that red cow, but won't none of them say a word anymore. Truth is, I kind of miss it."

She said his way with animals was magical.

He told her that before she showed up he'd been dealing with animals all his life without hearing a word from any of them, but the first time he met her was when that cow said *God bless you,* so it was Katie's presence, Bear insisted, that made the magic happen, without Katie he would've stayed being a dumb farmer the rest of his life.

She said, you were never a dumb farmer.

He said, you're the most beautiful woman in the world.

She said he was blind as a bat, her face had been rearranged by Cootie.

Will you hate him until the day you die? Bear asked.

The more I love you, she said, the less I hate anyone.

He told her he loved her.

She said she loved him, too.

They went on like this for some time, then she took his hand and kissed it repeatedly before turning to him and whispering in his ear, "I have something to tell you."

39

Into September then, and Jamaica gave birth. Katie was delighted with the litter, four females and two males, and told Bear it was a good sign, new life on the farm. But then POTUS died before September gave out. He'd been lying all morning on a red plaid mat that Katie had made for him, two pieces of flannel covering egg-carton foam. Bear had placed the mat next to a red building that caught the morning sun. It was POTUS's new favorite place. On the morning the dog died, Bear had walked past him several times on the way back and forth to various sheds. Bear didn't stop to check, POTUS looked okay, head down on outstretched paws, though it was out of character for him to be still abed when the clock was threatening noon. After lunch Bear came out of the house and saw POTUS still lying there, surrounded by animals in an agitated state, ducks quacking and guinea hens screeching, the Shetland pony snorting and pawing, cats murmuring their concern around what proved to be POTUS's corpse.

Bear waded through and knelt, lifting the dog by the scruff. POTUS's massive head lolled off the side. His tongue hung partially out of his mouth in a way that perversely reminded Bear of Carl Coote. Bear put POTUS's head back down on the big paws and smoothed the fur at that thick neck. I wished I'd known you were dying this morning, Bear thought. I would've come over and said good-bye instead of walking back and forth not saying a word, you were a good ol' dog.

Later that day Bear dug a big hole on a hill at the other side of the creek, just above the arbor where he and Katie were married. Doc Setton happened to be visiting and six volunteers were cleaning out buildings and these people, along with Bear and Katie and a wide variety of animals, formed the POTUS funeral. Bear thought it was altogether fitting that a dog like POTUS got a big turnout. (Jamaica was nursing and couldn't attend, though later that evening, her first night without POTUS, she left the whelping pen and stayed on his grave until her puppies' hungry cries finally called her back.)

Solemn as a color guard, Bear lowered his dog, wrapped in a blanket, into that grave. Bear didn't put a tennis ball or rubber toy in the grave, POTUS wasn't that kind of dog. He was a *shepherd.* When he had POTUS in the ground, Bear looked out at the assembled people and said he had a few words to say, which surprised everyone except Katie.

Shovel in hand, he told them, "This here's the first animal I ever buried, all the others what died on the farm I just dragged out in the woods or onto a high meadow for nature to take her course through buzzard and scavenger, but I'm burying this dog on a selfish reason: I want POTUS here close where he can keep an eye on things. I could tell you hours on end stories about ol' POTUS, how he laid up there on the porch and looked out over the farm like it was the Serengeti and he was a lion, which I think he resembled more than he did a dog . . . how he could break the back of a marauder that was after one of his newborn calves, but would carry cats around the yard in his mouth. The cats liked it so much they'd line up."

Bear looked down in the grave, then back up at the people around him. "Every summer he'd dig holes in the creeks and then when the creeks got low those holes would still have water and POTUS used those places to get cool. Even lying in the creek with only his head sticking out of the muddy water, that dog still had more dignity than the President of the United States. I raised him from a pup, there wasn't a day in that dog's life I didn't pet him. Now that POTUS is gone he leaves holes in my heart like them holes he left in the creek, but during dry spells the holes he left in my heart will fill up, too, with all I remember about him. He was a good ol' dog."

Bear began filling the grave.

The volunteers went back to their work whispering among themselves how surprised they were that Bear said all that. They were under the impression his vocabulary consisted of *yes, no, hi, bye,* and grunts. Someone speculated that Katie wrote the part about holes in the creek and holes in the heart and then made Bear memorize it. Another person said, she'll have to do things like that for him all the time unless she wants people to know he's retarded. Another person said, whatever possessed her to marry him I'll never know.

These volunteers—two girls and a guy from high school and three middle-aged women from the library—didn't realize Katie was following behind and listening. She thought, you have no idea who that man is. He reads constantly and fills tablets with words, he composes poems, he's magic with animals, and I'm the lucky one to have Bear as my husband, I'm the one who married up, not Bear.

When the volunteers turned and saw her, Katie told them, keep your hateful gossip off this farm. Go spread your poison elsewhere.

At the Briars Café the volunteers speculated on why Katie had spoken so harshly to them—it was more than just overhearing their gossip, in the past she'd never said a mean word to anyone, something else must be going on.

"I didn't want to say this," one of the middle-aged women said, "but my cousin works at the hospital and knows the doctor Katie goes to and . . . don't you dare tell anyone you got this from me, but she's pregnant."

All their eyes went wide.

"That ain't the worse of it, though." Best of the gossip, she meant. "Kate apparently *got* pregnant about the same time her fancy ex-fiancé came to town to get his little house back from her."

From around the table several delighted *oh-my-God*s were whispered.

Another woman suddenly remembered something and said,

"That ain't *even* the worst of it." Best of it . . . all eyes upon her. "When Bear was a teenager he got the mumps, they settled in his groin and while it don't matter much if just one testicle swells up, I heard both of Bear's got big as baseballs."

"Oh my God," they all whispered again, then quickly divvied up the check and made their excuses, they had to go, get to their telephones, buttonhole neighbors, tell someone, tell everyone, tell anyone who would listen . . . and believe me you'll want to hear this because guess what, Kate Renault out there at the animal rescue mission, now her name is Kate Long, she's pregnant and she *got* pregnant around the time her old boyfriend was in town *and* Bear is sterile as a steer.

40

Rains came hard in October and the Briars River overflowed three times in two weeks, but mainly the town of Briars was sopping wet with gossip about Bear and Katie and paternity. It was a village of a thousand people who had known one another all their lives. Few moved away, hardly anyone new moved in. The residents were forced to use each other over and over again. Your high school sweetheart married your best friend, then divorced and married you, while the respective first spouses eventually got married to each other and eventually divorced. Meanwhile children were dropped in and out of wedlock, fathered by husbands and ex-husbands and neighbors' husbands to the point that when those children grew up and started dating, their parents would say, "You're going out with WHO?" . . . and then have to think back fourteen or fifteen years to make sure a daughter didn't date her uncle or half brother. Any resident of Briars could visit any house in town and find something—a child, a spouse, a TV, a couch—that had once been in his or her house. In this closed-closet society, no topic was more compelling than paternity.

The gossip was caustic even among those closest to Bear and Katie, people who volunteered at the animal mission and now became prized guests at dinners and outdoor barbecues, where they dispensed insider information. If you knew a mission volunteer and saw that person at the gas station or grocery store, you'd raise your eyebrows to ask, anything new? And if the volunteer shook her head no, you were both disappointed: nothing new to tattle, no new gossip to hear.

In the subjects' household itself, strains were manifest, Katie and Bear both knowing what neither acknowledged, the topic carried around during the day like a package, delivered but unopened, and then taken to bed, where it was placed between them. They didn't have sex or say *I love you, I love you, I love you.* Eventually the atmosphere around their house became like before a storm when the barometric pressure drops so low you get that niggling headache and feel irritable and wish that whatever was going to happen would just please go ahead and happen. It finally did, one night at dinner.

"I ain't seen you smile for a long time," Bear said offhandedly.

She pasted a false, demented smile to the corners of her mouth and asked, "How's this?"

Bear said he didn't like it one bit.

She was looking at him and you could tell she was making calculations . . . trajectory, speed, distance to target. "Speaking of smiles, I assume you're familiar with the *Mona Lisa*?"

"I don't know her personally."

"Har, har. You're familiar with the enduring mystery of Mona Lisa's smile?"

He put the dishes on the counter and sat at the table across from Katie to hear why Mona Lisa was smiling.

"Paternity," she said.

Animation left his face and Bear sat there looking dull and unlit, his mouth slack.

She went on: "I read some studies that were done in England on DNA, and the researchers happened to discover that in a surprisingly large percentage of children, the mothers had become pregnant by men other than their husbands, but the married couples had raised the children as their own. The results were confirmed by studies of populations in other countries. The percentage differed according to the target group's level of education, social class, income . . . but it was always *there.*"

Bear picked up a fork.

"It's no mystery why men oppress women—because they can, because they're larger, stronger, biologically more violent. It's playground politics written every night in the home and all across history—the big mean kids beat up the little gentle kids. Men beat up women and rape them and leave them for dead. But the one thing men can't control is paternity. Even if the baby really is her husband's, the woman smiles because she *knows* what he can only hope and assume and trust to be true. The Mona Lisa is smiling because she's pregnant and knows who the father is."

Fingering his fork, Bear said nothing.

"Comments?" Katie asked archly.

"Why in the world would you want to tell me a hateful thing like that?"

Because I hate myself, she thought, and I can't stand this thing being unspoken between us, I want it lanced, I want it over with. But what she said was, "You know why, don't play dumb."

"Dumb?"

"That's right, *dumb.*"

He held the fork in front of one eye to see what she looked like behind bars.

"What're you doing?" Katie asked.

Bear grimaced. "See, I can smile like that there Mona Lisa, too."

She told him he was pathetic, and took off upstairs at a dead run, chased by Bear.

She got to the bedroom and slammed the door, shouting, "Don't you DARE hit me!"

He was shocked that she would think he was capable of striking her.

"I'm locking the door," Katie said.

Bear could've head-butted that oak slab off its hinges, but he stayed on his side and told Katie through the door that he loved her no matter what.

No, she didn't deserve that kind of love. Still feeling hateful, she told Bear again that he was *pathetic.*

He put his forehead on the closed door. "Please don't say that."

But the perversity of human nature prodded Katie to wound him as badly as she could, to find out how deep was his ocean. "Retard."

Bear wept to hear it from her of all people.

"Mouth-breather!"

"I love you, Katie."

"Trench-digger!"

"I still love you."

"I wish I had never married you!"

"Married to you is the best thing ever happened in my life."

"Don't cling to me!"

"Ain't nothing you can say will make me stop loving you," he pleaded through the door.

"I'm no good for you, we have to get a divorce."

"That won't stop me loving you, I'll love you till the day I die, and then wherever I am after I die, heaven or hell, I'll keep loving you from there, too."

She told him that was *sick*.

Bear placed his hands next to his forehead, which was still pressed against the door. "I love you."

"I don't love you."

"Yes you do, Katydid."

"Don't call me that, I hate you!"

"I love you!"

Pressing herself to the other side of the door so only that inch of wood separated them, Katie shouted, *"Just leave!"*

"Not in a million years—start counting!"

Okay then, she said, she was leaving him, first thing in the morning . . . no, *right now.*

"I'll still love you when you're gone!" He was crying openly, like a child.

"Leave me alone!"

"Katydid!"

She kicked furiously at the bottom of the door.

He patted with both hands near the top as if to calm that door down. "Please don't be mad at me anymore."

"I HATE YOU!" she screamed, kicking and kicking.

"I LOVE YOU!" he called back, patting and patting.

They emerged from that argument like homeowners after a hurricane, stunned by all the damage, resolved to make repairs. It was never mentioned again, the paternity box stored away, tied with string, harmless as an unexploded bomb. Katie and Bear resumed life in an atmosphere of cleared air—and lawyers.

Lawyers everywhere. A team of animal rights attorneys (along with volunteer law students and law clerks and law researchers) was on call to defend against suits brought in the wake of the mission's animal rescues, which might've been moral triumphs but were also patently illegal. One of the more spectacular of the rescues conducted that autumn involved a hunting ranch that had begun operation in the next county. For various prices (twenty-five dollars for a goat, six hundred dollars for a bull) you could bring your choice of weapon and kill your choice of animal—a few exotics but most of them common barnyard creatures. The hunting aspect was completely absent. The selected animal was herded toward the client, who waited in the shade. It should've been called a killing ranch, you paid for the thrill of taking a life. Volunteers rescued the target animals, which were being kept in appalling conditions, apparently under the theory that they were going to be killed anyway, what's the point wasting time and money properly feeding or caring for them. Deer were panic-knotted in corners of net-covered runs. Tusked pigs, before being herded out to a dirt road to be shot full of arrows and to die a drawn-out death, were chained to stakes and fed dead chickens, forced to drink from mud holes that had formed within the reach of their chains, kept apart so they couldn't touch or smell or groom each other, with no shelter from the sun and no treatment given to their infected, infested chain wounds. The volunteers released a variety of videos to television stations; the most damning were of "The Hunt." (The staff of the ranch had taken these hunt videos to sell to clients; the mission volunteers had stolen them from the ranch office.) One typical production showed two fat white guys looking ridiculous in their new camouflage gear, grunting with the effort of getting in and out of a pickup truck, listening seriously as they were told by a guide to get ready and be quiet because their trophy was coming toward them on the dirt road. The men checked their high-powered pistols and looked at each other nervously. Up the road a famished Guernsey bull was eating grass, lifting its head but not fleeing as the killers approached. When they were within twenty feet, they opened fire, not trying for fatal shots but apparently fascinated with the damage they could inflict, shooting the bull in the legs, the stomach, the ass (they laughed after that shot). The only danger the men faced was the possibility of heart attacks while following the bull at a fast walk. After an agonizingly long time (the men said on the video that they were splitting the cost of this hunt and wanted to make sure they got their money's worth), the bull died. Staff members from the ranch smeared blood on the fat red faces of the hunters, who made silly statements for the camera regarding the thrill of the kill and the magnificence of the animal they had just tortured to death. One of the assholes said he was getting back to his man-the-hunter roots. The cruelty depicted in this video was so banal and showed the hunters in such a shameful light that their personal businesses were hurt (one sold insurance, the other ran a gas station). The hunting ranch lost clients, filed for bankruptcy, and sued Animal Rescue Mission. When the owners realized that the mission's pro bono attorneys could keep the case tied up in the courts for years, they dropped the suit and the rescued trophy animals became permanent members of the mission's menagerie.

These successes came at a price. Prominent animal rights organizations spoke out solemnly against the mission's brand of rescue terrorism and the mission became a legal target of groups representing farmers and hunters and gun owners. More lawyers.

Whenever they had an attorney-free day, Bear and Katie worked on the farm and helped care for the rescued animals and made rounds to check on farms and households they'd visited previously. Katie would try to cheer Bear with stories and pranks when the seriousness of being sued and the lack of privacy weighed especially heavy on him. One morning she decided they should go around cussing all day, at least one cussword in each sentence. "Hell yes," Bear told her. "Okay, then," she said, "don't forget, you bastard." "I won't, you little piece of dog shit." Katie made it through until the afternoon, when she met with some potential donors and either forgot about cussing or decided the game wasn't worth losing out on a few sizable checks. That night in bed, Katie whispered, "Good night, hon." Bear whispered back, "Sweet dreams, bitch." This caught her off guard until she remembered the game and wished him sweet dreams too, asshole.

Bear always had fun with Katie but he was having the hardest time getting accustomed to all the people being on the farm. He'd come into the house and see a stranger checking legal papers on the kitchen table; he'd walk behind a building and find a couple college kids digging a hole for some project Bear wasn't even aware of. He learned to smile and nod, ask no questions, and keep moving. On many days the only opportunity he and Katie had for private talk was the time between going to bed and falling asleep.

"I see you're reading a lot of books about pregnancy," she told him during one of these half hours.

"Take care of you, take care of the baby."

"You probably didn't realize it, but you left one of those books open on the bathroom sink."

"Really?"

"Yeah, it was being held open with a tube of toothpaste and a jar of cream, almost like you wanted me to read it."

"Mmm," he murmured.

"The chapter it was open to was 'Sex During Pregnancy.'"

"Really?"

"Uh-huh. The gist of the message was, sex during pregnancy was just fine and dandy."

"That's what it said?"

She knuckled his rib cage.

"Hey," he protested.

"We can do it if you want," she offered.

He said not that way, coolly offered.

"How do you want it?"

"Like before."

"Do you masturbate?"

"Katie!"

"I might be the first woman you ever made love to, but I bet you're not a stranger to self-abuse."

He didn't reply for a while then said, "I used to have dreams and then there'd be accidents in my sleep."

"Wet dreams."

"Is that what you call 'em?"

"Who'd you dream of, some waitress from town?"

"No."

"A movie star?"

"The First Lady."

"Who?"

"See, in this dream, I had done something heroic, I don't always remember what it was, saving people in a crash or something, and the President was away on some trip, the Middle East or somewhere. So the First Lady invited me to the White House and after the official ceremony she took me to the White House bedroom and she said she was going to personally thank me. I started to reach out and shake her hand, but she said no, that's not how she was going to thank me, then she started unbuttoning her blouse. It was one of them real starched white blouses and she had on a black skirt. She was wearing a string of pearls around her neck but she didn't take them off. Everything else but not them pearls, I remember that part."

"I bet you do."

"And then, she took my hand and led me over to the big presidential bed and the First Lady said, 'On behalf of a grateful nation . . .'"

"Then what?" Katie asked.

"Then . . . she *thanked me.*"

"You know what I think?"

"What?"

"I think you made up that story to deflect me from asking about, from finding out your *real* sexual fantasies."

"That's what you think?"

"I think you're a clever and wily Bear."

Not enough, he thought, not nearly enough.

42

Almost November, then, when Bear drove a tractor up the hills and through the pastures to reach the highest and most remote meadow on the farm. Pulling a five-foot mower behind the tractor, he began cutting the two-acre field to rid it of brush and briars, weeds and trash plants. Keep down the weeds and grass will flourish, was one of the truths of grass farming. Bear should've done this meadow months ago, before the weeds set seed, but mowing pastures was a chore he had neglected in the wake of mission work.

The two-acre meadow was steep, just off the peak of a hill, and surrounded by forest. The top of the meadow ran at a leaned-over angle, and he had to be careful not to hit an outcropping and flip the tractor, a mishap that killed more farmers in this area than any other kind of accident. Keeping in first gear, Bear made a few swipes around the field's perimeter to acquaint himself again with the angle and to remember rocks and groundhog holes, to watch for any new hazards that could tip the tractor. Eventually he shifted into second and settled into the routine of mowing, circling the perimeter, cutting another five feet of weeds and woody growth, leaving mowed grass in his wake.

Bear was about a third finished, working on a center rectangle of weeds surrounded now by a wide border of clean-cut grass, when he saw Katie coming up the trail and walking out onto the meadow. Something wrong? He stopped, set the brake but left the engine running, and hurried to meet her.

She was carrying a thick red plaid blanket and wearing a peasant dress, plain white cotton, and over that she wore one of Bear's old tweed jackets. She had on long dangling earrings, little brass monkeys holding on to each other, hand in foot, three to an ear, the final monkey on each earring almost touching Katie's shoulder.

"Everything okay?" Bear asked worriedly as he searched her green eyes. "You feeling all right?"

She said she was fine, just wanted to get away from all the activity down there. "I need the exercise."

"Stay strong for the birth."

She nodded. "I thought I'd just come up here and read a book, watch you mow." Katie's face was colored from the exertion of the hike and also she had painted her lips red, had shadowed her eyes the faintest blue.

Bear said, "I'm glad you're here but there's not much to watch. I just go 'round and 'round."

"That's okay, at least I'll have you in sight."

They kissed lightly and Bear resumed tractor work while Katie spread the blanket at an upper corner of the field and began reading. She waved when a round of mowing brought Bear and the tractor nearby.

After dipping to the lower end of the meadow where he couldn't see Katie, Bear mowed the long side, climbed the steep end of the field, then turned to come Katie's direction again. Now she was on her back eating an apple; her legs were bent and the dress had dropped away under her to reveal her white panties. Bear changed gears from second to first and slowed the throttle. Absorbed in the apple and reading her book, Katie didn't acknowledge Bear, who mowed past at a snail's pace and then turned around to watch as his wife took apple bites . . . then he dipped again to the lower end of the meadow where he couldn't see her.

He mowed down there in a fast third gear, came up the steep end of the field, turned hard toward Katie at the far upper end of the field. She had gotten over on her knees, supporting herself on elbows. With one hand she held the book open on the blanket, the apple in her other hand. The hem of the white peasant dress blew around in the light breeze. Bear slowed from third to second gear, watching as Katie moved her knees apart for a more comfortable position, then he went down to low gear and looked as long as he could before he ran out of field and had to turn.

He raced along the lower route, turned up the steep end, his back tires kicking up dirt as he steered again for Katie. Now she was even lower on her elbows, even higher on her knees, still reading and still eating that apple. Bear skipped second gear and went right to first, throttling back. He shifted into the ultra-low granny gear, the tractor's big rear wheels turning more slowly than a clock's second hand. When Katie reached around and offered him what was left of the apple, Bear bailed off the tractor while it was still moving and hurried for her blanket.

"You want to finish this?" she asked from that position up on her knees, down on her elbows, looking back over her shoulder at Bear.

Accepting the apple, Bear knelt behind his wife.

"What're you doing back there?" she asked pleasantly.

He took a bite while looking at her white underwear, her legs, the dress hem blown by the wind up over her back . . . and said, "If you don't want me to do this you better say *hippopotamus* or whatever it is you say to make me stop, because otherwise . . ." His voice trailed off as he tossed the core.

"Otherwise what, sweetie?" she asked in a taunting voice.

"By golly . . ."

She laughed.

He pulled his pants down, then hers, working them off her legs while telling her again that if he didn't hear *hippopotamus,* he was going to start in, she'd been warned, by golly.

Katie put her forehead on the blanket and laughed softly . . . crazy love. Meanwhile the driverless tractor crept lentamente across the meadow, heading toward the bordering forest but traveling so slowly you'd think it was trying to sneak away without Bear noticing.

He was on his knees hesitating behind Katie and praying he didn't hear *hippopotamus.* He drooled a line of saliva in a sunlit string to Katie's bare back. Bear wiped it off, wiped his mouth, she cocked her hips, and Bear moved slowly like that tractor over there entering the woods in granny gear, making a ridiculously unhurried escape from farm work.

Katie turned her head and looked up over her shoulder at him.

Bear told himself to be easy, remember she's pregnant.

But then she said dirty words and squatted back against him.

While a few feet into the woods, the tractor edged its bumpered nose against a big white oak tree and Bear grasped her hips with both large hands.

That tractor was pushing, too, though at a laggard rate, one big rear tire turning slowly, digging up dirt without fuss, making a hole in the forest floor as the tree held firm against the tractor's efforts.

He kept pushing against her and she back against him. He ground his teeth. Then almost exactly like a big animal heart-shot, he grunted and shuddered.

She laughed that it was over so quickly. "You okay?"

He said he was, though in truth Bear's toes curled so tightly inside his big workboots that both feet got the muscle cramps.

In the forest, the tractor was going nowhere, nosed against that tree and still churning up dirt from that one back tire turning.

Eventually they were resting on their sides, facing each other. "You planted that one," Katie said.

"I'd like to plant a whole garden of 'em," he admitted.

"Do you realize that you got off your tractor while it was still running?"

He nodded.

"And it went off in the woods by itself?"

He nodded again.

She laughed. "You don't care?"

Speaking of the tractor as you would a trusted dog, Bear said, don't worry, it won't go far.

"I'll leave the blanket," Katie said, kissing him and picking up her book and striking out for home feeling that old familiar squish and drip while Bear tightened into a fetal curl and listened to his tractor grinding slowly, game without hope, against a tree.

43

In its middle, December turned unnaturally warm and at the full moon Katie woke Bear past midnight to tell him she was scared.

"Of having a baby?"

"Other things too." She said she had that old *koyaanisqatsi* feeling and urged him to tell her a story, show her a magic trick, do something to stop the universe from wobbling.

He thought a moment, then said, "I seen some tracks today, how about I show you?"

She said okay without even asking what had made the tracks.

"It's warm out and we won't need flashlights, either."

"Okay."

They set off through a light snow. Bear and Katie walked until she finally said she had to stop and rest.

"You okay?" he asked.

"It's going to be close to dawn before we get back," Katie said, then began crying.

He came around to look at her face. "What's wrong?"

She shook her head. How would you explain it? She was blue for no logical reason. Also, they'd walked too far. "You just kept going, another hill, another ridge."

As she continued crying, Bear feared she was losing the baby. "*Katie,* what's happening!"

"It's okay . . . I just need some time to rest."

"We should've never done this, *never.*"

"I'm okay."

"I'm *stupid*—"

"Don't say that. I just need to sit awhile."

He gathered some evergreen boughs and made her a soft

place. The night was clear, there was that moon, there were those stars, and although the temperature was in the mid-forties, there was no wind and, in the night's dead stillness, it didn't seem cold at all.

Snow reflecting moonlight cast shadows. You could see . . . up into trees.

Katie was holding his hand, squeezing and kneading it. "What have you been tracking?"

He kept searching treetops.

"Bear?"

He nudged her. "Up in that beech tree."

Katie had to watch his face to see where he was looking, then she followed his gaze. "What are they?" she asked, pulling on his hand to help herself stand.

"Barely people," he said.

"Oh my God."

They made their way to the beech.

Up in that tree were five children . . . no, wait, there's another, way up in the crown, and *that one* hiding on the far side of the trunk . . . seven children from infant to four or five years, all of them wearing dull gray sweaters and skullcaps like clothing from the Middle Ages, leggings and leather footgear, the children swaddled in homemade blankets with their arms free so they could grasp on to a limb—even the smallest babies stayed where they had been placed, nesting between limbs, in forks, next to the trunk. There might be more up there unseen from the ground, but Bear and Katie saw those seven who were watching back, looking down with big black eyes that glistened in the night light. It was difficult to make out their facial features, but this was no optical illusion, these weren't bunches of leaves or squirrel nests that an exhausted Bear and Katie mistook for children in a tree. The eyes were the clincher: you looked up in that tree and saw eyes looking back.

"*Barely people* put their kids in trees at night to keep them safe while the adults go out and collect ferns and bait," Bear explained to Katie.

She said it was eerie . . . then felt her fetus move.

"*Barely people* always leave sentries around a child tree," Bear whispered. "They're probably watching us right now."

Katie looked around and told Bear, "The Lakota called trees 'the standing people.'"

He said that was a good thing to call trees, he had named many trees himself.

"Is this true?" she wanted to know. It was an odd question. Katie meant, was it true what she was seeing right now with her own green eyes?

"True enough," he told her.

Children with big black eyes . . . up in a tree at night . . . in December. Katie said, "I don't think I can bear it."

"Don't be trying to get 'em down for a rescue."

"No, I wouldn't."

"*Barely people* can't be violent, it's not in their nature, you could walk up to a mother and snatch the baby right out of her arms and she still couldn't do you any violence."

"I'd never—"

"All they can do is cry that alarm—you heard it that time, remember? If we was to start climbing this tree to get those babies—"

"We won't."

"The sentries would put up the alarm and the others would come running but those babies wouldn't make a peep, it's in *their* nature to stay quiet and hide. If you was to take 'em home they'd all die in captivity."

"Bear!" Katie spoke sharply because apparently she wasn't getting through to him.

"One summer I was growing a whole acre of sweet corn and the raccoons got into it," he told her. "I kept trying to catch 'em at it, then one dawn I heard the dogs making a racket and I come out with my rifle and there in a sycamore tree about the size of this beech here, I see half a dozen baby raccoons. Cutest little things. They had big black eyes just like these *barely people* babies and they was holding on to tree limbs and tucked against the trunk just like these kids here—them little raccoon babies had been placed in a tree for safekeeping, too." Bear lifted his arms as if he held a rifle, pointing it at the children in the tree. "And one by one I shot the six of 'em out of that sycamore tree."

"Oh Bear," she said softly.

"They was small and fluffy like raccoon toys and each time one of them hit ground, POTUS and Jamaica would run over and tear it apart. One by one I shot 'em out of that tree. The ones that hadn't been shot yet just stayed there looking down like these babies here are looking down now." Bear lowered his arms to make the imaginary rifle disappear. "Everybody waited their turn to get killed. Groundhog babies'll do that, too."

"Let's go home," she urged him.

"I'm blood-soaked," he said softly.

"No, Bear, you're the best—"

"I'm blood-soaked with animals, killed too many, killed for good reason, killed for no reason, killed for fun, from the time I could stand on two legs I been killing animals, and now they don't talk to me no more."

"Let's go home," she said again.

44

Now into its third week, December stayed too warm for itself. Birds that hadn't left for the season thought about sticking around. Plants sent shoots up through the sun-warmed soil. The temperature was in the sixties during the day and barely dropped into the forties at night. Then an arctic wind turned as if noticing warm Appalachia from afar and funneled air that had blown across glaciers, air so cold it was blue, the temperature dropping from sixty-five degrees one day to twenty the next, then it was single digits at night, zero during the day, and a week before Christmas it got cold cold: twenty below and staying that way.

Everything was affected. Pipes buried three feet that had never given any trouble froze solid. The farmhouse wouldn't stay warm, wouldn't even get into the upper fifties, not even at midday with all the wood stoves going full blast. Katie worried what they would do if it got this cold when the baby was born . . . then she remembered the *barely people* children bundled up and left for safekeeping in a tree.

Plants that a week earlier had nudged up their green noses got them frozen off. Birds that had waited to fly south were screwed. Domestic animals fared according to how they were kept. Outdoor animals fed and watered properly can tolerate bad weather, and if they're given a place to get out of the wind and wet, they can survive just about any level of cold.

The job of providing this food, water, and shelter for the mission's animals fell mostly to Bear. Volunteers had stopped coming around, after a huge argument about the decision Katie and Bear made to slaughter some cows because there wasn't enough hay for the winter and the beef could feed all the dogs and cats and other carnivores, including one big Bear, here on the farm. Katie sent out letters explaining that the mission was fighting against cruelty to animals, their inhumane treatment, anything that subjected them to unnecessary harm or pain, but she did not think it was unnatural for cows to be killed for food. Calves on the farm were born naturally, suckled their mothers, never received growth hormones or chemical supplements, ran wild, grazed and frolicked on grass, drank fresh water from clean streams. Some of these yearlings would be taken for food, killed swiftly, suffering less than they would from predation in the wild, and then butchered with respect and gratitude, the way Indians and other native peoples treated the animals they took, not as trophies, but to feed their families. Katie convinced almost none of her critics.

Volunteers stayed away, lawyers left, donations dried up. Katie had spent most of her savings supporting the mission and for the first time in her life was authentically poor. Creditors called. Katie went to the feed store and was humiliated when the owner told her no more feed until she paid down her account. "Just 'cause you're running a animal orphanage out there," he said, "don't mean I'm in the charity business, too."

It got colder. Bear wrapped a scarf around his face, put on two pairs of gloves and socks, insulated boots, and a heavy canvas coat, then went out into twenty-below December and worked. He actually felt better than he had in the summer when all those people were around and Bear had become a stranger on his own land. Now he was by himself, taking care of animals, feeding out hay, silently criticizing those who had stacked it wrong in the new barn, didn't know to turn bales on their sides to aid airing and prevent strings from rotting. This was the first hay Bear hadn't put up all by himself, he'd never had help before.

In the middle of the cold snap, when Katie and Bear were wearing sweaters and hats in the house and a glass of water left by the bed would ice over by morning, Robert called one midnight, drunk and despondent, complaining that Bear never called anymore, that Bear was turning his back on him like everyone else now that Robert was bankrupt and divorced and out of work.

"I would never turn my back on you," Bear promised.

"Then why don't I hear from you?"

"Robert, we got twenty below here for the last week, I got to crawl under the house with a propane torch to keep the pipes open . . . make sure the animals get fed, keep their water unfrozen. You know how many animals we got to take care of now?"

"Oh, I'm sure your sanctuary is a great success, I know you've had stories in newspapers, you and your wife are heroes, no doubt about it."

"No, Robert, I ain't saying that."

"Of course, I'm the one who gave you the farm."

"I know you did, Robert." But this time, Bear did not reflexively offer to return ownership of the farm anytime Robert wanted it.

"I don't mean to harp on it," Robert said—and then harped on it some more. "I won't see my boys for Christmas, *she* has them off with her at her parents' house. I think she's going out with somebody, maybe he has a job, which of course would make him a hero, wouldn't it. I come in for an interview and people take one look and want me out of their offices. It's like they can smell the failure on me," Robert told Bear. "It's the end of the line for your big brother."

"No it ain't, Robert—it's just December."

December affected everyone. The normally effusive Doc Setton came over to the farm for a visit and complained that he had lived beyond what was necessary, his friends were dead, he was tired. When he took out a cigarette, Katie said she hadn't realized he smoked.

"Just took it up," Doc said.

"Everybody else in the world is trying to quit."

"I guess I can't smoke around you 'cause you're pregnant huh?"

"Doc, why are you being so combative?"

It was December and twenty below zero.

Before Doc left that day he told Katie and Bear about a rescue that was needed at a farm across the river. "The farmer, Martin Lonns, has apparently given up, doesn't go out of his house, won't let anybody come around to help . . . crazy or senile or just sick of this cold, I don't know. I was there before the weather turned and saw what kind of shape his cows were in, God knows how they're faring now."

❦

Katie and Bear bundled up and drove to the Lonns farm early that afternoon. The house, similar to Katie and Bear's, was built on a plot below the grade of the road so that as you drove in you got a chance to examine the roof and feel superior. Then you followed switchbacks down the mountain until you got down to where you were going and had to look up to where you'd been.

Bear knocked on the door. No answer, no barking. When he came back to the truck, Katie said she thought she'd seen some cows by the barn, lower on down the mountain. Standing at the truck door, Bear told Katie she should keep the truck running, he'd check the barn lot. She said she was coming with him.

"It's freezing out here," he told her. "Every little footprint in the mud is frozen like a rock for you to trip over. I wish you'd please just mind me once in a while."

"Mind you?" she asked, laughing.

Bear got in and shut the door. "When that baby gets born," he asked, "am I going to have to start worrying about it minding me?"

"It?"

"He or she."

"Minding you in the sense of obedience or minding you as in *you bother me?"*

Bear didn't answer, he was thinking of that dream he had about a little girl standing by his bed saying she was his daughter waiting to get born . . . then he said, "She."

"It's going to be a girl?"

Bear nodded. "Pretty as her mother," he said, reaching over to touch the small round oval part of Katie's face that was showing from her scarf and hat.

"Get out of here," she told him affectionately.

Exiting the truck, Bear was instantly slammed by how cold it was, colder than a well-digger's ass, his father used to say when Robert and Bear had to go out in this kind of weather to feed the animals and haul water that splashed out of the bucket and got on your pants leg. You could feel the frozen weight pulling on your trousers and banging against your leg as you walked. Robert did most of the work, Bear went along because he loved his big brother's company.

Thinking about Robert, Bear was smiling, but when he came around the edge of the barn his face hardened.

Katie had been right about seeing cows in the barnyard, there were eight in an enclosure about a hundred feet on each side, three of those sides a four-plank board fence, the back of the barn forming the fourth side. Warm weather preceding the cold snap had left the barnyard deep with mud, and the cows—Hereford beef cows—were in it up to their knees or higher. When the arctic air came in, the viscous mud froze solid as concrete. Well-fed cows would've kept moving to stay on top of the freezing mud, but these cows were starving to death and simply froze in place encased nearly to their sunken bellies in mud. You had to wonder how long had they suffered.

They were like statues placed in a grotesque tableau, Cows in Winter Mud, arranged in a seemingly random manner and stuck deep so they wouldn't fall over. Then one of the statues raised its head and leaned ever so gently to the left, as if to pull the front right leg free, while making a low-in-the-throat trombone groan.

Bear climbed the board fence. Launching out across the barnyard, he felt every hole and ridge in the frozen mud. It was like walking across an ocean that had been churning with breaking waves then got flash-frozen, each splash caught like jagged stone. Bear kept his arms out to the sides for balance and still nearly fell with every awkward step, turning his ankles, slipping, beating his way to the cow.

She stood between two others whose bodies might have given her a slight break from the wind. The cow was a young mother who looked as if she'd been suckled, though Bear didn't see any evidence of the calf. Bear slipped off a glove and rolled down the cow's lower lip, then pressed her gums, which were gray and showed no circulation. Forcing her lower jaw open, he put his hand in her mouth and grasped her thick tongue. It was cold. She won't be alive much longer, Bear thought; a cold tongue was telltale.

As he took a step back his foot caught on one of the ridges and he fell hard on his ass, bruising a leg from butt to knee.

How does a man let this happen to his animals? Bear wondered as he regained his feet. And how in God's name are we going to rescue this one? You'd have to chip away at the frozen mud with chisels or be careful using a chain saw, and even then you'd have to keep a chunk of the mud around each leg because if you tried to pull that leg free, skin and flesh would stick where it had been frozen. We'll have to get a dozen volunteers, Bear thought. The cow will probably go down once she's freed, we'll have to put boards across this frozen mud and then manhandle, pull, slide, winch, come-along her to a trailer. It'd be easier on all concerned to put a bullet in her head. Imagine a line from the right eye to the left ear and from the left eye to the right ear and where these two lines cross is where you put that bullet. Katie will probably want to try rescuing her, though. Then Bear thought, no, I'm not going to put it off on Katie, I'm the one who wants to save this damn old tongue-cold, mud-frozen cow.

He walked around to determine how bad her legs were stuck. It's amazing that a flesh-and-blood creature in this condition can still cling to life, he thought, she must be the world's greatest optimist. He saw a mound of frozen mud near her udder and, looking more closely, discovered it was actually her calf, lying there as calves will, turned in a tight circle, snout to tail, this one covered and stuck in mud like it had been caught by an arctic Pompeii.

Bear returned to the truck just as Katie was getting out. She said she'd become worried because he was gone so long—how are the cows?

He told her they were in a bad way, she didn't need to see it, being pregnant and all. "We'll go back to the farm and call some people to help, bring some equipment over here—"

"Bear, tell me."

"They're frozen in the mud still standing up."

"Frozen alive in the mud?" she asked.

He said one of them was alive, yes . . . but only barely. "You get back in that warm truck, let me check the house once more before we leave."

Bear walked to the door and knocked, no answer, but this time he tried the handle and found it unlocked. Pushing open the door to the kitchen, Bear hollered, "Mr. Lonns?" No answer. *"Mr. Lonns?"* The house was quiet, then suddenly someone turned on a television set and played it at high volume. Bear went in, crossed through the kitchen into the dining room and then the living room. Unbelievably hot, must be eighty or eighty-five degrees in here, not only was the central forced-air heat on high, but each room had electrical space heaters blazing away.

Martin Lonns was sitting in his underwear, a pair of long johns stained and threadbare. His hair sticking up wildly, he was unshaven and ripe in this overheated room; Bear could smell him from the doorway.

"Mr. Lonns?"

He was in his sixties, thin, with thick coarse black hair on the backs of his hands and sprouting through the weave of his long johns and growing not only from inside his ears but all over the dangling lobes, too.

When Bear went over and turned off the TV, the man dug out a revolver from between two couch cushions and waved it generally in Bear's direction. Sputtering was the best he could manage.

"Put that away, Mr. Lonns," Bear told him quietly.

He found his voice. "For rent, for sale, for free—get out

quick! *Get out! Get out!*" With a quivering hand he tried to pull back the hammer.

Bear stepped over and took the revolver. "Your cows are in bad shape."

"The Lord gives me dominion over cattle of the field—now get the hell out of here."

"Having dominion means taking responsibility—"

"I'm tired," Lonns said. "Wife gone . . . I'm tired of working, tired of being cold. Been feeding cows and supporting a family since I was eighteen years old, that's forty-five years now taking care of them, when's someone start taking care of me?"

Before Bear could speak, Katie came in with anger rising off her like steam. "Get his ass up off that couch and drag him to the barn."

"You went down there?"

She had. "I want him dragged out there to see what he's done, what he's allowed to happen." Then to Lonns, "Get up, old man, you're going to go look at your cows."

He made no move to surrender the couch. "Seen enough of them cows, don't need to see them no more."

Katie told Bear, "I want you to go over and drag him out by the arm. If he wants to get dressed first, fine, but that man is going to see what's become of his cows. I'm not going to let him claim he was sitting in here and had no idea what went on outside, I won't let him deny it ever happened." She loosened a scarf. "We're going to have to kill that one that's still alive, aren't we?"

"I'd like to try saving her."

Katie was surprised.

"With enough help we might be able to."

Lonns was staring at the dead television, occasionally grinning idiotically.

Katie snatched the revolver out of Bear's hand and pointed the gun at Lonns. "Get up, old man."

Lonns raised both hands and cackled like this was part of a skit from some stupid show—except where's the laugh track?

"Mr. Lonns," Bear said, "you better get to your feet."

He cursed them both.

Standing there holding the gun, Katie said it was a sin, what this man had allowed to happen to his cows.

Bear told her, "It happens more than you think. A person living out in the country all alone, he goes a little crazy, just gives up, sits staring at a wall or stays in bed and won't feed or water anything, won't shower or even get dressed. I used to go over and help people like that even before you showed up. You can't really blame—"

She insisted she could.

Lonns stood and shouted at her, "When do cows feed and water *me*?"

With the revolver still in one hand, she went over and pulled Lonns to the door, dragging him outside even though all he wore were those ratty long johns. Bear didn't have the heart to follow. He expected any moment now to hear a gunshot. I'll take the blame for killing Lonns, Bear decided, so Katie can stay out of jail and have that baby.

A few minutes later, she came dragging the old man back into the house. He was a fright, lips blue, eyes red, like a cartoon version of a man shivering. Snot had frozen on his face and he looked wild, like he'd seen elephants for the first time.

"He might not have learned anything," Katie told Bear, handing him the revolver, "but at least he can't deny it. American GIs liberating concentration camps were so outraged that they went into the local towns and dragged the German citizens out to the camps, forced them to march through and see the horror of it. Deny *that,* you rotten degenerates." Becoming enraged all over again, Katie reached for the revolver.

Bear kept it from her.

Lonns began gasping, then started choking, turning red and red-blue and purple. Bear led the man back to his couch. Lonns blubbered in a liquid way, his nose running and his mouth all drooly. To Katie's disgust, Bear wiped and comforted the old bastard, covering him with blankets.

As she considered the poor excuse for a farmer shivering under those blankets even though the room was stifling, everything piled up on Katie's mind, the debt, the loss of support for the mission, being pregnant, this cold snap. "I'm sick of all these farmers mistreating their animals," she told Bear. "People around here . . . Do you realize that except for Eddie Lancor, who unchained Old Bob and brought him in the house, we haven't had one situation where anyone's seen the light, changed their ways? This guy here, as soon as he gets some prescription medicine, he'll be back on his feet, starving his cows and kicking his dog—I found a collie whimpering under the porch, gave her a can of dog food from the truck and then poured out some water from those jugs we carry; she was more interested in the water than the food. So don't tell me this guy just gave up on life. When you got animals under your care, giving up is not an option."

"I've never seen you so mad, Katydid."

"Let's try to save that cow," she finally said.

They went home to collect their gear and call volunteers. They convinced four people to leave Christmas shopping for later, we have an animal to rescue. The six of them worked by headlights until 2 A.M. Against all odds, that Hereford cow lived through the extraction ordeal and was taken to the mission, where she would live for another fifteen years, walking each day in a stiff-legged gait but still sunny on life.

❦

On Christmas morning, Bear and Katie exchanged modest gifts, a pair of gloves, a sweater, and then the next day they heard that Philip Scrudde had died of a heart attack.

Two days later Bear told Katie he had to take care of some business, then went to the funeral. Although Scrudde had never been indicted or arrested, people believed the worst of him. When the preacher at his church requested a prayer conference with Scrudde, wanting to know the truth, Scrudde broke off from the church and stayed at his big house in town, not going out much, a small man who seemed to shrink with each passing day.

Bear was surprised there were so few people at the funeral; he counted a dozen but they included the preacher, who was obligated to be there, the guy who was going to sing gospels, and two people from the funeral home. If as big a deal as Scrudde drew only a dozen mourners, Bear thought, he'd be lucky to get three or four at his own funeral.

"Where do you keep hearing about these animals?" Katie asked him a week later when Bear brought home a litter of kittens he'd pulled out from under a porch.

"People just tell me."

"I think you've gone on more missions by yourself than the volunteers ever did as a team."

"I reckon." He didn't tell her about all the rescues, certainly not the one Bear made in February when Carl Coote sent a biker friend over to ask Bear if he'd drive to Coote's trailer and take care of his pet ground squirrel. Coote was going away to jail on a grand theft auto charge and there was only one person in the world he'd trust with his squirrel. "He says," Coote's biker friend told Bear, "that he's sorry."

The world began to thaw in March, got better in April, then the baby, Ruth Elena Long, was born in the good month of May.

45

In the year following the birth of Ruth, Animal Rescue Mission grew into a strongly funded, permanent organization that was able to pay Bear and Katie small salaries, the mission having finally found its audience, appealing to a large number of people who weren't strict vegetarians but who loved animals and hated any cruelty done to them. These people believed that it was probably more natural than unnatural for animals to be eaten by humans, a stand that continued to outrage most animal rights activists. To those activists, Katie quoted British writer John Berger: "A peasant becomes fond of his pig and is glad to salt away its pork. What is significant, and is so difficult for the urban stranger to understand, is that the two statements are connected by an *and* and not by a *but.*" To which the activists replied, you can't love a cow and still eat a hamburger. You should meet my husband, Katie told them.

Seeing the sanctuary filling so quickly, people would ask Katie what she intended to do when she couldn't take in any more animals—what's your plan for limiting the number of animals you accept, don't you realize you can't save every animal in the world? Katie would tell them, "We don't have to save every animal in the world, we have to save just one, and by saving that one, we save them all." People didn't understand, didn't realize it was written.

At one organizational meeting held on the farm, someone maneuvered Bear up to the front of the room to thank him (the tone was unfortunately patronizing) for being the mission's "quiet strength." Everyone knew that Bear went out on private rescues, returning to the farm banged up, cut by wire he had removed from a panicky horse's legs, scratched by a cat he pulled all hiss and spit from a hole, kicked by a cow, bit by a dog whose name he didn't know . . . and he came home with all manner of creatures he'd saved, a lamb, a bird, a pony, a turtle.

While Bear was uncomfortably front and center, someone asked him, as a lifelong farmer, what his philosophy about animals was. A veteran of these debates, Katie feared that Bear was being embarrassed and, with Ruth in her arms, she came toward the microphone to rescue her husband.

But Bear was already responding to the question, speaking with a heavy country accent that he almost never used with Katie: "Iffen you gotta heifer a steer, least don't laugh when he pees on his tail . . . is my philosophy."

People looked at one another as if Bear had spoken in ancient Greek; some snickered.

By this time Katie was at the mike and she wasn't about to let it go at that, Bear made to look the fool. "My husband almost never says anything that's not worth listening to," she said, sounding awkward and patronizing to her own ears. Then to Bear, so others could hear, "You said 'heifer a steer'? I don't know what that is."

He replied directly to Katie, though aware everyone in the room was listening. "Sometime they get an infection in their . . . you know." He swept a hand down to indicate, in the most general way possible, nether regions.

"Penises?"

He nodded. "And the infection is so bad it closes up and them steers can't pee, which is to say they can't void their bladders and it gets to where they like to die." Bear was using *like* in the rural Appalachian sense of inclination—the steers were inclined or about to die. "Which gives you two choices: you can hurry 'em to slaughter whilst they suffer from that swollen bladder or the doc can come around behind and make a cut under the steer's tail and dig in and find the urethra, then pull it out—the urethra is the pee tube, the doc pulls it out sort of backwards so it comes out under the steer's tail like a heifer's does and the doc ties it off there. Well, that ol' steer is happy he can pee again but he still thinks it's coming out like normal from underneath, so he don't know—like a heifer knows naturally—to swish his tail aside when he pees and that's why he ends up peeing all over hisself. Now, I seen more than one farmer nudge his buddies and laugh when a heifered steer pees on its own tail, but my philosophy is, iffen you gotta heifer that steer to save its life and stop the pain, okay, but at least have the common decency not to laugh when he pees all over his tail."

The college kid who edited the mission's newsletter printed a story in next month's issue, "Bear's Philosophy." Bear cut out the article and carried it in his wallet along with six photographs: POTUS as a puppy, Katie, Ruth, Katie and Ruth together, Robert's high school graduation portrait, and a much-folded faded picture of Bear, Robert, and their parents.

When the mission had grown into an official organization with rules and procedures, staff members asked Bear to record the rescues he undertook on his own: where he was going and what animals he was saving and the intervention's results and so on. He always nodded and said he would write the reports, but he never did. Staff members complained to Katie, who explained that her husband had been making these private forays for years, please leave him alone.

One time he brought home teenage felons, a sullen group of four, three boys and a girl, all of them pierced, tattooed, their hair dyed jet black or black-green, nervous smokers who wouldn't look you in the eye but cursed under their breath and were obsessed with death and the dark sciences. Deputy Miller had arranged for them to do community service instead of jail—they would go work at the mission. But the Gothic teens had already informed Bear they had no intention of cleaning out cages or picking up dog shit and you can't make us, you can jail us or kill us but you can't make us. Bear said he had something special in mind for them and put the kids to work playing with puppies. He called this canine socialization, a term Bear had overhead mission staff members use. Each teenager got a separate litter to socialize. The teens tried to stay cool and tough and totally unimpressed, but after half an hour with puppies running and yipping and licking and grabbing a shirtsleeve pretending it was prey and then suddenly collapsing in puppy exhaustion, the teenagers became children again. Two of the four returned to volunteer after their mandatory community service had ended. Katie told Bear that his puppy program worked miracles, and maybe the mission could bring in the clinically depressed, cancer patients, the suicidal, surround them with puppies and see if it helped. Bear said it wouldn't hurt.

The canine socialization program was taken over by volunteering psychologists and Bear was politely asked to stop feeding the puppies because he tended to overdo it and they became little butterballs barely able to waddle.

After that Bear concentrated his formidable energy on raising Ruth. Sometimes Katie would come upstairs of a morning and find Bear sitting on a chair outside Ruth's room.

"What're you doing, hon?" Katie would ask.

"Waiting for Ruth to wake up."

"How come?"

"So I can go to work."

When Ruth was two, Mr. Lancor died and his daughter brought Old Bob to the farm. The daughter said her father lived well beyond the doctors' predictions and everyone in the family agreed that the reason for this was that he became so devoted to Old Bob. They loved each other and were inseparable, and maybe this is what got Mr. Lancor's mind off his problems, or maybe it was the power of love that extended his life. "My father was real clear," the daughter said, "where he wanted this dog to go, so here I'm bringing Old Bob to you along with a check for two thousand dollars, it's what Daddy wanted and nobody in the family said a word against this check even though they fought over his other stuff like every couch and tool chest was made of pure gold."

Old Bob wasn't a surprise because Eddie Lancor had become an avid supporter of the mission over the last couple of years and often told Katie and Bear he planned to make sure his dog came to them eventually. The shocker was when another man's daughter drove up and brought out another black dog that was being "willed" to the mission: Mitchell.

Katie couldn't place him but Bear remembered right off. "This is Mr. Noyles's dog."

"Devil Noyles," Katie murmured.

Bear nodded.

Even though the daughter was standing right there, Katie didn't pull any punches. "After we saved his starving horses, he sold them both to slaughter, mother and daughter."

Bear nodded. "Surprised he wanted Mitchell to come to us."

Noyles's daughter, who had her father's pinched expression, said she was surprised, too. "Daddy hated you two for coming onto his property and shaming him by feeding them horses, but when he died we found a piece of paper in his Bible saying what he wanted done with certain things. Mitchell should go to those people who fed my horses, that's what Daddy wrote, so that's what I'm doing, though I don't otherwise have any truck with the lot of you."

Because Mitchell and Old Bob arrived at the farm during the same week, they threw in together like two Americans in foreign France and became best buddies, making their rounds, taking turns peeing on the corners of buildings and the tires of unfamiliar vehicles. It got to be one of the most familiar sights on the farm, two old fat black gray-muzzled dogs walking together, napping together, peeing together the way devoted bachelors will.

One puppy had been kept out of the last litter from Jamaica and POTUS, the others given to good homes. Bear and Katie named the big male Veep. He turned out to be less a chip off the old block than an understudy to Old Yeller—a big goofy puppy who got tangled up in his own legs and barked ferociously at geese but then ran yelping when they hissed at him.

Veep tried to keep up with Old Bob and Mitchell on their rounds, but the two elders didn't have much patience for rambunctious youth. Often, one of the old dogs would pee on something significant and Veep would step forward to smell it just in time to get anointed by the other statesman; then Veep would look around like someone was playing a joke with the garden hose, his tail wagging because he loved jokes that involved the garden hose.

Bear didn't think much of the dog, didn't figure he lived up to his breeding, but Veep was devoted to Ruth, which in Bear's opinion covered a lot of territory.

Jamaica, the old female shepherd, died when Ruth was three. Jamaica was buried next to POTUS, whom she'd loved beyond measure. Ruth attended the funeral and put flowers on the grave. The girl was shielded from little that went on at the farm and at age three knew more about birth and death than some people understand by age thirty. Lots of dogs came to the funeral; Old Bob and Mitchell sat together, of course, and lent a solemn air to the proceedings until Veep, who even at age three still acted like a puppy, began digging for a beetle, jumping around and barking and eventually knocking into Mitchell, who bit the German shepherd without preamble or apology, causing Veep to yelp, after which he settled down and the funeral proceeded without a hitch.

❦

Katie and Bear with daughter Ruth lived in a domestic bliss wide and deep enough to dilute most of life's dramas. People ask how you're doing and they want to hear you're struggling, on the road to recovery, trying to understand, hoping for the best . . . they don't want to hear you're happy. Saying "I'm happy" makes you sound like you're an idiot. But Bear and Katie and Ruth were happy.

The vet, Doc Setton, had given up his practice and said he was enjoying life while waiting to die—smoking three packs of cigarettes a day, though he didn't smoke around Ruth. After the girl went to bed, Doc would light one cigarette after another, drinking wine and speaking of the old days.

Katie told him he should quit smoking.

"Why?" Doc asked cheerfully. "Because they'll kill me when

I'm a hundred? I might be the only man in this country who *took up* smoking at age eighty but I enjoy the habit, nasty as it is. Here's a quote for you: 'If alcohol is queen, then tobacco is her consort. It's a fond companion for all occasions, a loyal friend through fair weather and foul. People smoke to celebrate a happy moment, or to hide a bitter regret. Whether you're alone or with friends, it's a joy for all the senses. . . . I love to watch the flame spurt up, love to watch it come closer and closer, filling me with its warmth.' That's from Luis Buñuel, a Spanish filmmaker, in case you didn't know."

Katie asked, "How'd he die?"

"He died at eighty-three, so whatever killed him took its time."

Katie offered her own quote: "'A custom loathsome to the eye, hateful to the nose, harmful to the brain, dangerous to the lungs . . .' That's from James the First of England, written four hundred years ago."

Doc turned to Bear, who'd been sitting there with a serene smile, doing what he usually did when they had guests, just listening to the others talk. "You want to jump in with a tobacco quote?"

"L.S.M.F.T.," Bear said without hesitation, as if he'd been waiting for the cue.

Doc Setton and Katie, who'd each had several glasses of wine, exchanged looks and laughed.

"Lucky Strikes mean fine tobacco," Bear said as he stood and went into that silly poignant dance of his, pirouetting in a dreamy manner, singing softly with the rhythmic tap of his feet, "L . . . S . . . M . . . F . . . T . . ."

Later that evening, while Bear was upstairs checking on Ruth, Doc mentioned Bear's strange performance and said it had been years since he saw him acting like that.

"There was a time," Katie said, "that I really thought he was mental. Please don't ever tell him I told you this, but Bear used to hear animals talking to him and he'd talk back, they'd have conversations. In fact"—she looked at the doorway to make sure Bear wasn't there—"he told me he still goes out to that red cow we have, you know, the ancient one, twenty years old or whatever. He loves that cow and claims she used to talk to him 'in a kindly fashion.' He says he still goes out there and speaks to her but she never says a word back to him."

❦

The time between going to bed and falling asleep was still their sanctuary from a busy day. Sometimes Bear and Katie would lie on their sides under the blanket face to face, touching each other. She would tell him he had the best, kindest, most loving face she'd ever seen. He told her he loved everything about her from earlobes to toenails and if he owned one of them scales they saw the other day in a jewelry store— A carat scale? Katie asked. That's it, he said, if I had a carat scale I'd use it to weigh the sleepy grains in your eyes, you're that valuable to me. On and on it went between them, to a degree that would make you gag if you weren't one of the participants, telling each other repeatedly *I love you,* saying it as a mantra, *I love you, I love you, I love you,* until the words themselves produced a comforting soporific effect, leading Bear and Katie to sleep in a warm nest, *I love you,* covered by feathers, *I love you, I love you.*

❦

Old Bob and Mitchell slept close, too. They'd taken over that large red flannel mat Katie had made for POTUS. The two old dogs looked so much alike—fat, black, shaggy, gray-muzzled—that newcomers to the farm couldn't tell them apart, though in fact Old Bob and Mitchell had strikingly different personalities.

Having been raised on a farm where he was allowed to roam, Mitchell was the more worldly of the two, while Old Bob, kept chained for most of his life, had a gentler and more sheltered personality.

Devotion they once gave their men was now pledged to each other, so that when Mitchell woke up one night with an anguished whimpering and quick kicking of his legs, Old Bob got concerned and asked, what's wrong . . . you're not dying, are you?

Mitchell said he dreamt he was chasing rabbits.

You used to chase rabbits? Old Bob asked.

Are you kidding me? I chased *everything.* Didn't you?

No, I was chained.

Mitchell said he was never even put in a pen, he had free run of the farm and beyond.

Beyond?

Oh yeah. There was a female who lived on the farm over from mine, Mitchell said, and every time she'd come in season I'd go there and breed her. Up that hill, across a ridge, down another hill, breed her, wait till we came unstuck, maybe breed her again, be home by the time the man was up, nobody ever figured it out. I can't even tell you how many litters of mine she had. I like to breed. They don't call it being *in heat* for nothing. How many times did you breed?

Old Bob said he had never bred.

Not even once?

No, I was kept chained.

Not me, I had free run. Go ahead, name an animal and I'll tell you if I chased it.

Deer?

Deer? You gotta be kidding. I chased so many deer that if all the deer I chased were put in one forest, it'd have to be the biggest forest you ever saw. You never chased a deer?

Old Bob said no, he was chained.

Mitchell asked him for how long.

The first nine years of my life.

Good God, Mitchell said. How'd you get unchained?

Old Bob admitted he didn't know what brought it about. One day my man came out in the rain and took off that chain and next thing I know I'm living in the house with him, I'm even sleeping in bed next to him.

Now it was Mitchell's turn to be impressed. He said he'd never been allowed in the house.

Never? Old Bob asked.

Not once. I slept in a shed and got fed on the porch.

Old Bob said that during all those years he was chained, he was fed dry food pellets, but when he got unchained and let into the house, suddenly he was given really great food that came out of a can or right from the table.

From the table?

That man fed me whatever he was eating. I mean, he would take a bite then put another bite on his fork and give it to me.

Mitchell was even more impressed. The two of you would eat off the same fork?

Yes! He was a great man.

Sounds like it.

Remembering how his man smelled, Old Bob wagged his tail and told Mitchell, I miss him.

Hey, name another animal, I'll tell you if I chased it.

Squirrels?

Squirrels? You're kidding me, aren't you? I know you're kidding me. If all the squirrels I ever chased were put in one tree, it would have to be a giant tree.

Old Bob said, I see them around here and think about chasing them but I'm too old.

Mitchell admitted he was too old for chasing squirrels, too. But when I was young, he said, I chased everything.

Groundhogs? Old Bob asked.

Groundhogs? Are you kidding me? If all the groundhogs I ever chased were put in one hole—

It'd have to be a big hole?

❦

Ruth was coming five.

If you love two people as much as I love Bear and Ruth, then you can't begrudge how much those two people love each other, Katie kept telling herself as Bear and Ruth went everywhere together and had long discussions and laugh sessions you could hear from the next room. Katie spoke to Ruth as mother to child, but Bear talked to the girl as he would to a best friend.

One summer day, Katie watched out a window as Bear and

Ruth stood together looking at a shed. The top of the little girl's head came above Bear's knee, and both of them had their hands on their hips. They've been looking at that shed for the last fifteen minutes, Katie thought peevishly. Why don't they come in here and spend some time with me, what could possibly be so fascinating about some old shed?

"I'm going to paint that shed," Bear was telling Ruth.

"That's what you said last week," she pointed out.

"It was true last week and it's true today."

"You ain't going to paint that shed."

"Don't say ain't. And I *will* paint that shed."

"When?" she asked.

"I don't know."

Ruth made a little raspberry sound. "You're not going to paint that shed."

"Yes I will."

"What color?"

"I think I'll paint that shed red."

"It's red now."

"That's the shed ol' POTUS was laying against when he died."

"I know, you told me a hundred times. What color was it then?"

"Red."

She thought a moment before saying, "It sounds to me like that shed is always going to be red."

Ruth and Bear had occasional disagreements, as friends will. One time she put a scarf around Veep's shoulders and a blue bonnet on his head. The bonnet was tied under his chin with a red ribbon. When Bear saw this he told her to take that scarf and bonnet off that dog. "His father had more dignity than the President of the United States," Bear said, "and I won't have a son of his dressed up in froufrou."

"He doesn't care," Ruth said.

Veep sat there with a goofy grin on his face, so devoted to her that she could sew thorns on his head, he wouldn't mind.

"Well, I care. German shepherds are supposed to be guardians, not playthings."

"He's a wolf."

This gave Bear pause. "A wolf?"

"I'm Little Red Riding Hood and Veep is the wolf that ate my grandmother and now he's dressed up in her clothes pretending to be my grandmother and I'm going to say, 'What big teeth you have, Grandmother.'" Ruth grabbed the dog's lips, pulling them apart to show off his big teeth. Veep wagged his tail in delight at her touch.

Bear thought about all this, then said, "Well, I guess it's all right if he's supposed to be a wolf. 'What a big dumb goofy expression you have, Grandmother.'"

"That's not in the story," Ruth pointed out.

Bear and Ruth stayed on the farm when Katie traveled to conferences and fund-raising meetings. Ruth never had need of a baby-sitter and went everywhere with Bear. Eventually he took her on his private rescue missions. When Katie asked her daughter about them, the little girl turned an imaginary lock on her lips and threw away the imaginary key.

Katie worked hard every day, hiring and firing staff, organizing volunteers, raising money, and making tough decisions about the stands the mission would take in position papers. Bear's position was he didn't ever want Ruth out of his sight.

She was in his sight, but not by his side the day a farmer, drunk and angry, came to get his horse back. The animal had nearly starved to death, but the farmer was ranting about the palomino having been his pet; he hollered to volunteers that he adored that horse and wanted it back, and meanwhile he was going to kick as much ass as he could, you goddamn bunny-huggers.

Bear was on an overlooking hillside clearing weeds above POTUS's grave when he saw the farmer, who had an ax handle and a length of logging chain. He was raving, swinging the chain in a circle around his head, using that ax handle on anyone within reach, and in fact he managed to knock down a couple volunteers. People were shouting for Bear and running for cover, when Ruth, curious about what was happening, stepped out into the yard. Like a silverback, Bear charged off that hillside, bellowing, but he was too far away to affect the outcome.

From around the house came Veep, positioning himself between Ruth and the drunk. Witnesses later said that Veep was so aggressively focused on the threat to the little girl that the dog was actually vibrating, all puffed up, taking slow steps as his predator eyes locked on that man, who, upon seeing the dog's profound *intensity,* got sober quick, dropping ax handle and chain and running for his truck. After that, Bear never again criticized Veep for being foolish.

Ruth wore overalls or jeans, didn't like dresses, while Bear still wore items from the apparently inexhaustible supply of dress clothes, slacks and coats and vests, in the attic. They'd set off across a field together, holding hands or not. Bear would kick at a pile of cow manure and Ruth would run off and find a pile of her own to kick. The idea was to spread the manure around so it would fertilize the pasture instead of killing grass by staying in solid clumps.

Bear explained to Ruth what they were doing, he explained everything to her. "When people call farmers shit-kickers, it's because they see us doing this."

"I'm a little shit-kicker," she sang.

"Oh geez, Ruth, don't say that in front of your mother."

"Why?"

"*Shit*'s a bad word."

"*You* said it."

"I know, but I was just trying to explain why people call us that. Please don't say it in front of your mother."

"Okay."

"She'd kill me."

"I said okay."

Ruth turned five in the good month of May. Then, in another awful June, it was confirmed that Bear had the fast cancer and he died six months later, cold December.

46

Robert came to stay at the farm for the last three of those final six months. If you saw the two brothers together and were told, one has come to comfort the other as he dies from cancer, you'd assume Robert was the one dying, Bear the one doing the comforting. Robert, just into his forties now, had become gaunt and haunted by life's defeats while Bear was radiant about having his brother back on the farm at long last.

Even though Bear was in and out of the hospital, alternately being killed by the cancer and poisoned by the anticancer efforts, he still got happy around Robert. Remember that time I saved you from a beating when that jealous boyfriend came looking for you, remember when we was cutting down that big oak tree and the wind caught it, remember . . . ?

Katie tried not to begrudge them their memories, though she would've preferred to spend these last months alone with Bear and Ruth, just the three of them. He got out of the hospital at Thanksgiving and came home to die.

The Saturday after Thanksgiving, Ruth was upstairs in the bedroom talking with her father. Katie and Robert were in the kitchen with coffee.

"I knew something was wrong with him last spring," she said. "He would whimper when he moved around in bed at night. I knew he had to be hurting because that man never complains about anything."

"Even as a little boy he was stoic," Robert said.

"I let it be known when people don't do things the way I want them done at the mission, when animal rights organizations would rather stand on philosophical ceremony than get down in the trenches and rescue abused animals . . ." She started crying.

Robert reached across the corner of the table and put his hand on hers.

"If something's wrong, I complain until it's made right," Katie continued. "But your brother never complains, never."

Robert agreed, then took his hand back and drank some coffee. He was hollow-eyed and needed to put on thirty pounds.

"When you were growing up," Katie asked him, "did you have a neighbor who fed hay to her family and got carted away to an asylum?"

Robert looked astonished. "That was our mother!"

"Your—"

"I guess she thought Bear and I and our father acted like animals so, one mealtime, she went around putting hay on our plates and—"

"Bear always said it was a neighbor woman."

Robert shook his head and wondered how Bear, a man he thought was simple and straightforward, could, in truth, have so many turns and complications. "Sometimes when I walk past that bedroom and see Ruth with her father," he said, "I wonder what they talk about. It seems like they never stop talking."

Katie was nodding. "Ever since Bear was diagnosed, he's been having these intense talkfests with Ruth." She sipped at her coffee, which was no longer hot. "I hate to admit this, but a few times curiosity got the better of me and I lingered by the door to listen, eavesdrop. I thought Bear was probably trying to impart all his wisdom to her. I could understand that. You find out you're going to die and you want to tell your daughter everything you would've told her over the years about life and love and doing right. So I thought he would be instructing her to follow the Golden Rule or . . . you know, to thine own self be true, turn away from bitterness, trust your heart, remember I'll always love you . . ." Katie started to cry again, then resolved not to; she was weary of crying. "But instead, you know what I heard him saying? 'Change your oil every three thousand miles, it doesn't matter what the manual says.'"

Robert laughed softly as if coughing under his breath, it was that mannerism of his.

Katie continued, "'Never race a cold engine,' he told her. He said almost all the wear in an engine is caused in the first few seconds before oil starts circulating and people who race a cold engine are ignorant and deserve our pity."

"Automotive advice is what he's imparting up there hour after hour to a five-year-old?"

Katie shook her head. "It was other things too. But always practical stuff. He told her never get a pocketknife with a stainless steel blade, always pick one made of high-carbon steel that can be sharpened correctly. He told her to store rifles and shotguns with the muzzles on the floor on a piece of cloth, that way when you pick the guns up they'll be pointing safely at the ground instead of at your head, and also any oil left in the barrels will drip toward the muzzle instead of back into the firing mechanisms . . . as if she has pocketknives and cars and guns, as if she'll remember any of this when she's old enough to drive or . . ." Katie was crying in spite of her pledges not to. "And what the hell does 'righty-tighty, lefty-loosy' mean?"

Robert laughed again in that soft way of his. "Something our dad used to say . . . you turn a nut or bolt to the right to tighten it and—"

Katie said, "The way he's dying is bad. I wouldn't let any animal brought to our mission die in pain with no hope of living. It's wrong."

Robert agreed, but neither one of them knew what to do about it.

"He told me once," Katie said, "that he was afraid no one would show up at his funeral except the preacher and the vet and you if you could get time off work."

Robert winced. "I suspect he'll get a pretty good turnout."

She was shaking her head. "A few curiosity-seekers. The locals hate us. I'm burying him on the farm."

Robert agreed with this, too.

❦

There were a few good days left in November. On one of them, Bear asked Katie and Robert and Ruth to come to his room because he had a new poem for them to hear. "It's called, 'I'm Not Going to Kill Anything Anymore.'" No one commented, so Bear went ahead and recited it:

I'm Not Going to Kill Anything Anymore

I'll go around and spring all my mousetraps,
Pick up those ant pellets I put down,
Close that Roach Motel.
And free every bee from a yellow trap I hung in a tree,
  a trap so cruel
 It's got pictures of flowers on it.
And won't never kill another groundhog,
Won't gas 'em,
Shoot 'em,
Or dig 'em up with a shovel while they're trying to
  hibernate.
From now on I'll let moles tunnel all they want,
And wasps sting,
Little flies buzz 'round my wooly head.
'Cause I'm not going to kill anything anymore.

Ruth clapped but told Bear she squished a spider in her room last night and its guts came out *yellow.* "You leave them spiders alone," he said. Ruth replied that she'd leave spiders alone if they stayed off the wall above her bed. Katie and Robert, meanwhile, were too bewildered to say anything . . . of course Bear isn't going to kill anything anymore, he'll be dead within a month.

It got worse the first week of December when the weather turned cold and a decision had to be made about medication. Doctors couldn't stop Bear's pain completely, but to dull that pain they gave him an amount of opiate that put him in a mental fog where all he could do was sleep and murmur, little aware who was with him, much less what was being said. The doctors had informed Katie that Bear wouldn't live until Christmas and the decision she had to make was this: Take him off the pain medication so he can talk, can say good-bye, or let him die in a painless fog.

She and Robert were at Bear's bedside. Katie said she didn't know what to do. "I want to talk to him, but then I think it's selfish for me to trade his pain for my need to say good-bye."

"If you're asking me," Robert said, "I think my brother would like to say good-bye no matter how much it hurts."

Hearing this in an opiate dream, Bear felt a weight lift.

We're almost finished.

It was the nineteenth of December and Bear was off the pain medication; nobody outside the family was allowed in for a visit. Ruth, Katie, Robert took turns with Bear because when they came in together he would just lie there and look at them, listening to them talking among themselves, never saying a word. But when each was alone with him, Bear talked.

He told Robert it was almost worth dying just to get him back here to the farm, then added, "Guess what, Robert . . . I said *almost.*"

Ruth sat on a small red chair next to his bed, the five-year-old listening with the rapt attention of a rabbinical student. "Thought leads to action," he told her, "and action leads to habit and habit leads to character and character is destiny." "Okay," she said. He raised an arm and moved his finger in an arc. "A point moved through space forms a line, a line moved through space forms a plane, a plane moved through space forms a solid." She thought he was talking about spaceships, that kind of plane.

When Robert, overcome with curiosity like Katie, eavesdropped by the door, he heard Bear telling Ruth, "The best way to double your money is fold it in half and put it right back in your pocket." Robert thought, I wish somebody had told me that. Bear said, "In a fair fight, a monkey will always beat a dog." The little girl replied, "Really?" Bear confirmed it.

Robert had to leave, he couldn't bear to hear more.

When Bear and Katie were together, he told her he loved her and Katie said it right back to him. She told Bear that magic has gone out of the world. "People believe in science now, not magic or poetry. When boys and girls fall in love now, they probably don't give each other flowers or rhyming words, they probably do little experiments, chemicals in beakers, because no one honors magic or poetry. When we go out into space we take lab rats instead of haiku."

Bear smiled listening to her, he had absolutely zero idea what she was talking about.

She told him he carried magic within him, that's why animals talked to him and why he could take her out on a winter's night and find little *barely people* babies up in a child tree. Katie leaned close to him and begged for the truth. "Did that really happen?"

He patted her on the back as Katie said, *I love you, I love you.* She asked him if she'd reached a million yet. Bear said, you're almost there.

One time Bear asked Robert if he remembered the most megahurts Bear ever took.

Robert didn't. "Five or six?"

"I got up to seven once, it left that bruise I showed you. Guess what, Robert."

"What?"

"Inside my belly right now? It's ten thousand megahurts. And the worse part? Saying uncle won't make it stop." He looked up at his brother. "Close your mouth, Robert."

The twenty-first of December began zero cold. Katie came into the bedroom at 6 A.M. with coffee. Bear was dead. She called for Robert.

"What is it?" Robert asked, entering the room.

She was standing there holding both cups of coffee. "Make your brother open his eyes, I want to tell him something."

Robert went to the bed, bent over Bear, then looked back at Katie. "Hon, he's gone."

"I didn't ask for a report on his condition, I *asked* you to make your brother open his eyes, I have something I need to tell him."

To his credit, Robert turned back to the bed and leaned over Bear again. "Brother, open your eyes . . . Katie has something to tell you."

But of course he didn't open his eyes.

Katie put the coffee cups on a dresser and moved in next to Robert to grasp her husband by his shoulders. "Bear? Bear!"

"He's gone, hon."

She turned and gave Robert a ferocious look. "Go out and get the dog."

"What?"

"Go out and get Veep, bring him in here."

"Why—"

"Robert, will you just do what I ask!"

He went outside and put a collar on the big German shepherd and led him into the house, past Ruth at the breakfast table ("Hey, Veep, what're you doing in here?"), up the stairs, and into the bedroom where Katie was waiting, sitting on the bed holding Bear's face in her hands, talking to him.

"Here's the dog," Robert said.

Katie came over and knelt in front of Veep, who licked her with slavish affection. "Now listen to me. You are the son of the dog that Bear loved more than any animal on earth," Katie explained while holding Veep's massive head. "I want you to go over there and tell him to open his eyes, I have to tell Bear I love him."

Made nervous by Katie's emotional state, Veep lifted his paw to shake hands.

"DID YOU HEAR ME!" she shouted at the dog, who began whining and pulled away from Katie to try hiding behind Robert.

"I'll take him back outside," Robert said. "He doesn't understand, he thinks you're upset with him."

"I am! He refuses to talk to Bear, all the animals around here used to talk to my husband, why won't they talk to him now?"

Ruth came in and asked what was wrong.

"Honey," Robert said to her, "would you please take Veep outside for me?"

"Come on," she said, grabbing the German shepherd's ear in a death grip and pulling hard. Tail wagging, that dog accompanied her down the stairs like he was taking the road to glory.

Katie was shaking Bear and pleading with him to open his eyes.

Robert grasped her arm.

She looked at him with a panicked expression. "Go out and get the old red cow, she'll talk to him. *Please, Robert, please.*"

"He's dead."

"Bear said I had almost reached a million, I wonder how close I was." She pulled away from Robert and grasped Bear's face. *"I love you."*

"He knows, hon."

"BEAR, I'LL ALWAYS LOVE YOU!"

"You have to go downstairs and tell Ruth."

"BEAR, OPEN YOUR EYES!"

"Come on, hon." Robert was moving her as gently as he could toward the door.

"BEAR!"

While Robert led her away, Katie reached for Bear with both arms. She begged for another hour with her husband, another minute, then, at the doorway she shouted, "LOOK! He's opening his eyes, he's trying to sit up!"

Horrified, Robert turned . . . but Bear hadn't moved, he was dead.

"Bear . . . Bear . . . ," Katie continued, and downstairs Ruth asked what was wrong. When Katie told her that Bear was dead, your father is dead, she screamed in that piercing manner of little girls.

47

Katie hired a local carpenter to nail together a box. Bear's body was put in, and the box was placed in the smallest room in the house, a room designed specifically for this use and called, appropriately enough, the coffin room. They opened all the windows in that room and kept the door closed, and Katie wouldn't allow anyone to visit or mourn Bear until she got her way about burying him on the farm. It took three days to bully and browbeat the officials, but finally she was allowed to plant Bear on the same hillside with POTUS and Jamaica and the other animals, in a pretty spot that overlooked the creek and the arbor where Bear and Katie were married. Robert dug the grave himself, using shovel and prybar on the frozen ground and taking twice the time it would've required Bear to dig half the hole—Katie thought she was going to have to go out and help.

There had been no wake, and Katie wondered who would show up for the funeral on Christmas Eve. She was counting on Doc Setton, Miller, and some of the volunteers, but she didn't think any of them would start arriving as early as they did, at the very beginning of this crisp clear windless day, thirty degrees. You had to squint, the sun was so bright.

People brought food. The first arrivals parked around the house. People coming later parked along both sides of the county road. Katie was astonished. Eventually mourners were parking so far away that older people and those with young children had to be shuttled in, it was too far to walk. Upon arriving, people spoke to Katie and Robert, said hello to Ruth, and took their food inside. Coffee urns were set up. People visited, helped themselves to food. Katie didn't have to take charge, the process fell into place on its own.

By 10 A.M. five hundred people had arrived and Deputy Miller called the state police to direct traffic at the highway where the county road turned off and bottlenecks had formed. Doc Setton suggested that Katie start a receiving line where people could pay their respects, then maybe some of them would go home, leaving room for newcomers.

Three chairs were brought from the house and placed down by the creek for Katie, Ruth, and Robert. They couldn't be expected to stay standing to greet everyone who was here, though stand they did.

People were surprised there was no coffin to look into or at least to look at, Bear already buried, but an orderly system eventually developed: you got in line to greet the wife, the daughter, the brother, tell them how sorry you were and what a great man Bear was, then you crossed the little footbridge, walked up the hill, said a prayer or something at Bear's grave, and then you could get something to eat and go home.

But the gathering had become a kind of reunion and few people went home. The day continued as it had begun, crystal-clear sky, blinding sun, no wind, in the thirties, new people arriving . . . by two in the afternoon there were a thousand.

Katie and Robert finally sat down. Ruth had gone off somewhere with Veep and friends.

"Do you know all these people?" Robert asked at one point.

Katie said she didn't know half of them, not a third of them.

Strange things began to occur among the mourners. Some of them looked nervous, burdened, as they made their way up the line toward Katie. When they reached her they would blurt out some contorted confession of animal neglect. They would praise Bear's understanding, hug her, shake Robert's hand, and make their way anxiously toward Bear's hillside grave as if they had one more apology to deliver.

Robert and Katie kept looking at each other: Who *are* these people?

One man must've weighed 350 pounds. He wore overalls under a shiny black suit coat, sweating in this thirty-degree weather, actually wringing his hands. When he reached Katie, he knelt heavily by her chair as if she were a priest who could absolve him. In fact, he pinched the edge of her coat and pulled Katie close to whisper in her ear, taking longer than any of the other mourners, finally finishing whatever it was he had to tell her and struggling to get up off his knees. Robert had to help. Then the man hurried across the bridge and heaved himself up the hill to Bear's grave.

(Robert later asked her what that was about and Katie said the man's accent was so thick she had a hard time understanding everything he said, but she thought it went something like this: He used to organize dogfights and also trapped bears and baited them with the dogs. "When he said he used to bait bears I thought he said he used to date Bear and it took a while to recover from the shock of that before I understood what he meant, that he used to engage in bear baiting, siccing dogs on bears and letting them fight it out to the death." Apparently during one of Bear's private missions, he went to this man and told him that what he was doing was wrong. The man said he told Bear to go to hell but Bear kept returning, showing the man how to dress his dogs' wounds and techniques for training the dogs in the religion of *come, sit, stay,* helping out around the place however he could. He said Bear never criticized him personally, never called him names, just kept assuring the man that he himself knew that what he was doing was wrong. At one point, Bear put his hand on the fat man's chest and said, "You know it's wrong, right there in your heart is where you know it's wrong." The man said he kept telling Bear to go to hell, but then one night, about 3 A.M., the man woke up—he said it felt like there were worms or beetle bugs in his chest—and next morning he released a bear he was keeping chained in a shed. He never baited another one, never let his dogs fight again. "But your man kept coming over to visit me, missus," the fat man told Katie, "kept helping me with the dogs, talked to me. He was a good 'un. I found Christ and lost all this weight." Katie blinked at that last confession.)

As the fat man made his way back down from the grave, he waved at Ruth and she hollered, "Hey, Roger!"

Katie and Robert exchanged looks about that, too.

At least a dozen people Katie had never met made references to how Bear had helped them or helped a family member or friend. One little old lady in a black bonnet from the last century told Katie that Bear gave her parakeet a vitamin solution from an eyedropper and saved its life. Katie thought, my husband who could pick up the back end of a truck, who offered to kill men on my behalf, went out on missions saving parakeets with an eyedropper?

When Katie saw Carl Coote in line, she called Robert over and said, "That's the man who smashed my face, I don't want to talk to him."

Robert went to Carl and told him to leave. "Hold on a second, will you," Carl said, cutting ahead of others to kneel in front of Katie. "I know I ain't welcome here and I'm leaving soon as I tell you something. Bear took care of my pet when I was in jail, sent me pictures of Henry, told me in a letter how the little guy died of natural causes so Bear buried him. Bear also told me it should be written across my chest, how sorry I am for what I did to you. You think it'd be all right if I walked up and told the big guy good-bye?"

Though she still refused to speak to Carl, Katie nodded her consent.

At 4 P.M. it was growing dark and the mourners' line showed no sign of ending. Katie asked Robert if he would let people know she intended to say a few words up by Bear's grave, and then afterward she would continue receiving people down at the house. Robert agreed and reminded Katie he wanted to say a few words, too.

They were just organizing this maneuver when the blast of

unmuffled internal combustion shattered peace, someone racing down the county road, making his way among the parked cars and mourners, a huge black motorcycle that caused people to wince and cover their ears, it was so punishingly loud. As bad as that motorcycle sounded, its rider looked even worse. This guy had to be six and a half feet tall, broad shoulders, big belly, long hair, scraggly beard, wearing a tiny helmet like a little black pot overturned on his massive melon head. The rider stopped the motorcycle near where Katie and Robert were receiving mourners and got off with the grim determination of a knight dismounting to continue battle afoot.

Even people who knew nothing of motorcycles could see this one hadn't come off an assembly line. It had been chopped, lengthened with black-pipe extensions, made lower than what seemed practical, a motor big enough for a truck, everything painted powder black and put together with heavy welds and oversized bolts.

The biker was dressed in black leather, jacket and pants and boots and belt. A big silver chain anchored his wallet to his wide belt, though one wondered who would be so foolish as to attempt stealing anything from this Viking. That was the word written in red script across the back of his black leather jacket: *VIKING.*

He was tattooed everywhere you could see skin, even on his face. One facial tattoo said *slash* and had lightning bolts around it. And even without the tattoos it was a frightening face, nose bent and eyes hooded and teeth bad. He had a scar that ran straight from the hairline above his left eye, dribbling across that eye onto his cheek below. This wasn't a dashing dueling scar, thin and white, it was an ugly red worm of a scar that had caused his eyelid to lose its lashes and wrinkle like thin plastic exposed to heat.

Everyone had stopped talking to watch him. After angrily throwing his little helmet back toward the motorcycle, the Viking looked around until he saw Ruth and then made for the little girl with intent.

Four farmers stepped out of the crowd and put themselves

between Ruth and mayhem. They were old guys in their fifties with big bellies, the kind of fat white guys who get made fun of a lot 'cause they dress goofy and can't dance, but with half a ton of them between the girl and the motorcyclist, she was safe.

Or maybe not. The black-leathered Viking stopped at this protective circle and raised his arms to reach between the farmers. One of them took out a big folding knife. People braced for the fight, the blood, then Ruth wriggled through the farmers and leapt up into the Viking's outstretched arms. Katie gasped; it was like seeing her daughter embraced by a grizzly.

You could tell the Viking was trying hard not to smile as Ruth traced a line down the red scar that crossed his eye. "Guess what, Butch," she said. "Bear's dead." The big man nodded and whispered something in the little girl's ear, then handed her a white card. Ruth kissed him on the cheek and got down. The Viking turned to Katie.

"You Bear's woman?" he grumbled.

She nodded.

The rider extended his hand, clad in silver-studded leather with the glove's fingers cut off. Katie accepted a white card like the one he'd given Ruth. Scribbled in blunt pencil was a telephone number, including area code, and two words: *The Wolf*.

"Katie," he growled.

Startled, she looked up from the card.

"Any man speaks against you, raises a hand to you, call The Wolf night or day, twenty-four, seven."

Without further loquacity, he got back on his motorcycle, clasped helmet to skull, kicked the engine into life, spun around in a tight circle that shot gravel at everyone, then took off as rudely and loudly as he had arrived.

(Robert would also later ask, who in the blazes was that? But Katie didn't have an answer, didn't know how Bear and Ruth had met the biker or why she and Ruth were being offered The Wolf's protection. "But I did take the card away from Ruth," Katie told Robert. "I was afraid she might get mad at some little boy from school and then she calls The Wolf and next thing you know they're finding pieces of the little boy all up and down the interstates.")

Now it was dark. On that hillside, standing next to Bear's grave, Katie held a stone in her hand and words in her heart. She looked out at a thousand people on this Christmas Eve and wanted each of them to understand *everything* she felt about Bear. She wanted to tell people that living with Bear made her feel protected—not just a sense of physical safekeeping but spiritual protection—that his heart and soul were so good and honest and straight they provided a karmic shield that allowed nothing to harm anyone Bear loved. She wanted the mourners to know that Bear was magic, that he was a poet. She wanted to explain that in a changing world, Bear stood like a tree, that back in D.C. everyone she knew was hot to be hip while Bear stayed the same year after year, or if he changed it was to spread his canopy, deepen his roots. The man was steadfast. His wallet contained no driver's license or credit cards or insurance papers, nothing but photographs of people he loved and a clipping of an article titled "Bear's Philosophy." Katie wanted everyone to know what that philosophy was, and the details of heifering a steer and having the common decency not to laugh when it pees on its tail.

But when she opened her mouth, all that came out was his name, which Katie said over and over until little old Doc Setton stepped up to comfort her.

Robert was next. At least he could be counted on to deliver a powerful eulogy—Robert was famous as an orator. It was said that his high school commencement speech had parents weeping and students standing on their chairs cheering. Stone in hand, Robert looked at the thousand people standing in the cold on Christmas Eve.

"He was my brother," was all Robert got out before he too broke down, his most articulate gesture placing his stone next to Katie's on Bear's grave.

People waited for what might happen next.

Giving Katie to Robert's care, Doc went to the grave and said a few words about how he admired Bear as a farmer, how gentle he was with animals, how skilled he was in growing grass . . . then Doc put his stone on the dirt and suggested that anyone else who had anything to say could step up here and say it. Then we'll all go down to the house, he said, as many of us as can fit in there, and have coffee.

One tall farmer—imagine Ichabod Crane in a green barn coat and bright red watch cap—acted as if he'd been standing here just waiting for an invitation to speak. First he stilt-walked his way to the creek and found a stone, then he stilt-walked up to Bear's grave. "Told me once!" Ichabod shouted, presumably referring to Bear and speaking loudly out of eager nervousness, "he could talk to animals. I believed him. Iffen he was to say he swapped Bible stories with wiggle worms, I'd take it as gospel and strike down any who said otherwise." He put his rock on the fresh earth and walked back down the hill with the self-satisfaction of a man who'd come to say his piece and, by God, had said it.

Katie had no idea who he was or why Bear had admitted to him what she thought was his secret, talking to animals.

There was a rush now to collect stones from the creek and then get back in line to wait your turn to speak in public about Bear and put your rock on his grave. People are hungry for death traditions. They also sensed magic here on Christmas Eve, were glad they stayed, became imbued with a sense of privilege, and felt superior to those who'd left early. Robert would later describe it flamboyantly as the kind of pride that must've swelled in archers at Agincourt on the feast of St. Crispin.

A young woman stepped up to the grave and testified that Bear took a raccoon out of her attic.

An old man said Bear came over and helped him with a milk cow that was down, back legs split apart, then once they got that cow on its feet, Bear came in the house and fixed some plumbing. And he loaned me twenty dollars I never paid back, the man admitted. He put his rock on the grave then went over and offered a twenty-dollar bill to Katie, who shook her head.

"Please, missus," he begged.

"No," she said, "it's not necessary."

He kept holding the bill in his trembling fingers and Robert rooted for Katie to take it and then she did, the old man thanking her profusely.

A stunningly beautiful blond woman, dressed like a New York model and wearing high heels up that hill, held her equally beautiful and blond three-year-old daughter dressed in red velvet who laughed and threw kisses until the mother whispered something and the little girl, smiling to light up the evening, shouted, "Bear got my dog Chipper"—she had to listen to her mother for the next part—"out of a hole!"

Where are these people coming from? Katie wondered. How did Bear find them?

One of the formerly sullen teenagers to whom Bear had assigned canine socialization duty declared Bear way cool, put a stone on the grave, and went down the hill, high-fiving two other pierced teenagers who waited in line with stones and stories.

In the dark, people brought out candles, flashlights, lanterns. It was colder now—but still no wind. They told their stories into the night even though it was Christmas Eve. People had things to say about Bear and wouldn't feel right, *especially* on Christmas Eve, not to say them when they had the chance.

A big guy who said he was a truck driver with a bad alcohol history confessed he kicked a dog to death in a drunken rage outside some tavern. "I stomped and stomped and my buddies all watched, some of 'em laughed, some told me to quit, but I just kept stomping. It was a little yellow stray dog that would follow me home from the tavern most days, but I came out that particular day and stumbled over it waiting for me. Being drunk and all and mad at the world, I kicked that dog to death. Bear heard about it and came over to talk to me." He wasn't sure he could continue. A powerfully built man with a bull neck and massive hands, he wasn't accustomed to speaking out like this and also he was ashamed of himself. "Never criticizing, Bear just talked to me about dogs and how they love you even if you're ugly and stupid and no one else in the world loves you, a dog would be happy for the privilege of licking your hand. Dogs love you even if you're drunk and want to kick them to death. They don't understand why you'd do it, but that don't stop them from loving you. Bear said he thought that little yellow dog was waiting for me in heaven, just like he used to wait outside that tavern, no hard feelings. I told Bear if that dog had any sense he was waiting to bite me, but Bear said no, dogs jumped across some big canyon to cast their lot with man, come thick or thin. A dog will refuse food to stand by the man he loves, Bear said . . . a dog loves a man like water runs downhill, just can't help it." The truck driver was crying openly now. If you told men who used to drink with this man that he got up in front of people and cried over a dog, they would call you a goddamn liar. "I ain't had a drink since Bear come to see me. Every day I get off work I go around picking up strays, keep 'em at my house until I can find 'em homes. What I wanted to say about Bear . . ." He looked at the stone in his hand and didn't say anything more, he'd already said it all.

A ten-year-old boy holding his father's hand was crying, too, afraid about standing up in front of everyone like that truck driver—see what it's done to him? Bear had caught the boy beating on a cat with a board, but he didn't holler at him, he just told the boy things about cats, how they got tiny purring engines inside them that run on love instead of gasoline and how hearing a cat purr was a little like sitting on God's lap, that kind of contentment. Bear taught the boy to fix a cat's wounds, how to hold a cat so as not to hurt it, but so you don't get scratched too bad, either. As the boy continued crying, his father said, son, you don't have to do this, we can go home. But the boy insisted he was going through with it, he was old enough to know what he owed.

Katie was astonished. She'd thought their victories had been rare and isolated, but now she looked out at a candlelit procession winding down the hill and across the creek and even past the house, a line of triumphs—Bear's eulogy.

She woke the next morning with five seconds of joy, thinking it'd all been a dream. Then came reality and Katie felt hammered, like she'd been on a bad drunk, though she'd had nothing to drink except cup after cup of coffee. The last of the people hadn't left until just before dawn.

She dressed and stepped out into the hallway, past the other bedroom and a snoring Robert, down to the kitchen where Ruth was eating a bowl of cereal and playing with a little basket made of reeds.

Katie reached out touch her daughter's head when something scurried across Ruth's shoulder and down her arm.

"Damn!" Katie exclaimed, pulling her hand back. "What was that?"

Laughing, Ruth retrieved the salamander and showed it to her mother.

"Where'd you get it?"

"On Daddy's grave."

"What?"

"They brought a whole bunch of them."

"Who did? You've been out there already this morning?"

"I saw them."

"Who?"

"They're gone now."

"Show me."

They both dressed in winter clothes and Katie instructed the girl to put the salamander in the basket and bring it along.

Up on Bear's grave, on top of the mound of stones, were a dozen small baskets like the one Ruth had in the kitchen: crudely woven of various grasses, some with lids on, some open. Around the baskets were flowers and berries and clumps of moss, sprays of ferns. "How did they get flowers and salamanders this time of year?" Katie wondered aloud.

"I let a bunch of them go already," Ruth told her, referring to the salamanders. "They squiggle between the rocks and bury themselves in the dirt. Can I let them all go?"

Katie wasn't sure she liked the idea, but she allowed Ruth to release the rest of them. Then Ruth told her mother, "When I came out, those people ran away with their little babies holding on like monkeys."

"Barely people."

"Who?"

Katie shook her head. "Your father's family."

"Hey, Mom, guess what."

Katie lifted Ruth into her arms. "What, honey?"

The little girl looked like she was keeping a secret bigger than she could hold. *"Guess what!"*

"What?"

"Merry Christmas, that's what!"

Coda: Bear

Robert moved out of the house the day after the funeral and rented a room in town, but he went back to the farm almost every day and worked as a volunteer. People speculated that he and Katie were having an affair, but the truth was that Robert—divorced, out of work, his two boys in college—stayed around the farm for the same reason all those animals were at the mission, for sanctuary. Also to comfort Katie. He walked with her and read from C. S. Lewis's *A Grief Observed:* "No one ever told me that grief felt so like fear. I am not afraid, but the sensation is like being afraid. The same fluttering in the stomach, the same restlessness, the yawning. I keep on swallowing."

Robert took whatever jobs he could get in Briars, eventually went on salary with the mission, and worked every day with Katie. People continued to gossip about them, but people were wrong. Katie and Robert never even kissed. But, as the saying goes, they grew in love.

Two years after his brother died, Robert asked Katie if she would marry him. She replied that she'd been waiting for this, but Robert couldn't tell if Katie meant that in a good way, waiting in eager anticipation, or a bad way, dreading it.

"If I marry you," Katie told him, "please don't ever think I'm grateful I finally got the 'good' brother, the handsome one, the smart one, because I know who the good brother was, he was my husband for nearly six years."

Robert said he couldn't agree more. You'll never get an argument from me on that, he said.

"He was magic, he was a poet . . . and, Robert, as much as this might hurt your feelings, you come in second, you always will."

He claimed that coming in second to Bear was an honor.

"I don't know what you see in me," she said.

"I love you," he replied, which pretty much clinched the deal.

Two years after they were married, they had twin boys, and two years after that, a third son. Katie was forty-two and would on occasion think about life's arc: to be damaged by illness and then at the hands of men, but then to marry a magical man, give birth to a daughter, marry another wonderful man, have three sons—if you didn't call it crazy love, what would you call it?

Eleven years old when her third half brother was born, Ruth was tomboy and tyrant: fearless, strong, loyal, loving. She gave adults the impression that the three boys were impositions upon life itself, but the truth was, she loved them and told them secrets, dragged them around the farm, and generally treated them as if they had been created for her amusement, benefit, and protection. Sometimes Ruth came back from an expedition in the forest with the boys and they would have strange, wondrous, guilty, chagrined looks on their faces as if they'd seen elephants or had been robbing convenience stores. They might have mud deep into their ears and even on their teeth, odd scratches and marks on their legs, pockets ripped, socks missing, and might be carrying salamanders and hellbenders. If the boys were in especially rough shape, a blackened eye or a missing shirt, Robert and Katie would question Ruth, who of course feigned innocence. Then the boys would be lined up all wide-eyed and close-mouthed. During the interrogation they were like little commandos—we ain't telling you nothing about Ruth. If pressed by their father or threatened by their mother, the boys would turn imaginary locks on their lips and throw away the imaginary keys.

(When the three boys grew up, smart, independent women fell in love with them. They were prized by these women because they genuinely, truly liked women, not as sexual mysteries to be solved but as chums and mates and pals. They treated women lustily as the occasion arose, but also with the kind of ingrained respect that bomb disposal experts have for TNT. All this was a legacy from their big sister Ruth.)

Because they were so similar, Ruth and Katie had clashes that would clear the house of all males. To torment her mother, Ruth would sometimes lift a fork in front of one eye to see what Katie looked like behind bars. Katie, catching this, would say that Bear used to do the same thing—*what does it mean?* Ruth wouldn't say.

In other words, they were a family: loved one another, talked, argued, fought, made up, went on trips and missions, worked around the farm, took care of animals, crazy love diluting their disappointments and celebrating their victories.

When Ruth was thirteen and the youngest boy two, she took him out to see Red Cow, twenty-eight years old, a celebrity of longevity, and the last of the animals from Bear's era—POTUS, Jamaica, the ducks and cats, Old Bob, Mitchell, even goofy, lovable Veep, all dead now.

Katie and Robert were watching from a gate as Ruth sat on a footstool rock and stood Joey between her legs, then called for the cow by rattling a bucket of sweetfeed. Red Cow was making her slow way toward them when she stopped and suddenly began trumpeting and tromboning in the strangest manner. Then she went crazy, bellowing and charging the two children.

Horrified, Robert and Katie scrambled over the gate but were too far away and couldn't do anything but shout, disbelieving their eyes as they ran. That lovable, gentle old cow had turned berserk, attacking the boy.

Everyone was screaming but the cow kept stomping and trumpeting, it was a nightmare.

Robert got there first, kicking the cow away and lifting Joey, who was wailing. He searched the boy's face for injuries and opened his mouth to look for damaged teeth. Katie came running in and snatched her son away. "He's okay," Robert said. She didn't believe him and put Joey on the ground, lifted up his shirt, turned him over, pulled down his pants, turned him back over, jerked off his shoes and socks, examined his feet, counted toes, then checked hands and fingers.

Not a mark.

Joey's only injury was to his composure. He cried because he was scared, but he didn't have a scratch.

The two adults couldn't understand it, they'd clearly seen that cow stomping the boy. Then Ruth spotted the snake's body. "Dad, look." She usually called him Robert but slipped at times of stress like this.

A fat copperhead lay near the rock where Ruth had been sitting. It was the color of newly minted pennies. Its body had been smashed to pieces by the cow's hooves.

"We're going to call a vet," Katie announced. "A copperhead that big could kill an old cow."

As Katie held the little boy and patted his back to make him stop crying, Robert and Ruth examined Red Cow for bite marks. Ruth told Robert, "Guess what? This cow was trying to warn us to move away from that snake, she was running over here hollering, 'Move, move, move!'"

Robert laughed softly. "Moooove, mooooove."

"No, Robert, not *moo,*" Ruth insisted. "My dad raised cows all his life and he never heard one say *moo.* They trumpet and bellow and sound like trombones but they don't go *moo.*"

"Your father knew more about cows than any man alive," Robert said. Then he told Katie he didn't think Red Cow had been bitten but they should probably get a vet out here anyway.

"Red Cow talked to us," Ruth insisted. "She told us to move because she saw the snake and we didn't. Don't you believe me?"

Robert thought a moment. "Actually, I do." You could tell he was speaking the truth, not just placating her.

Katie had loved Robert before this, but loved him more after. She asked Ruth, "You staying out here, hon?"

Ruth said she was.

"Me too," Joey said, struggling down from Katie's arms.

"Do you think it's all right?" Robert asked Katie.

"I think they're probably safer with this cow than they are anywhere on earth," she said, as they set out for the house.

Red Cow was greedily into the sweetfeed as Ruth scratched

behind a floppy ear and little Joey worked a hand into that bucket for a taste.

Ruth thanked the cow for saving their lives, then asked, "What did you and my dad talk about?"

Robert and Katie overheard the question but were too far away to catch any reply.

ACKNOWLEDGMENTS

For past support, for support while writing this book, for material, for commiseration, and, not least, for sheer foot-stomping, eye-watering, laugh-stupid entertainment, here are the players I'd like rotating at my table if heaven turns out to be a poker game and I should be so lucky:

Joshua "Mad Dog" Martin
Matthew "Snake" Martin
Bob "The Observer" Neff
Ed "Death of Russia" Lockwood
Larry "The Bear" Abrams
Michael "Iron Mike" Watt
Mike "Brother" Snow
Ambrose "Have Pen, Will Travel" Clancy
David "Smoke and Mirrors" Rosenthal
Bob "The Sicilian" Dattila
Jon "Colonel" Mallard
Don "Chopper" Bordner
Jason "Doc" Amar
Phil "The Artist" Gill
Gregg "MIA" Downey
Bob "Fire on the Mountain" Parker
Curtis "The Old Man" Martin
Jim "The Rabbi" Betchkal
The Cruthis Brothers
The Old Gang

About the Author

DAVID LOZELL MARTIN'S previous novels include international bestsellers *Lie to Me* and *Tap, Tap,* and the critically acclaimed *The Crying Heart Tattoo*, *The Beginning of Sorrows,* and *Crazy Love*. He lives in the Washington, D.C., area.

Also available from

David Lozell Martin

"Triumphant... profound...hilarious... respectful."

—*The New York Times Book Review*

"Engrossing and quite radical...a blast."

—Patrick Anderson, *The Washington Post*

"Martin's talents in the saucy lowlife-comedy genre are abundant."

—Richard Bernstein, *The New York Times*

Available wherever books are sold or at www.simonandschuster.com